PROPHECY OF BLOOD & FLAMES

Book One of the Aurorian Trilogy

There is Promise in the Light.

Lacie M. Lou

Overcaffeinated Author Publishing LLC

This is a work of fiction. Names, characters, places, and incidents either are the product of the author's imagination or are used fictiously. Any resemblance to actual persons, living or dead, events, or locales is entirely coincidental.

Identifiers: ISBN 978-1-963955-00-2 (paperback) | ISBN 978-1-963955-01-9 (ebook) | LCCN 2024905141

Book Cover by David Gardias

Chapter Illustrations by Lacie M. Lou

First edition 2024

Dedication

To anyone who has ever read a fantasy novel and not seen
themselves come to life on the pages.
I didn't see myself represented in novels either, so I wrote one.
And, I wrote it for you, too.

Cire

S TICKING TO THE SHADOWS, I creep down the stone hallway, away from my sleeping comrades getting much needed rest after a long journey, my own mind too restless to sleep. The path I take is familiar from many nights spent sneaking away to the secret library.

I find the hidden door with ease, pushing it open slowly, listening for the sounds of boots echoing on stone before inching it just enough that it lets out a low, ominous groan. I hold my breath, my heart rate increasing. Even after dozens of trips to this forbidden room, my heart skips like a frightened animal at the sound of the door finally giving in, allowing me to escape into its depths among the hidden knowledge it locks tight.

My excursions to the library started by chance one evening when I couldn't sleep, and I found myself wandering the temple. Then, my heart would race with just the fear of being caught outside the barracks, a punishable offense– if you consider losing a meal's rations a true punishment. Now, I risk far worse by breaking orders and reading forbidden knowledge.

The Aceolevia Temple's library holds all the secrets of the past, information that the High Priest couldn't bring himself to burn, but considered too much of a threat to let it remain loose in the world. If you let them, older Morei warriors will share stories about their excursions into the villages and cities of Hevastia to collect forbidden texts.

If only my work were as simple as collecting texts of the Old Ways.

I shudder, remembering the mission I just returned from. The sounds of the villagers screaming in terror still echoes in my ears and the images are burned into my eyelids, fending off any chance of restful sleep.

I run my finger down the spine of a well-worn book.

Will this be the book I read tonight by waning candlelight? I think to myself, a soft chuckle rising in the back of my throat.

These books and scrolls are my preferred company to that of my regiment, a boisterous group of men in bloodstained clothes. The past year or so, hidden away in this treasure trove of knowledge, have made me think of myself as separate from the men I was raised alongside, a scholar who would rather fight with words and knowledge than with blades and brute strength, or magic.

In the beginning, I believed the Haematitian Council–I thought what we were being called to do was right. I wore my uniform proudly, gave my body to the cause without a second thought. We're touted as the sole protectors of the True Faith, the final line before the plague claims us all, the guardians that will ensure another Great War never comes to be.

With every year, every village left smoking and in ruins, every unsuccessful "cure" brought back to the Council, my resolve has chipped away.

What if we are wrong?

I keep my worries to myself, these kinds of thoughts are not to be shared with anyone. I have heard rumors of other temple guardians or priests who have spoken against the Haematitian Council, never to be seen or heard from again. I shudder at the thought of ceasing to exist. It is a fate worse than being among the walking dead of our regiment.

The scroll I pick up is covered in a thick layer of dust, careful to unroll it slowly, its age showing in its fragility and torn edges. I brush my hand over the page, trying to make out the words hidden beneath the dirt and debris, frowning when I realize this particular scroll is unsalvageable, lost to time and the blatant disregard of the Haematitian Council.

The next scroll is different, the sides are embossed with gold. Unrolling it, I notice the parchment is thicker, and excited chills travel across my arms and down my back–I know in my gut that this scroll is more important than the many poems and short stories I have read here.

Mother Odora

Before there was life on Odora, there was nothing. Odora existed only in the twinkle of the largest solari Arryn's inner being. In a burst of passion and fiery breath, Odora was born from Arryn's center. She was to be his Amorei for all of existence, his one true love.

Odora was unlike the other solari. While Axuna, Uzelia, and Lunei were fiery, hot-headed and uncontrolled, Odora was softer and gentler than her three sisters. Her beauty was more subtle than that of her sisters who all circled Arryn's powerful light. It came from the softness of her glow, the depths of her joy which radiated her inner beauty to the surface. In her light grew flowers, flowing rivers, and rolling hills, a new world was born on her surface. This world was the opposite of the hot, uninhabitable beauty and fiery passion of the fellow solari of Arryn's inner circle.

It was not long before her sisters became jealous of the attention Arryn showed Odora, of how he shined his light in the most spectacular way for her, and her alone. They tried to trick Odora, telling her that the life she grew and cherished disgusted Arryn. Odora was wise and knew they were trying to trick her, she would not listen to them, and continued to grow beautiful plants for Arryn to shine his light on.

The others were not dismayed, and they continued to search for a way to rid themselves of her presence. On a trip to visit Arryn, Lunei, the smallest and most jealous of the solari, encountered a cold chill she had never felt before. The chill spread slowly at first, and she tried to contain it, afraid of what was happening. She called to Arryn, begging him to warm her with his brilliance, to save her.

As she continued to shiver, the chill spread from within her to her surface, cooling her fires and dimming her light. As her light dimmed, the smallest solari became enraged at Arryn and especially at Odora for taking his light away from her. She became dark and barren. As she continued to orbit Arryn, drawing ever closer to Odora, Lunei plotted Odora's demise.

Patiently Lunei waited for her opportunity, and as she passed her sister, Lunei rammed herself into Odora. The impact sent Odora flying away from Arryn, just within his glowing warmth. Lunei laughed gleefully for she had won, not realizing that in her attack on Odora she had also set herself apart from Arryn's inner circle. Arryn was left surrounded by the two oldest sisters, Axuna and Uzelia, who were wise not to let him know of their trickery, blaming Lunei for Odora's loss.

Odora and Arryn wept for the loss of each other, for it seemed hopeless they could ever find one another again. Eventually, Odora's tears spilled to the surface of the world she had grown. From each tear sprung a child, eight in total. Each gifted with an essence of Odora herself, a magic to be used wisely. Overjoyed at the discovery of her children, she divided the surface into kingdoms, one for each of her children and granted them eternal life so she would never be lonely again.

Odora's children were named for their gifts: Soran (Elemental), Keladone (Time), Raephe (Blood), Aerethia (Illusion), Opulia (Healing), Leomaris (Attunement), Meltise (Caster), and Laiken (Metamorphosis). As centuries went on, her children began to create life of their own, content to spend their time among their creations, finding companionship and joy in the beauty of their work. Odora bestowed her children free reign over their kingdoms. The siblings lived in harmony with one another and with their people who worshiped them.

That all changed the day Soran chose to forsake his eternal gift of life with his Mother Odora for the love of a mere mortal named Hevastia. Odora begged and pleaded with her eldest son to forget Hevastia, to stay true to his nature and to honor his gifts, but Soran was stubborn and chose to turn his back on his mother's wishes. At the time of

Soran's unexpected death, Odora summoned her children to her side, forbidding them to ever walk the surface again, convinced their work was evil, and that love only breeds jealousy which begets pain and suffering. Mother Odora refused Hevastia, Soran's half mortal lover, at her door, and turned her away from her children.

The children of the other deities all continued to worship their god or goddess, waiting patiently for their return. In order to keep their magic alive, each deity's direct descendents, the god-touched, would walk among their people as the conduit to their magic, a living key.

I finished unrolling the scroll, and hastily scrawled at the bottom is a short note. I squint, holding the parchment as close to my dying candle flame as I dare, trying to make out the words.

Our Ladyship's influence will return, walking the surface among Her people, god-touched and blessed with power. Born of blood, but filled with spirit, forged from fire, tested by shadows. She will overcome the darkness that pervades the land and restore Her glorious light in the hearts of Her people.

The bottom of the scroll is torn, the rest of the note, missing. There are those that still worship Lady Hevastia, the sovereign goddess and namesake of our country. They are known as practitioner's of the Old Ways, believing in the return of Hevastia, that she would be the one to restore our land and rid it of the plague and dark beasts. The Haematitian Council believes only in the True Faith, the doctrine that the strength to overcome all manner of obstacles and atrocities lies within us, and that sacrifices must be made to further our strength and aid us in the battle against the rising darkness.

I have read other accounts from the Old Ways sequestered away in this dark, dank room. When the Haematitian Council announced the True Faith, all remnants of our former goddess and her practices were gathered and presumably destroyed. Worshiping Lady Hevastia is a punishable offense, and I would know—my duty as a Morei guardian is to travel our land and deliver the message of the True Faith through demonstration of our might and power. *Tithes* are collected from every village or crumbling city we 'visit,' in order to further our strength and honor the True Faith.

My eyes scan the scroll once more, and I think to myself, *This is the second mention of a god-touched walking among us, the first in an account of the last princess of the land, Atrya. Is the princess miraculously still alive?*

The sound of boots shuffling along the stone and the soft tap of a sword against chainmail pulls me from my thoughts, and I quickly reroll the scroll, extinguishing my candle in the next breath. I inch closer to the door, not daring to close it fully or it will alert the patrol to my presence. I can only hold my breath and hope they are as unobservant as they always are, wandering past the cracked door without stopping. The sound of boots recedes, and I breathe out in relief.

Another night not caught by the guard.

It brings a smile to my face knowing I've once again broken the rules under all of their noses.

I wait several more minutes, cloaked by the darkness, before slipping out of the library and closing the door behind me, wincing at the low moan as it shuts firmly. I follow my steps back to my barrack bed, and close my eyes.

The horn sounds as I drag my eyes open, the groans of my comrades echoing across our small barrack room. We hustle to dress in uniform and assemble in front of the barracks. Kai stands next to me, eyeing me closely, and I frown.

"What is it?" I hiss, trying not to draw any attention to myself.

His sharp eyes lock onto mine, with no hint of suspicion. "You appear tired, that's all."

I chuckle and quip, "Well you would be too if you were kept awake by your snoring."

He flashes the faintest smirk, before the sound of heavy footsteps echoes down the hall, and my attention is pulled in the direction of the small contingent walking toward our regiment. High Priest Marius is flanked by his guards, walking purposefully.

"Gentlemen." High Priest Marius stands tall, his beady eyes glaring down his long nose. He stops in front of Kai. "Are your men ready to accept their mission, Captain?"

Kai stands taller and nods his head. "Yes, High Priest." Everyone falls into line, standing tall.

"Excellent." The High Priest turns away, flicking a hand in impatience. "I need you to travel to the Ventemere Mountains, our scout has identified a potential threat hidden within the mountains. I need your men to go there, cleanse the village, and bring back 'the cure.'"

I grimace internally, trying to keep my face a mask of practiced indifference.

"As the Right Hand of your Excellence's Will, we proudly accept responsibility for maintaining order and safety in the land.

We will leave at once." Kai's words are well practiced, this is our fifth mission in as many months. But duty trumps our men needing rest.

I duck my head to conceal rolling my eyes. With each success, he gains favor with the High Priest and Priestess, distinguishing himself apart from the rest, from me.

High Priest Marius nods his head in approval before walking off, his guards forming a tight box around him, a dark red spot in a field of silver armor.

Kai turns sharply to our group. "Men, gather your supplies. The Ventemere Mountains are a several weeks long journey from here. Time is of the essence."

Eliana

*T*HICK SMOKE FILLS THE *air, choking the breath from my lungs. My eyes and lungs burn, but I push forward trying to find my way out of the darkness. The heat of flames presses in on me from both sides, and I walk faster, stumbling on the uneven ground.*

My boot catches on bricks from a broken wall, and I come crashing to the ground, cutting my hands and knees on the shattered stone. I cry out in pain, clutching my right hand close to my chest. I crawl forward, shuffling, the sound of scattering stone echoing into the darkness. My fingers brush over something crunchy–I've made it to the edge of the village, to the fields surrounding my home. The scorched grass crumbles under my boots as I stand, my home now up in flames.

Tears run down my ash-coated face. My people's screams of terror and pain follow me, and my heart clenches. The white-hot flames climb higher, consuming everything, their light illuminating the ruins of my home.

I bolt upright, a scream rising in my throat. My room comes back to focus and I sigh with relief, sagging back against my desk. *It was only another night terror.*

The light of my candle's tiny flame casts an eerie glow in my room, throwing shadows to every corner and behind the sparse furniture. Sighing, I put down my quill, and stretch my arms over my head. There's movement out of the corner of my eye, and I snatch my quill, brandishing it like a dagger. The candle's flame flickers in the breeze of my shuffle and I realize the movement was just the light glinting off my dressing mirror, not my mother or some monster sneaking in to surprise me. My heart pinches at the thought of my mother checking in on me like I'm a small child. I just had my eighteenth birthday–I'm hardly a child anymore. A half-hearted laugh escapes my clenched teeth and I shake off the feeling of being watched.

Writing by candlelight is against the law.

I imagine her standing in front of me, ever present and always nagging me. She would chide me, her dark eyes full of mock concern. Then she would brandish her own quill or a wooden spoon from the kitchen, a challenge in her eyes, and a half smile on her face.

But, mother is not here, and it's just me in my small room. I want to brush off my paranoia, but the story I recorded this evening and my most recent nightmare still linger fresh in my mind's eye. The traveler was an avid storyspinner, painting a grotesque and frightening tale.

There's nothing to be worried about.

My fingers brush over the stack of parchment, each page a story from a neighbor–a familiar face–but some are like tonight's tale, a story from the rare traveler that finds our small, hidden village. The grandiose, colorful tales these travelers bring is always the talk of the village for days after they leave, usually bringing some brightness to our rather dull, routine lives. But this story in particular will be spoken of in hushed tones, childrens ears covered, and behind closed doors lest the elders hear us spreading panic amongst the clan. I thumb through the top of the pile and pull out a few pages that I should have burned.

It has been 3 moon cycles since the last traveler stumbled upon our village, thirsty and in need of rest. The land beyond my small world is rumored to be overrun with monsters, and the unforgiving terrain makes it nearly impossible to find us, and for us to leave. The storyteller, Jasath, was a merchant who peddled handmade wares from the far stretches of Hevastia in exchange for other unique goods he could trade in his travels. My eyes wander to the stone holding my parchment down, a smooth rock painted with an intricate, swirling knot—I traded Jasath a written story for it.

Three weeks ago when he learned I was a scribe, and also the only daughter of the chieftess, he pulled me aside and promised me more stories in exchange for room and board. Bellaema, my mother, was not inclined to grant such a request–lingering guests are not tolerated in our village. She says it is for our protection but I believe it is to keep us ignorant. Jasath paid me more than I bargained for with the news he shared.

Jasath of Windemere
Traveler, Merchant-Trader
The tale I wish to tell is not a happy one, it is a warning to all who live here that the mountains will not protect you forever. Our land is dying, the plague continues to spread leaving nothing untouched by its dark stain. There is no final death. I have seen with my own eyes the lost rise from the ground and walk again. It is no longer only the dark monsters in the shadows we must fear, but our own loved

ones may come back to haunt us, torture us, and remind us that we are forsaken people of a cursed land.

My travels have taken me many places, the feeling of dread I carry in my heart I have sensed far and wide, it is in the heart of every child of Hevastia. The mothers toting children in busy marketplaces, the farmhands in small villages, the men and women of every corner know to fear their arrival. Where their power extends to, disturbing and frightening horrors follow.

Dark beasts haunt our lands, they kill without prejudice. Their hunger is bottomless, their thirst for blood, for violence, unquenchable. Shadows of the night, you will not see them until they wish it, until it is too late to even scream. Devouring all in their path they leave rot, ruin, and a country beaten and broken.

The Haematites are coming to 'cleanse' each village and city of Hevastia. They promise to eliminate the blight that threatens to end our existence, that continues to weaken us. Traveling all of Hevastia, their minions seek that which does not exist. They say that blood is the cure. Every village and city must 'tithe' to the Haematitian Council or perish in the spreading darkness.

I warn you, do not allow yourself to continue in ignorance, I implore you to fortify your minds, hearts, and walls. Guard against the monsters of the night, and the monsters who will come before them, promising deliverance from death and darkness, and only bringing more of it.

"I thought you got rid of that blasphemous tale," a familiar voice says from behind me, and I flinch at the tone of my mother's words. "Jasath is delusional from long spans of travel alone, he cannot be trusted to share news of Hevastia with us. And I will not have you encouraging this fear-mongering amongst our people."

I straighten my shoulders and turn to stare my mother in the eyes. "But what if it is the truth? Or at least partially true? Should we not ensure we are prepared?" I hear the whine in my voice and know that my words will not penetrate my mother's rockhard mind. When she has made up her mind there is little point in arguing. But my fear emboldens me and I press on. "We know so little of Hevastia and what has become of it. What if we are a target of the Council?"

I think of our neighbors and friends who follow the teachings of Lady Hevastia faithfully. We are magicless, but not faithless. The perverse magic of the Council is disturbing and dangerous. Everyone in our community openly worships Lady Hevastia, our sovereign and our land's namesake. All of us are at risk from the Council for that crime alone. It is no secret that they do not tolerate "practicing" the old magics of the world, what they call the "Old Ways." We have heard tales from other travelers that across the land villages and cities have been ransacked by the Council's Morei guardians for harboring those loyal to Lady Hevastia's teachings. I know my mother believes us to be untouchable. Her voice taunts the back of my mind. *Who would go through the trouble of traversing the Ventemere Mountains?*

"Please, mother, listen to reason. Think of the struggles we had this harvest season—the terrain has been more unforgiving than years past. This is a sign. Jasath's words ring with truth."

"Eliana, my star, it is our responsibility as the leaders of our village to keep our heads on our shoulders and not get lost in some tale. When I asked you to be our scribe, I intended it to bring you closer to our people, to ground you to our life, our history, not to send you frollicking in the dark fields of your imagination. You must give up the notion of the world beyond our clan, we cannot help them. We can only protect our own as we know how to."

I bite my tongue and swallow the sharp remark. Hopeful, I look into my mother's aging face and beg her with my eyes to listen. "Is it so wrong to want to help them?"

She touches my cheek, and smiles down at me, her eyes crinkling in the corners. "No, my star, it is not wrong to want to do right by others. It is that very strength which you carry so closely in your heart that will make you a capable chieftess of our village. But, strength can only extend so far, we need it here, with us." She touches my cheek one more time before stepping away and retreating to the door.

Her shadow recedes down the hallway, and I listen for her door closing. Alone once again, I turn back to the parchment in my hands and decide that I cannot get rid of it just yet. Jasath's words linger in my mind, nagging at some far buried part that I cannot access.

My mother's reminder to be loyal to the clan, to forget the notion of the world beyond our land, burns a little hotter tonight, a steady heat in my veins that grounds me to reality, and connects me to our people, to this place I call home. Everyone has a place in our village, everyone has a purpose, and mine is to be my people's history keeper, and someday their leader. If only it were so easy to stay rooted where you are planted. I close my eyes and wish for sleep to find me easily tonight.

The morning chill nips at my exposed toes, I can tell that the three solari–Arryn, Axuna, and Uzelia–have not yet risen, their warmth not yet kissing the air. With a grunt I push off my blankets, and gingerly place my toes on the ground. I pause, listening for my mother down the hall–her faint snores are the confirmation I need. I have enough time to sneak away before morning training. My muscles ache from yesterday's sessions. I don't pretend to know my mother's motivations for increasing my training. I wonder idly if it is due to the increasing risk of monsters in our hidden valley, but I push that thought out of my head. I cannot waste a rare chance to slip away.

I pull on my boots, my coat, and grab my satchel with my drawing supplies. Slipping out of the door, I gently close the door behind me and duck into the lane beside our house. It does not take me long to sneak to the edge of the village, through the gate, across the rolling fields that surround our village, and over the short rock wall that marks our land. The steep mountains surrounding us provide plenty of protection–we are a well-hidden valley.

The solari are just beginning to peek through the highest mountains as I climb one of the animal trails that leads out of our valley and into the rocky terrain of the mountainsides. Most trails have long since been abandoned, their paths broken by stubborn plants that push through the rock and toward the warm suns. This trail is freshly turned, the young plants broken and trampled beneath small paws or hooves. I make a mental note to keep my senses sharp, instead of lulling into the usual daydreams I escape into on my hikes.

Up the mountain's side I climb, careful with my footing as the path narrows. I know I will reach a decent resting spot soon. This trail is familiar to me–I've climbed a similar path on this hill before. The trail opens to a cliff overlooking a large, lush green field of flowers and tall whispering grass.

I long to run my hands through the soft leaves as they dance in the breeze, but my wanderlust is practical by nature, and cautious by necessity. It's unsafe to wander too far from the village–even before Jasath's warnings it would be horribly risky to travel so far alone. I swallow down a rising bout of fear at the thought of the horrible beasts Jasath painted in his stories.We are all forbidden from leaving the village–we do not leave our sanctuary, ever.

Turning the corner of the hill and I sigh in relief. The cliff sits undisturbed, as if it has been waiting for me all along. I settle against a large rock, my legs dangling over the edge. The breeze ruffles the small hairs that frame my face, and pull at the pages of my sketchbook.

My concentration on capturing the solari rising in the sky above the field is broken by a twig snapping behind me. The hairs on the back of my neck rise, my skin covered in prickles of adrenaline. Another twig snaps, accompanied by the low growl deep in an animal's throat.

Breathe. You can do this, it's probably a young laseron, a mountain lion, overly confident from inexperience. When I stand up, it will flee as they always do.

I slowly put my quill and notebook down, and stand, pulling my dagger from my boot as I straighten to my full height. I'm tall for my age, certainly bigger than a small *laseron*, they barely come up to my knee and are usually quite skittish.

It is to my chagrin that when I turn around, it is not a *laseron* that crept up behind me.

The beast staring me down is lean and powerful, like a *laseron* but twice its size. I don't recognize it. Its fur is of the darkest night, but it is not glossy like that of a healthy animal. Instead it is matted down and oozing puss and blood. The growl continues to pulse from its large throat, cutting past its bared teeth, yellow and chipped. My hand slickens with sweat, I tighten my hands around my dagger but it feels pathetic in my hands compared to the large fangs prepared to sink into my flesh.

I send a quick prayer to Lady Hevastia, and an apology to my mother, not that she'll ever hear it. My boots grind into the rocky cliff, and I brace myself for whatever the beast will do next. It snarls and paces back and forth, careful not to come too close to me or the edge of the cliff, but never far enough for me to make a run for the steep mountain trail and the village far beyond it.

I never let my eyes leave the beast's, so I know the exact second it has made the decision to lunge. I duck and roll as it leaps toward me, its claws catching my hips, raking deep tracks into my skin. I cry out in pain, but force myself back to my feet, favoring my uninjured leg. It resumes pacing, toying with me, calculating what to do next.

Not sparing a second for it to make its next move, I palm my dagger, weighing it in my hand, as I angle my body. I will only get one shot at the beast's neck. I hurl the dagger with as much force as I can, and not bothering to see if it struck true, I turn around and run, limping as fast as I can down the steep trail. My only hopes are my impeccable aim, and that it's not so easy for the large beast to trail after me. My breath comes in short gasps, I can feel myself weakening from blood loss, my legs threaten to buckle under me. The beast trails me, slowly, patiently, as if it too can sense the fight leaving my body.

It feels like the better part of a day as I stumble down the mountain, lazily hunted by the prowling creature, but in truth it has been only a few minutes. Ahead the trail widens, leading to the wide plain of the valley and the village. I am so close to safety, but will my neighbors be able to stop this beast? It must be one of the monsters Jasath spun tales about—we have nothing like this in our valley.

I continue running as best as I can, but as I glance back for the beast, I miss a large rock in the path. My body hits the ground, my breath sucking in and out, hissing in pain. I am too afraid to look over my shoulder again, but I must get back up and face the beast if I can no longer outrun it.

There's a pained grunt and the crash of two large animals colliding. Dread sinks into my stomach. *How is it that my luck is so bad there are two of them?*

When I turn around it is not another beast but something far worse. A man is attacking the beast with lethal precision, and no remorse. His sword slashes at the monster, leaving severe gashes with every strike. I should feel grateful for him saving my life, but all I can see is the uniform he wears, and the insignia on the right arm – a blood red shield. It is with a fear worse than death that I realize he must be part of the Haematitian Temple, and if he is so deep into the mountains it can only mean one thing.

The Morei guardians are in the mountains, they've found us.

I find within myself some deeper, inner reserve of energy that I did not possess when fleeing the dark beast. I pull myself up and turn my back on the man, the monster, and I take off running for the village as fast as I can.

I need to warn my mother, we must prepare everyone immediately.

Cire

THE VENTEMERE MOUNTAINS ROSE up to greet our regiment this morning as we passed into the long shade they cast on the fields laid at their feet.

What secrets do you hold?

I wonder to myself, searching the rocky mountain terrain for the pass that will take us to the rumored "Hidden Village of Bellamere." I frown at the idea of getting lost in the unforgiving terrain, tasked with tracking down yet another tithe for the Council. Behind me are the grumbled sounds of pain and complaint as the rest of the guardian regiment catches up to me and our captain, Kai.

We were badly beaten in last night's attack, the third on this journey. The monsters are thick in these parts, as if it is not enough to risk encountering the regular predators of the wild, we must also protect against dark beasts. The Council continues to promise that the solution to our problems is almost within hand, and with every rumor of someone practicing the old magicks, another guardian regiment is sent out to "cleanse" the unfortunate village and return with the "cure" to the dark plague.

It feels as though we are chasing ghosts.

My stomach turns at the thought of more pointless slaughter, but it is all I have come to know. My body almost itches for another beast to appear from behind a boulder and give me an excuse to draw my blade and take out my frustration. And yet, I secretly, desperately wish to never draw it again, for it is a wretched thing only capable of delivering death to the innocent.

Kai waves me over, and I increase my pace to catch up to him. He is so steadfast in his devotion, so sure of our cause, and I want to believe in it as well. There is no doubt in his heart that we will succeed in our mission, and his resolve, his morale keeps us all going on these long stretches of ruthless marching. Through all the pain and suffering met at the end of our blades.

"There is an animal trail to the right, it looks freshly trodden." He does not need to voice the rest, I know he means to suggest one of us scout it to make sure there is not a beast ahead, or that perhaps it is the trail to the hidden village. I groan internally at the thought that it is another dead end, like the many we have encountered in this unforgiving terrain.

Ever the dutiful soldier. "I'll go ahead and clear the way for the others."

"Thank you, Cire. Your brothers thank you."

I fight to suppress an eye roll, they would only thank me if I was able to convince Kai to stop dragging them to the far corners of Hevastia chasing rumors and hellish tasks for the Council. I grab my sword, Light Breaker, and my bow and arrow, hoping to get lucky and snatch a few small animals on the way for dinner. The boisterous noise of my comrades echoes in the ravine we've been trekking through for the past half day as I pick my way across the rocky mountainside, careful to keep my footing sure as I ascend.

The bottom of the path is wide, and the underbrush here is much thicker. I know as I climb it will narrow as they always do. I push aside a rather large dried bush when twigs snap. Something is moving quickly. I unsheath my sword, Light Breaker, and plant my feet, letting it run right to me, unsuspecting of the danger it barrels toward.

I have to collect myself from shock when a girl falls at my feet having tripped on a rock hidden by the brush. I refocus on the trail at the sound of another twig snap. Right behind her is a nasty, large, black beast–deranged with its matted, blood crusted fur.

I step forward, eager to take on the monster in front of me and hungry in my desire to work out some frustrations on it.

A low growl sends a chill down my spine as it locks red, cloudy eyes on me. I swing my blade, making sure to keep back from the beast, dancing close to slice its shoulder and gliding away in the next blink to keep out of reach of its swinging paws. It growls and lunges at me, barely missing my calf. I sidestep away and yell at the beast, goading it to come closer. The beast snarls, yellow fangs on full display.

It lunges again, I bring my sword down on its neck, slicing clean through. Annoyed at the black, thick blood coating my sword, I wipe it clean on a mossy patch.

It's at that moment I remember the girl fleeing the beast, and turn around to find the trail empty save for me. The girl must have run off to leave me to fight the beast.

Where did she come from?

I pick my way around the dead beast, careful to keep my footing on the path as it winds up and into the rocky mountainside. This path is not well traversed, so it most likely does not lead to the village, but curiosity guides me farther up the mountain, interested in knowing what brought a girl into the unforgiving terrain alone.

My breath catches in my throat when I round a tenuous curve in the trail, my eyes taking in the Thessimis Fields dancing in the mountain breeze below. The small cliff is just enough space to sit and take in the view. My boot snags on a finely detailed leather strap of a satchel, its contents haphazardly discarded. I pick up the notebook, flipping through the pages. My hand stops on a drawing of a beautiful, skillfully sketched flower, a variety that must be native to the mountains.

So this is what brought you all the way up here.

I close the notebook, sliding it and the broken quill into the pack before slipping it over my shoulder. Under the pack there is a deep red smudge, dried out in the breeze coming from the edge of the cliff. The beast must have gotten a chunk of her flesh–a faint trail of red mixed with thick drops of black blood stains the soft moss and rock.

I touch the black blood, thick like mud and rancid smelling. *She must have gotten a chunk of its flesh too before they found me at the bottom of the trail.*

I trek back down the trail, stopping only to kick the dead beast once more for good measure – you can never be too sure with these dark beasts. The red blood trail picks back up where the girl tripped, leading me away from the trail and the dead monster and toward a different trail that disappears deeper into the mountains.

Kai is indifferent to the news of a lone monster, it is not anything we have not seen before. "And what of the girl?" he asks me, again, his eyes landing on the satchel gripped in my fist.

"She ran off while I was attacking the beast." He hisses in a breath, ready to reprimand me for being so careless. "She was injured, her blood has left us a clear trail. If she is one of the lost villagers, she will lead us right to her people."

The words taste bitter, unfulfilling in my mouth. When Kai smiles at me, a knot twists in my gut.

Just one more ghost. Finish hunting this last ghost and then I can rest.

Our regiment finds new energy at the prospect of being close to our target, many of them eager for a fight, though I wonder if such simple mountain folk will be much of a challenge. I hope for their sake we can end this quickly. It is the same prayer I say every time we are near a village, hopeful that, just once, it will be different.

The men around me busy themselves with sharpening their swords, fletching new arrows, and preparing for a fight. I find a large rock separate from the practiced rhythm of my comrades and the noise, taking some solace in the quiet space I tuck myself away into. I pull out my own sword, letting muscle memory guide the whetstone in my hands over the blade as my mind drifts to my thoughts, preparing for what I must always do.

The Haematitian Council must not know, or simply not care, that they have lost the love of the people. I grew up under the Haematites' shadow my entire life, and I believed that the Council was truly keeping the needs of our people in their hearts, but doubt has crept into mine. Our people live in squalor. They scream in terror as we approach their gates. In my heart I know this cannot be right.

As a child of the Aceolevia, our studies of our people's history were limited, filtered by the elder guardians and acolytes of the Council. With no history but the story spun by the Council and elder guardians, I walked the path of the True Faith, swore an oath to protect Hevastia's Heart and serve as a trusted hand of the Council, a Morei guardian. My obsession for knowledge, and my pursuit of a deeper faith are the very reason I have so many cracks in my devotion to the Council's mission.

The various journals discarded in the darkest corners of the Aceolevia's library hold forgotten stories of a different Hevastia from another time– a land that was healthy and vibrant, and the people were joyous. There are even more that recount the pain, fear, and struggle of the era of the Great War.

Those stories I understand, I live them first-hand as we fight our own people to maintain the Haematitian Council's slipping grasp on power and their dominion over Hevastia's Heart.

A few contain poetry from long-dead soldiers, temple acolytes, and courtesans from the old kingdom, the emotion tangible in the worn pages. Those are my favorite, my mind travels back to the library where they lie hidden.

Independent study of combat or strength conditioning is encouraged by the Council, but I would be punished if they ever found out that I frequent the sealed library.

I have read the tales, the scattered accounts of the prophecy of the one true queen, of Lady Hevastia's chosen, and I believe. I believe she is out there. Every village we march to, I search for a sign of her.

The men I have followed across the continent and back march and fight because of orders, because their family's livelihood depends on their blind obedience. I will no longer be led astray, I know Hevastia's Light shines on me. She will lead me to the lost princess, our true queen.

Kai's hand on my shoulder brings me out of my thoughts, and back to the present. "Are you ready to lead us into another victory?"

I flash what I hope is a convincing smile, and slide the whetstone along my blade one more time. He reaches out his arm, and I take his forearm in my hand as he pulls me up, and gives my arm one last squeeze.

I can see the excitement, frenzy building in his eyes. Kai delights in our bloody work, and selfishly I wish I could join him in the fervor as I once did. It would be easier if I was ignorant and willing to blindly obey.

"Almost, I just need to pack up my things." His eyebrow twitches, just the slightest, the only sign he will give that he heard me when I know his mind is already in the village, visualizing his glory. I, too, am visualizing myself amongst the thrall of the battle we march to, but in my mind I am practicing how to feign my punches, throw my swings so they glance off bodies rather than cutting through.

That is, if it comes to a fight. I think back to several other villages where the citizens put down their arms once they realized the might of the Haematitian Council was upon their doorstep.

I slide my sword into its scabbard, tucking all of my daggers into their respective places, though I know I will not be throwing them today. It is all for show, I must march in, showing my full strength, and artfully use none of it when "attacking" the villagers. The horn sounds for us to fall into formation. The Council's will must be obeyed. The men chant our credo.

We are the Morei, the Haematitian Council's right arm. No one shall escape our righteous deliverance. Kneel and be saved, for the Council sees all and saves all who need to be cleansed.

Eliana

M Y HEART RACES, BEATING furiously as I sprint to the village as fast as I can. My focus is singular, I can picture her face as I push my body to take just a few more strides. *Just a few more. You're almost there. Don't give up yet. Need to find my mother. Need mom. Mom.*

My lungs threaten to give out before my injured leg does, and I vow that if we see the end of this day I will train harder than I ever have before–I will wake up earlier, I will quit daydreaming and I will commit to my people, to my place at my mother's side.

Tears stream down my face as the gate to our village grows larger. With each passing wheeze of my lungs, I pump my arms and legs harder to keep myself from falling to the ground and passing out. One of my best friends, our apprentice blacksmith, sees me. I can see her eyes register shock at my blood soaked leg and my desperate sprint to the safety of the wall and the gate.

"Naomi... find my ...mother... I must ... tell her ... something ... hurry" I gasp for air between words, trying to project my voice to carry across the light wind that is a permanent part of life in our valley. A gift from the high mountains to have such fresh air.

I relax when she nods and takes off running deeper into the village, disappearing around the corner of a hut.

My knees finally give out as I cross the threshold of the gate. The gravel bites as it digs into my skin but I barely feel it. My heart pounds in my ears, drowning everything else out, and my head feels heavy with exhaustion and blood loss.

Two familiar boots stop in front of my eyes. Strong hands come under my arms and lift me, gently cradling me between two bodies, helping me walk to a bench outside the blacksmith shoppe on the edge of the village.

My mother's worried eyes fill my vision and I suck in a deep breath, holding it for the count of three to calm myself and keep from crying or talking in such a rush she can't understand me. I must remain calm for my people, I must display strength.

"My star, what is the matter? Why are you injured? What happened to you?" The unspoken question of *'Why weren't you safely in the clan's lands?'* hangs silently between us. But it will have to wait.

"Mother, I was out on a walk in the mountain trails when a beast as dark as midnight attacked me. I tried to fight it off, but it caught my leg." Her eyes drift to my injured leg, the blood drying on my pants and boots.

I swallow, take another breath, and continue.

"I fled down the mountain, and I saw—I saw one of the temple guardians that the merchant warned us about. He was wearing a uniform, and he attacked the beast with a large sword. I didn't wait to see who won, I ran here as fast as I could to warn everyone."

"Did you see more than just one man?" My mother asks, no sign of questioning my story, just asking a simple, but weighted question.

"I only saw the one, but he could be scouting ahead of the rest." Fear settles in my chest.

What if he is a sanguinar, a blood mage? We're all in great danger.

Her eyes darken, the only sign that says she believes what I say is true. My shoulders sag in relief, I made it in time. We can escape with our lives, no one knows these mountains like our people do. Like I do.

"I can take us to safety, I know a different way out of the valley, one that is difficult to find if you don't know where it's hidden." I say it with a lot more confidence than I feel inside.

"Naomi, Brynne, gather everyone in the village market. And fetch Pyria. Eliana needs help for her injury."

Naomi leaves, hurrying to find her family and neighbors. Brynne hovers, wanting to say something. She reaches out to me before dropping her hand and following my mother's orders. Her eyes convey everything I need–*I don't want to run, I want to stand and fight.*

I swallow the rising tide of fear churning in my gut. Brynne has always been the most brazen of us, and normally I wouldn't so readily agree with her. But I don't want to hide, I want the Haematitian Council to regret ever entering our hidden sanctuary.

"Thank you, mother." She gives my hand a little squeeze, "Don't thank me yet, my star. We will need to have a talk after I address our people, there is much I must share with you." Her voice is stern, showing only a hint of the storm of concern I imagine is brewing under her skin.

I broke our one law—never leave the village lands. Her lip quivered when she gave me a half-smile and I know she is just as afraid as I am.

Pyria arrives, carrying a small basket of her medicinal herbs and supplies. She kneels down beside me and pulls back the shredded scraps of my pants to see the three, deep gashes left by the monster. She clucks her tongue under her breath, her head giving a little shake.

I wince when she applies the herb paste to my wound, drawing a circle over the gashes—a rune for healing—and wrapping it in *pamu* grass to keep my wounds protected. She mouths a prayer to Lady Hevastia, a healing rite. When she's done she pats my knee, and offers me her hand.

"Thank you, Pyria." She smiles, and helps me limp to the village market, my mother having gone ahead to help the elders and families with children. Pyria lost her voice long before I was born, many of the elders used to tell tales of the village—one was a story of how Pyria and her sister came to lose their voices. I wish I could remember it now, if only out of gratitude for her help. Her story deserves to be written down when I have the chance.

Everyone has gathered, the small village market a swirling sea of colorful fabric humming with the sound of hushed whispers—parents consoling scared children, young warriors conspiring amongst themselves about why we are gathered. All of their whispers stop when they see me. A few even gasp in shock. I catch Brynne's eyes over the sea of our friends and family and she gives me a small, reassuring smile.

When it is time for me to assume the responsibilities of chieftess, my mother will ask me to choose one of the eligible clan warriors as my Champion. The Champion's Rite is a place of honor in the clan as my right hand advisor, and to some chieftesses, a life partner. I have no interest in a partner, but Brynne has been an excellent friend to me, and a fierce protector of our people–she would make a strong Champion.

I smile back at her, hoping it doesn't look too much like a pained grimace, though that is the best I can muster right now. A few knowing elbows are thrown at her from her comrades, playful shoves, and I can see her blush behind her hands. A small blush colors my cheeks as well. I grit my teeth and keep walking to stand beside my mother. Her voice turns everyone's attention back to us at the front of the marketplace.

"Friends, the time we have feared has arrived. Many of you will recall the merchant's warnings from a few days past. His words were not the first signs of the darkness's spread to our village. Our warriors have found signs of monsters prowling in our valley, our crops have been suffering from sickness. This morning, my daughter was attacked by one of the monsters and fought valiantly."

A few faces in the crowd began to gaze back at me with hope despite the somber message, encouraged by my bravery. My mother pauses for a breath, while I hold mine. "A Morei guardian came to her aid, it is unclear why. But we do know that means they are in the mountains. We must leave our lands behind until the threat of the Haematites passes."

At just the mere mention of the Haematitian Council's guardians, fear spreads through our clan. A low murmur ripples through the crowd, a few of the mothers weep, clutching their small children to their chests. Brynne and the other warriors grow restless, one of the older warriors palms a dagger letting it roll in his fingers.

"Everyone, please, I know I dismissed the merchant's claims. In truth, I was blinded by the security we have had for generations, hopeful that the mountain would continue to hide us. But the Haematitian Council is persistent, darkness is spreading, and it will not stop." She pauses for a breath, holding her hand up to silence those in the crowd who are ready to shout. They all take a collective breath, myself included. My mother has a way with the people that I have never been able to replicate.

"We will be fine. We are made of the same essence as the stone and air that guards our valley. We are resilient. We do not bow." My mother places a hand over her heart, and everyone does the same. "Lady Hevastia will protect us."

I place a shaking hand on my mother's arm. "Mother, there's something I need to tell you." She continues to talk, and I hesitate to interrupt her again.

Facing the gathered crowd, I make eye contact with my best friends–Brynne, our fiercest young warrior, a strategist, and Naomi, the blacksmith's apprentice and genius inventor. They both wear the same knowing smirk, and their attitude gives me the confidence I need.

I step past my mother, raising my arm to draw everyone's attention to me. "There's another way." My voice breaks but I press on. "We can fight."

One hundred pairs of eyes are on me as I slowly step forward and face my people, my friends and family, the only world I've known. My mouth dries up, the words are stuck in my throat.

Can everyone see my choking up here, unable to say what must be done, what will destroy our sanctuary?

My mom's heavy hand falls onto my shoulder, her eyes are steady and she gives me the confidence I need. I swallow, gathering just enough spit in my mouth to talk, without it being a whisper carried on the wind.

"We have an advantage, the Morei guardian allowed me to flee and we must not waste that opportunity–we have the knowledge that they are approaching. We will not be caught unaware. We can fortify the village, create a fortress that protects our homeland, our birthright." I pause, taking a deep breath for confidence. "In fact, Naomi, Brynne, and I have already begun preparations for this exact moment–we are not entirely defenseless.

"The walls have already been restructured so that they can topple with the simple pull of a stone. We can construct towers to scout for their arrival, repurpose items in our own homes to be used as weapons with the help of our blacksmiths. Lady Hevastia has gifted us the opportunity to demonstrate her might and strength, if the Haematites want to bring their dark shadow into our land I say we show them the brilliance of our Lady's Light." My voice crescendos as I raise my arms in a battle cry.

My people roar with applause, they stamp their feet and beat their chests, answering my battle call. My mother flinches at the sound but she takes my hand and raises it above our heads. We both wear brave smiles on our faces, and I stand up taller, swallowing down the throbbing ache in my leg.

I will be brave for my people. I repeat this mantra in my head as I walk away from the village market, following my mother to our home.

Her posture is sure and tall, she seems confident in our preparations to fight. As we walk my eyes wander to all of the huts along the road. They all have flower boxes in front of them, sprouting vibrant, hearty mountain lace, our clan symbol. It is a small purple bloom that delights in moonlight, preferring to grow in the dark shaded crevices of the mountain, a guardian of hidden things.

I curse under my breath, realizing I lost my sketchbook in my panicked scuffle with the black beast. It is a petty thing to mourn the loss of something so small, but those sketches are as much of a journal as I would allow myself to keep, the only proof that my adventures outside the village were real, not a figment of my imagination. My snarky side sighs in relief, I can play off to my mom how many times I have broken the law, she need not know it's been happening for months.

We reach our home too quickly, a pit deep and wide forms in my stomach. I embarrassed my mother, and if it were not for the more imminent danger marching toward our lands she would need to address my slight, my abuse of my position and privilege. *I'm sorry* forms on the tip of my tongue, but my mother's expression as she closes the door silences my apology, and extinguishes any argument I could muster. She looks devastated.

"Mother?" I ask, tentatively, like a small child. The gravity of my call to arms slowly seeped into my skin, a rock in my gut. "What is it?"

The storm behind her eyes is roiling, her inner turmoil begging to be unleashed, but she breathes deeply and sighs. "My star, there is so much to say and so little time."

I find the apology in me afterall. "Mother, I'm sorry. I know I messed up, I broke the law, and when we are safe again I will face any punishment you see fit to give me."

She shakes her head at me. "There is nothing to punish. That is not why I must speak with you." She motions to our dining table, the dishes sitting in place, left unused from the breakfast meal she was preparing before I brought panic down on us all. "Sit."

I sit on the chair, taking her hands in my own. "Mother, you're worrying me, what is it?"

She squeezes my hand. "I need to entrust you with something. It has been handed down through the generations of chieftesses. The temple seeks something long thought to be lost, but it has not been lost, merely hidden out of sight, biding its time until needed. Hiding here, in our village." She takes a deep breath. "Our village was chosen for a very special reason, to guard something until the time came for it to be wielded against the darkness, to bring back Lady Hevastia's Light."

"What is it that we protect?"

"We cannot speak of it now, but I promise when the time is right we can discuss it more. You have my word. I need to entrust you with a very special artifact. Do you swear to protect it?"

There is genuine fear in my mother's eyes, but what she says is not making sense. "Of course." The words slip from my mouth, and I can hear the nervousness, the suspicion in my tone.

My mother is normally a very rational, bold woman, molded by her duties and the weight of so many souls resting on her shoulders. She barely tolerated my love of myths and folklore as a child. For her to believe this is true, it must be. There's no way she would participate in any sort of delusion if it meant risking her people.

"You must not open it until you are safely away from here. Do you understand?" I swallow down my questions and nod my head. She stands up, walking to her room, and rummages through an old trunk, returning with a worn piece of parchment tied and sealed closed. "This holds some of the answers to the questions brimming in your eyes, my star. I am sorry we do not have more time."

I give her a small, encouraging smile. "It's okay mother, I will guard this with my life."

"I know you will, Lady Hevastia has gifted you her strength." She pulls me in for a fierce hug, and I fear it may be the last time.

"It seems inappropriate to say, but I am excited to stand by your side in battle. Brynne has a brilliant strategy for defending the gate and concentrating the majority of the battle there. Calculated damage will need to be taken, some buildings will be lost but nothing we can't rebuild before winter, or wait until next spring."

My mother cuts me off with a stern look before sighing deeply. "In any other situation I would be equally proud to have you at my side, but I need you to stay far away from this fight. You must lead the evacuation of our people who are unable to fight, take them somewhere hidden and safe–I know you have found a few of those places outside our lands." She gives me a small, knowing smile.

"How did you–" I ask, my mother's laugh cutting me short.

"A mother always knows her daughter's heart. That is why you must promise me you will obey your chieftess, and lead our people away."

"But mother, what about you? What about the battle? I should be there."

Another stern look passes between us, my mother's eyes burn with a fierceness I have rarely seen. It sends shivers down my arms.

"You need only worry about helping everyone evacuate, okay?" Her words sound so final, like a goodbye. She squeezes my hands again, before ushering me away to pack. I hesitate at the doorway to my bedroom, and see her sharpening her war ax at the table. The deliberate strokes of the whetstone on the blade are methodical. It has been so long since she has needed to use such a daunting weapon. In my training we mainly spar with weighted wooden sticks.

Turning away from my mother, I tighten a fist and vow to keep her safe. My larger leather satchel is far more plain than the one I made for myself this year, a gift for my eighteenth birthday. The parcel from mother lies in the bottom, covered by a new sketchbook, and my spare dagger. I strap my sword to my belt, slip a new throwing dagger into my braid, tuck my favorite dagger in my boot, and wrap myself in a lightweight cloak.

May Lady Hevastia guide my steps, though I walk in darkness, I am never far from Her Light. Bless my blades to smite those that walk in Her shadow.

The marketplace was quiet before, but now it is roaring with noise as everyone regathers. Walking among them, their belongings are tied together with scraps of clothing, some have the packs strapped to their backs, but most have them stacked on the ground, all waiting for me to lead them to safety.

Young children lean against their parents hugging their knees. Murmurs of reassurance ripple through the crowd as parents console their littles ones, and everyone waits with nervous energy.

I hug my satchel a little tighter to my body and give everyone my best smile as I touch those I pass, feeling them lay their hands on me in reverence, as they do my mother. Many smile back, but it never reaches their eyes.

My mother moves through our clan ahead of me, their arms reach out eagerly to touch her and steal comfort from her strength. She walks with an assured purpose, and her steps don't falter. The battle ahead weighs heavily on my mind, I cannot believe it does not weigh on hers.

"Today, some of us will step beyond our sacred clan land for the first time. They leave behind our home, not for forever, but so that they may return when it is safe to do so. Our land will welcome them back, it will not forget the years we have sown into it, the tender care with which we have treated it. Our people are of this mountain, one with this mountain, and it has valiantly protected us for these many years." I pause, my mouth threatening to become dry again. I take three deep breaths, breathing deeply in, holding and then releasing.

"The time has come for us to return the mountain's gift, to protect our land as it has protected us. It is no small task to raise arms in defense of our land, our people." A few in the crowd shake their heads in agreement. Our warriors gaze at me and my mother, resolute in their hearts.

I swallow, a nervous chill running up my spine, and nausea rolling in my stomach. "I humbly ask who of us is willing to fight the Haematites, and allow the rest a chance to escape the Council's long arm of darkness? Who will stand in Hevastia's Light and protect us?

My mother is the first to answer my call, raising her ax above her head. The warriors raise their weapons as well, linking arms with one another. Brynne's eyes shine with tears but she holds her sword proudly above her head. More followed–the blacksmith, his apprentice and my friend, Naomi, our baker and his son, all of the farmers and their many children.

Soon there are almost thirty willing to stand and fight, the remaining seventy of our clan will follow my lead down the mountain and to a cave I found on one of my first hikes many months ago. I thank the stars for that fortune, it is enough space to keep us dry and warm until it is time to return.

I try not to think about what happens after I lead them to the cave. I will not be waiting until the battle is over to return to our village, I will return to fight alongside our people. *Hopefully mother will forgive me for breaking my promise.*

Our remaining clan elder, Mythica, steps forward with a candle and faces our people. "Chieftess Bellaema, Eliana, our guiding star, and our brave warriors and protectors ask for protection and strength from us. Please join me in praying to our Lady Hevastia for sanctuary and deliverance from the darkness that threatens to snuff out our Lady's Light."

"May Lady Hevastia guide my steps, though I walk in darkness, I am never far from Her light. Bless my blades to smite those that walk in Her shadow."

Mythica begins the prayer and soon everyone's voices blend into hers. A deep rumble ripples through our clan and into the hearts of all who promise to stay back, to stand and defend us. Mythica and my mother walk down the line of warriors and volunteers, drawing runes on their faces, arms and chests using red clay and white paste from weeds that grow along the stream.

Each rune is a different element–the two triangles for the mountain's strength and fortitude, the rolling waves of water for endurance and swiftness in battle, the cloud of air for strategy and intelligence, and the sparks of fire for fierceness and power. Before the loss of magic one hundred years ago, these runes would have been more than symbolic, they would have been badges honoring the wearer's real magic, signifying the power of their given element. But there are no longer any blessed among us, just the damned that march to our doorstep.

When the prayer ends, everyone says their goodbyes to their families and loved ones. I ache to say goodbye to my friends, to thank Brynne and Naomi for being so brave, but my mother holds me back.

"That was well said, my star. You will make an impressive leader some day." She pulls me into a tight hug, and her arms tense, hesitant to let me go. "It is time for you to walk a new journey. You will never be far from this land or our people."

I am not sure what she means by that, but a small part of me thinks she knows what I intend. I try not to flinch at her words, opting for a small smile. "Thank you mother, I hope to make you proud." I hug her fiercely and step back, pulling my satchel across my body. "May Hevastia's Light protect you."

I lead everyone out the back of the village and to a small trail tucked between a thick copse of trees. I hold the branches back for everyone to pass, and look back to the village one last time. My mother has gathered our warriors, blacksmiths, and farmers into a tight circle. Her back is to me, but I still give a small wave.

Cire

I BEND DOWN AND see the blood trail pooling in larger drops as the girl slowed down, exhaustion and blood loss threatening to take her down. I lead the regiment deeper into the mountains as they tower over us, casting the trail into an eerie shadow. The path widens and my heart clutches at the site of the beautiful valley that unfolds before me. A golden light shines down catching the mountain breeze rippling through the tall grass as it brushes up against rows of neatly plowed and maintained fields. It's a hidden paradise.

Kai nods his head in approval, his eyes barely registering the view, still only concerned with the looming fight.

"Excellent work, brother. You have made your brother's in blood proud. I will include your invaluable service in my report to the Council."

I clench my fist at the mention of the Council, and the thought of receiving their praise yet again. Kai seeks glory and recognition. He would burn down a hundred villages if it meant any amount of praise from the Council.

The hidden village of Bellamere sits stoically in the distance, a small but foreboding presence that grows larger with each step forward. Surrounding me is the metallic *shing* of swords being drawn, the whisper of arrows being pulled from the quiver and notched, and the steady rhythmic feet of the regiment as they march into battle. I pull Light Breaker from its sheath, Kai mirroring my actions and drawing his dual blades, Virtue and Faith.

The village grows larger as we march up the hill in the center of the valley. We steadily approach the gate, not bothering to hide our advance.

My mind jumps to the girl on the mountain. There is something special about her– she's different, bolder than most girls her age, and with much better aim. I recall the dagger wound I found in the neck of the dark monster. Only a dagger thrown with lethal precision could leave such a clean wound–a reminder that while they may appear to be simple, sheltered mountain folk, I worry my comrades and I will soon find out they are anything but.

As Kai and I near the gate, there's a flash of black hair to my left and unexpectedly the village wall comes tumbling down around us, sending large rocks careening on top of some of the men flanking my left side. The noise of boulders connecting with armor resounds as they crush the first line of guardians. There is a short cry and moans of pain. Kai's grip on his swords tightens, and his face is murderous. He was not anticipating any difficulty, and the rock wall crushing some of our regiment has him on edge.

I pity their deaths, but I am grateful it was quick. The crumbled wall slows us down as we have to pick our way over the rubble, careful to maintain a watchful eye on the village. The shadows of the mountains do not reach into the village, but the high solari in the sky cast dark shadows from the huts.

There's a glimpse of auburn hair and I turn just in time to miss a lump of hot metal being thrown at my face. I drop my body to the ground, the rock wall biting into my knees and hands as they cut on the sharp stone. I hissed in a breath.

The screams of another Morei guardian erupt behind me, his arm hangs limp at his side, the hot metal collided with his shoulder guard fast enough that it broke his shoulder and melted through to leave a nasty burn. More chunks of glowing metal are launched at our tight formation, throwing it into chaos as more guardians are struck by the molten metal, the smell of burning hair and skin in the air.

"Burn this wretched village to the ground." Kai's ferocious bellow carries through our regiment, everyone answering the cry. He sprints deeper into the village to confront whoever is attacking our men. I run in the opposite direction, toward where I saw the auburn-haired girl from the mountain scurry off to. I round the corner of a hut at the edge of the village and go tumbling.

I groan, the ground smacking into my body, knocking the air from my lungs. The prick of a knife is a cold weight against my throat, and when I glance behind me it is the same girl from the mountain. Her auburn hair is pulled into a braid but a few strands have fallen loose and hang across her face, partially blocking her blue eyes.

Stars, she's beautiful. I wish I knew her name.

Her blue eyes harden when she recognizes me, and although she hesitates, she removes the dagger and sheaths it back in her boot. "I suppose I should thank you for warning us."

She holds out her hand, and I take it, letting her pull me to my feet. "What?"

She gives me a cocky half smile. "You let me go, because of that my people were able to prepare. Your men won't be leaving here alive." Her voice is resigned, determined, and a chill spreads down my arms. She is not what I expected her to be.

"Why didn't you?" I mimic slicing my throat.

"And draw your blood? Not a chance. My mother might not believe in the tales but I won't take the chance."

"So you're not going to kill me?" I ask, dumbfounded.

"You saved my life earlier today, consider this the favor returned. If we ever meet again don't expect the same reception." She glares at me, shakes her head, and turns her back to me as she walks along the wall of the hut, toward the center of the village.

I want to offer her some sort of praise on how her clan was able to prepare, but it feels wrong on my tongue. A loud crash sounds from a few huts away and the mountain girl takes off running toward the sound. I grab her wrist and pull her away, but she slips through my grasp forgetting about me in her limping gait toward the smoke and the fighting. Her leg is stained red from an injury.

Blood. If she stumbles into the wrong guardian she will be dead on the spot.

I run after her, and soon the sounds of battle can be heard bouncing off the stone huts sitting innocently around a large town square now turned to ruin in the rubble of the explosion. The burning building was a shrine of some sort. Dried flowers in clay vases and statues of Lady Hevastia, the namesake of our country, the goddess of the Old Ways, are being eaten by the ravenous fire.

She pulls a small sword from its scabbard, climbing into the wreckage, shouting for someone. I hesitate to follow her in, but I don't see anyone else, and she might need help. I catch up to her as she crawls through a small gap between collapsed walls. I can't fit, so I press my ear close to the hole, listening. The stone is warm to the touch. My eyes blink rapidly, trying to adjust to the burn of the smoke clogging the air, making it harder to see and breathe.

Someone beyond the wall chokes on the smoke and ash, their coughing carrying on the soot-coated air. Suddenly a hand is gripping the stone wall. Their knuckles are bloody, and one finger is bent in an unnatural way—if these are their only injuries they are very lucky.

I step back as a different young woman in dented, soot covered armor pulls herself through the hole. She stands to collect her breath until she notices me, and in one smooth motion I am on the ground for the third time today, her fist connecting with my jaw.

"That is for being a filthy *sanguinar*."

She pulls back, her hand going for the sword at her belt before thinking better of it. I notice her armor is too big, hanging awkwardly off her lithe frame, hastily strapped to her with new leather straps against old, dented metal. Encased in the metal sheet she is not an easy target to draw blood from.

Very clever.

I chuckle, unable to hold back the laughter of her insane boldness. "I guess I deserve that." The mountain girl slips through the hole and notices me over her friend's shoulder.

"You're still here." She frowns. She holds out her hand and pulls me up, again.

"I'm not here to fight, I want to help." I take a deep breath. "Call a truce for today, okay? What's happening out there—it isn't right, and I don't want any part in it."

She hesitates, clearly not believing me. There's a battle waging in her mind, her eyes staring off, squinted in concentration before she sighs and waves me to follow her. I stop short when the tip of her dagger pokes into my chest. She gives me a fierce look.

"Don't make me regret this." She grabs her friend's hand. "C'mon, Brynne, we need to help the others."

The girl in armor hesitates, but she follows my mountain girl as we run deeper into the village, the huts covered in thick ash, the smell of smoke and blood thick in the air. Up ahead is the ringing of swords colliding, and I pull ahead of them, motioning for them to stand back.

I peer around the corner and see my brother Kai engaged in a sword fight with a burly man swinging a large sword. The two of them are not the only ones locked in a one on one fight. Our second in command, Borlius, is in a fist fight with a young man, and up ahead a strong, tall woman swings her ax in an impressive duel with our largest fighter, Virstar.

More still are fighting with their magic, drawing power from the blood that runs red across the ground littered with the dead and the injured, who moan in pain. Walls of dirt fly up to defend guardians as the villagers continue to pelt them with molten metal clumps. A scream of agony splits my ears as one of the men manning the catapult is lit on fire by Sefrina, a fire-mage. The blood on her chin glows in the light of the flames. Before another one can take his place she launches another fireball, enveloping the contraption in flames and rendering it useless—the villagers main defense now gone.

Another scream erupts from behind me, and my gut clenches in fear thinking something has happened to the mountain girl.

Turning, her friend locks frantic, panicked eyes with me as Virstar's twin brother, Kristir, slits her throat. My mountain girl screams again, throwing a dagger and hitting home, its blade finding purchase in between Kristir's eyes before he can even summon his magic in defense. He and the warrior girl drop at the same time, their swords clattering on the stone path.

I expect to see fear or remorse in my mountain girl's eyes but there is nothing but brutal, determined rage.

She shoves me aside, adrenaline easing the pain of her injured leg, as she runs to the aid of the woman with the ax. I sprint after her. The other woman lets out a strangled battle cry, as Virstar brings his sword down heavily on the ax, knocking it from her grip.

The auburn haired girl is almost to the other woman when Borlius throws a small ax from his belt at her back. His aim is near perfect with the aid of the air magic he controls, there is no way he could possibly miss.

I conjure a portal in my mind's eye, trying to concentrate on somewhere safe, and when I am sure enough that it will hold, I place it right into her path, she runs through it, not even seeing it, and I snap it closed.

The ax travels through the air where she was moments ago, and sinks deeply into the shoulder of the tall woman. With her ax gone, her sword arm injured, she's not fast enough to draw her sword up to defend herself, and Vristar's falls in one long arc onto her neck.

My yell is guttural, feral as I lunge at Virstar. But my arms catch air, and instead there are arms gripping me as we both tumble into another portal not of my making, carrying us away from the battle.

Kai

MY BLADES CUT THE lowly farmer down with ease, I regret not drawing our little skirmish out more, if only to give myself the practice. The red blood pools below one of my swords before being absorbed. I take a deep breath in and out, basking in the essence of the man I had just slain as it shoots through my body, giving me added strength.

I pivot, searching for my next target, an eighteen year old girl—soft brown skin marred by soot and a bright fire burning in her deep blue eyes.

A stump of metal is grasped in her bleeding hands. The lump is the beginnings of a crude sword, but in an ambush it does better than bare fists. Her horrified eyes lock with mine over the dead man's body, and she screams at me.

I smile, showing my teeth. It must frighten her because she shifts her weight and takes a shaky step backward, into a half crumpled wall, caging herself in. Her hands shake, but she stands her ground, determined to be stupidly brave to the bitter end.

I strike without warning, and she manages to swing her crude weapon up in defense, blocking my blades from kissing her shoulder. My blades dig into the soft metal and one of them sticks. I struggle to pull it free, and in my distraction I catch a boot to my gut.

I scrabble to catch her foot, dropping my free sword. She drops the clump of metal–taking my sword with it–and tackles me to the ground, her fist connecting with my nose. "This is for Borielle, my mentor." Another punch.

Her punches barely sting, but in her rage there is little I can do to fight off her manic attack, alternating between punches and nails raking my face, clawing for my eyes. When I've had enough, and she's effectively worn herself out, I bring my own fist to her temple, knocking her out. She slumps against me and I shove her off, her face scraping in the dirt and crumbled stone shards.

My boot braced against the metal lump, I yank my sword out, gathering the other from the ground, and turn, ready to finish her off. I raise my arm and hesitate as another young girl, not much older than the one at my feet, sprints past me, intent on rescuing the woman locked in battle with Virstar.

Behind the girl, a familiar blonde head dashes behind her, blocking her path from attack, chasing after her. The portal takes shape in front of the girl's path, and I know at that moment that Cire is making a choice that I cannot save him from.

Unless I am fast enough.

Eliana

I OPEN MY EYES to see nothing but green grass. It's a welcome change from the suffocating ash coated air of my village. Reaching out my hands, I touch it, and it's so soft. My heart twists with panic at the thought of my home up in smoke. I clench the grass in my fist.

I blink a few more times, but can't get the throbbing behind my eyes to stop. It's the same feeling I get when I stand up too quickly, and gravity sucks my blood to my feet. The world around me warbles, shadows and colors throw themselves in confusing, disorienting swirls.

Ugh my head hurts. Where am I anyways?

The quiet hum of the wind and the sweet smell of flowers in the air tells me that I'm definitely no longer in the mountains. Covering my eyes with my hand to shield from the blinding light of the solari high in the sky, I see mountains rising far off in the distance.

There's an apple sized lump above my right eye, that sting to the touch. I stand up, dusting myself off.

How did I get here? Where's my mother, my village?

I whirl around, trying to find a sign of anything or anyone familiar, trying to make sense of everything that just happened.

And that's when I spot it. This giant, terrifying monster just twenty feet away. Its fur is matted, and a deep shade of burgundy like no bear I've ever seen. Small spines protrude from its back. It's down on all fours, with its snout rummaging in the grass, making deep rumbling, growling sounds. Through the swaying blades I can see canines the size of my finger, and I do not want to see the rest of its teeth. I bite down hard on the urge to scream.

It hasn't noticed me yet. Lady Hevastia, save me.

I curse myself for losing my sword, the dagger still tucked in my boot is nothing against a beast with a hide so thick. Backing away slowly from the beast, I edge back into the thicket behind me, hoping the additional coverage will make me harder to spot. And that maybe it's too big to fit into the thick brush.

Where even am I, what happened to the village? And what happened to my mom? Oh stars, Brynne.

Tears fall freely down my cheeks as the horror of watching Brynne's throat being slit replays across my mind's eye. Taking three deep, calming breaths, I try centering myself and focus on gathering my surroundings. From my hiding spot I can see an endless sea of rolling grass swaying gently in the breeze. The field is dotted with the most beautiful flowers I've ever seen in hues I cannot name.

It's a beautiful, and peaceful place, aside from the big beast standing so near. But even the beast does not seem all that threatening after observing its continuous snacking on the grass. Way off in the distance I can see what appears to be my small mountain range to my left, and an enormous forest to my right. But there's nowhere to hide in the tall grass except this thicket of thorny flowers.

I curl into a ball. The adrenaline from the fight is wearing off, and every twinge of pain and soreness verberates in my muscles. Hiding in the thicket, there's nothing to distract me. My mind runs through scenarios, trying to determine what choice I made that led me here.

If I had run faster could it have made any difference? What will happen to everyone without me there to guide them? How could I let them down? I promised my mother I would be there for them.

I shudder, trying to block out the smoking rubble of the temple, the crumpled walls of the village gate, the broken flower pots and crooked, kicked in doors of my friends and neighbors huts, and all the ways I led that destruction right to them. The fabric of my pants is scratchy against my forehead, but the small bit of pain is enough distraction from the blackness threatening to swallow me whole.

I replay the day again, and again. My eyes grow weary from seeing the weight of my choices burn into my very soul. I remember the space in front of me shimmering before being sucked away from my mother.

I was so close.

Tears fall down my cheeks, leaving hot trails of shame down my soot-covered skin. In my heart, I know she is gone, that everyone I loved is gone or so far out of reach. I hug my knees tighter. I never should have trusted that guardian. I should have killed him when I had the chance. It's his fault they found us.

It's my fault for not being strong enough to protect my people.

My favorite dagger feels heavy in my hand, its weight a strong reminder of the burden I carry, the wrong I must right. I know when I meet the Haematitian guardian again he will watch me put this dagger between his eyes.

My thumb traces the well worn groove of the blade, my nail catching on each word inscribed in the blade, our clan's prayer.

Bless my blade to smite those that walk in Hevastia' shadow. Blessed is Her messenger, the Guardian of Fate, and the deliverer of Her people.

Mother always said that we were the last of the old faith, our belief was our protection and strength. And, that someday when the time was right, Hevastia would return, born of blood and forged from fire to deliver our cursed land from shadow and restore her glorious light in the hearts of her people and the land.

If that is true, I hope she comes soon, before there is no one worthy of being saved.

The dagger fits snuggly back into my boot. My eyes roam the horizon, but there is nothing except my new friend. The beast seems to be gentle despite its imposing size and spines. I pick a few berries from the bushes around me and crouch low, and unimposing in the grass. I lay the berries one by one in a line, coaxing the large beast toward me. Its nose susses out the sweet treat, and it eagerly lumbers along, sucking down each berry while searching for the next. Soon, it's right in front of me, casting its shadow over me with its large frame. The beast watches my hands patiently, waiting for more berries.

"Patience, friend, there are more where these came from." It huffs at me in agreement, or maybe anticipation. Carefully, I slowly extend my fist, uncurling my fingers to expose three plump berries in my hand. The snuffling of its nose is a low grunt as it hunts out my prize. To my surprise, its nose and tongue are unexpectedly soft and gentle.

"Haha, you're so soft." A laugh escapes my mouth in wonder. The sound momentarily spooks the beast, but it quickly recovers, nudging my shoulder with its giant head for more treats. My outstretched hand hesitates before I ruffle the thick fur on the top of its head right behind its ears, and a deep rumble travels from its throat. I pull my hand back, nervous I upset it, but it places its head back in my hand, so I continue to stroke its fur.

You need a name, friend.

Its eyes peer deep into mine, and I feel like I'm being sucked into the depths of its stare with a sudden pull as if our soul-energies meet and stitch together. It's a feeling unlike anything I've ever experienced. Confused, I continue to pet its head as it lays it softly in my lap, content to be fretted over.

I whisper softly in its ear. "You shall be called Vendeekta for your strength, and your gentle but treacherous nature. And, for the vengeance I wear like armor, and the name written on my own heart and blade."

Another deep grumble ripples from its throat in agreement, and I rest my eyes, safely tucked into the warmth of Vendeekta. The tears fall freely, warming my cheeks and wetting her fur.

I wipe my eyes on my sleeve, sucking in a deep breath. I'm not ready to open my eyes again to a world where my family is lost to me. The sniffling must alert Vendeekta because her large head shifts in my lap, and I stroke her ears. A deep rumble ripples down her throat, and I know she is happy to be comforting me.

I trace a double ended arrow on her forehead, with the symbol for star and bear at either end. It's a very simple rune, but tracing the familiar lines brings me some comfort.

"You and I are bound," I tell her. "No matter where we may roam in this world, we will always be connected to one another. We will always be able to find our way back." I laugh and sniffle again.

Vendeekta nuzzles my hand and I give her an extra good scratch behind her ears. "I will take that as an agreement."

Stretching my arms above my head, I notice that the solari are lower in the sky. It's time to move on and find shelter for the night. Vendeekta rises from the ground and shakes the dust from her thick coat.

"We can leave soon, girl. There's just one more thing I need to do."

Broken twigs bite into my knees as I kneel in the thicket to dig a small hole under the thorn bush. My fingers claw at the packed ground, and soon I have a shallow hole big enough for the blessing ritual.

I painstakingly twist blades of grass into little figurines, knotting the head to hold them tightly in place. Thirty in total.

The small grass figurines shake in my hands as I pick them up one by one. Tears cascade down my face once again as I stare at the likeness of my mother, woven from the prairie grass that dances in the light breeze around me. I painstakingly coiled it to resemble her holding her ax high above her head, the call to arms for the battle still fresh in my mind.

How could that have been just today?

There is a grass effigy for each of my fallen clanspeople, for those I could count as lost and those I can only hope are still alive. An army of thirty small grass people lay at my feet. Tucked at the center of each where a heart would be is a single seed of our clan flower. My fingers shake, and my lip trembles as I am rocked by another wave of grief. I lay each effigy in the shallow hole, taking care to line them up nicely, in neat rows.

"Lady Hevastia I humbly ask that you welcome these warriors into your service. They fought valiantly for your Light and your love. Send them to the Beyond for their hard earned rest that they may revisit our world, once again reborn in your evershining Light."

I sprinkle the loose dirt over the hole, praying the warrior's rite over each as they disappear, secured into their final rest. I can only hope that this will work, that their souls will not wander the world lost and bereft of peace because our people are not there to properly bury their physical vessels. The lone hole I dug sits separate from the rest. Beside it lies another effigy, larger than the rest and crudely made.

"Lady Hevastia, forgive these misbegotten souls that they may find rest in the Beyond."

I lay the effigy of the fallen temple guardians in the hole, one to capture the souls of the many lost, and I bury it like the rest.

I will avenge my people's deaths.

I tuck the promise into my heart, wrap it around my wrists like bracers, and don it like armor.

My people are strong, and resourceful. The mountain cave will provide ample space and shelter for them to ride out this coming winter. They will rebuild stronger than before, rising from the ashes of our warrior's sacrifices.

I know that if I returned now they would weep to see me safe, wrap their love around me and lift me up to lead them. But I failed them, and I can't go back just yet. I cannot return to them without assurances that they will be safe. There is no safety so long as the Temple remains in power.

My mother was a strong chief, her shoes are still too large for me to fill. Better they think I am lost than to face their disappointment. As surely as I wear vengeance like armor, I wear the shame of my mistakes like a shroud I wish to hide under forever.

A gentle nudge sends me out of my thoughts, Vendeekta's warm brown eyes gaze expectantly into mine. It's as if she is saying, *Are you ready yet?*

I glance back one last time as we leave the thicket. My heart warms at the thought that anyone who passes by will wonder how the mountain lace bloomed in a straight line, and while they may not know how it got there, the land will remember my people's sacrifice and keep them safe.

Vendeekta aggressively shoves me from behind, and I stumble as we walk. I step out of her path to give her more space, but she headbutts me again. "What is it?"

Her head tilts in her impatience and she bumps against me again. Her front legs bend down, and she bows. "Are you ... offering to let me ride you?" She huffs in annoyance, as if to say, *Was it not obvious?*

I climb on her back, mindful of a few scars on her shoulders, and tuck myself in along her spines. She shakes a bit and I almost tip off her back. Gently I grip the soft wrinkles of fur on her neck and hold on as she lumbers through the field, cutting through the tall grass easily, and snapping the branches of small bushes like they are nothing.

When I'm comfortable with her gait, I sit up and watch the forest grow larger and the mountains grow smaller. My stomach tightens at the idea of traveling even further from home, but my body hums with excitement at the chance to see more of the world I've been so cut off from.

My hands reach for the solari in the sky, and for a brief moment, I feel completely free.

Cire

M_{Y BODY HITS THE} ground, tumbling hard. I feel the punch of a tree trunk that knocks the air from my chest. Coughing and spitting dirt, I glance up at the tree that stopped my roll. The gnarled limbs and charred bark are unmistakable, I know this tree well.

My muscles tense in fear. I am back to the village of Wildewell. It lies just at the outskirts of the territory surrounding the Aceolevia, the Haematite's Temple. The crunch of another pair of boots on the loose gravel brings dread rising in my gut.

Kai emerges from the remaining wisps of fog by his feet as they are blown away in the breeze. The soft tresses of his mahogany hair are blowing in the breeze, partially obscuring his eyes, but the set of his jaw lets me know he is pissed off.

He clears his throat. "Very odd, I didn't see you much during the battle." His words taunt me. He wants me to explain myself but there are no words I can say that will satisfy him or the Council.

He only waits a few breaths before continuing. He's never been very patient. "Where were you?"

I stand up, my eyes never leaving him, as he paces in front of me. "I was doing the Haematites' bidding, searching for the rumored mage of the village."

His laugh sends a shiver down my spine. "Is that what you would call your actions? I seem to have witnessed something else entirely." He laughs again. "Searching for her, you say?"

He strides closer to me, his rant just getting started. "From where I stood, it seemed like you were helping her. You used the traveler's stone–you let her escape. Why would you do that? What were you thinking?"

His next words are a solemn reminder of how different we have become. "We have orders, Cire. You have duties–to me, to the Council, to the True Faith's cause."

I have a fight of my own brewing. I step closer to him, my chest puffed in anger as I spew words dipped in hatred at his heart.

"You think our 'cause' is noble. It sickens me–it is not noble. Your bloodlust is not noble. It's an obsession that drives you, and would have driven all of our men into early graves. It was only a matter of time."

I wave my arms at the graves peeking through the low hanging mist that clings to our boots, a mournful shroud. "Is this what your ambitions had in store for us?"

"Do not speak of ambition as if you had none of your own." He crosses his arms.

"Do you know what you have done? You swore an oath, you are honor-bound. *You betrayed us*. And for what? A simple girl from the mountains?"

He shakes his head in disappointment, anger rolling off his shoulders as he lists all my "transgressions."

"It's the princess, Atrya." I say it with as much composure as I can. I need Kai to take me seriously. "She's just as we heard her described, don't you remember?"

"You can't be serious?" Kai's eyebrow darts up. "You're throwing your life away, everything we have worked tirelessly for, over a bedtime story? That girl is marked for death, she is the *tithe*." His eyes are twin flames, burning holes into my own. "Her life is no longer her own. She must be dealt with. You saw to that just moments ago when you turned your back on your brothers, on your Morei, and pushed her through the gate. Word will spread that you spared someone, that you ignored the tithe. She must be captured."

I grit my teeth and stand my ground. I will not cower again, I will not follow blindly as he continues to. *If I cannot convince him, I will have to stop him.*

My hand rests on my sword hilt. "There are books that I can show you, to explain to you the signs of *Her* coming. There is a prophecy."

He opens his mouth, but I cut him off with a glare. "You could have left me to die, the honor-bound, loyal 'brother' I've grown alongside would have, if something didn't make you doubt.

"And the only reason you would have doubt is because you saw Her, too. You understand, you just don't want to admit it. You don't want to face your choices." I swallow. "Our choices."

"Cire, honestly. The legends are a farce. A warm thought of the faithless. The work we do to maintain order—that is what is real. All those women were meant for a greater purpose, their sacrifices served the same purpose that we are sworn to.

"Our life, our choices are not our own. Those villagers made their choice when they turned against the True Faith. Their existence cannot be permitted, for as long as they live the plague will spread, and our work will never end. Don't you long for peace?

After everything we have done for the Council, how could you turn your back on our life's work?"

He gestures in the general direction of the Aceolevia Temple. "There is still a chance to redeem yourself and save us both. We must find her, and turn her over to the Council, as we have all the other nameless girls across Hevastia. Then you must beg the Council for mercy."

I shake my head, tightening my grip on the hilt of my sword strapped to my hip. "Never." The word sounds like a growl. "I will never turn her in. If you so much as look at her—I will kill you."

I have known Kai for nearly my entire life, from when we were orphans abandoned by our families to be raised by the Temple. Kai is stoic, headstrong, and very assured. He is never shocked, but my words cause him to stumble as if the pain of my betrayal cuts deeper than any sword ever could.

"What?" he bites out.

"Turning her over is not an option. The Haematites will destroy her, nothing will change and Hevastia will continue to suffer, and we will continue to suffer our miserable, dishonorable existence. Is that what you want?"

His shoulders stiffen. His jaw is tight, his eyes tear into me. "The Council will have your head for this. They will make me watch you suffer and they will torture her for the pleasure of it. How can you ask that of me?"

His question hangs between us, but I have no answer that will satisfy him.

"You cannot return home." He mumbles it to himself, his eyes focused beyond the village and into the hills behind us. He does not mean Wildewell where we have not lived for some years now, but the temple barracks we share with our regiment. The thought twists my gut to see how deeply the Haematites' reach is into my brother's heart.

Kai sighs. "She is your responsibility. I will not follow you down this path, Cire. You're on your own."

"Please, Kai."

"You should probably search for her. When I return to Aceolevia, I will have to tell the High Priestess what happened in Bellamere." His words are clipped, distancing himself from me as he makes his choice. There's a fierce sadness lingering in his eyes. "I can't forsake our oath, not even for you, Cire."

"The Thessimis Fields. She had a drawing of them in her notebook, that's where I sent her." I pull it out of her satchel, and flip through a few of her sketches, my thumb catching on the last drawing she was working on.

The likeness of the Thessimis Fields is unmistaken, and from her view on the mountains she could see the entire plain. I point to the picture.

"She was scouting on the mountain when the dark beast attacked her. That's when I found her notebook."

Kai takes the notebook from me and flips through it himself, landing on a page much farther back in the notebook where an intricate knot is sketched, its loops interlocking with one another so tightly it is difficult to distinguish one from the next. But the depiction is near perfect, it's Hevastia's Heart.

"As if you needed more proof, how could a sheltered girl from the mountains sketch the ruins the Council keeps hidden in the Aceolevia Grand Temple?"

"How do you–" Kai is at a loss for words, he just shakes his head slowly in disbelief. "If she is 'the one' the Council will never let her live, Cire." He hands me back the notebook and walks away, leaving me behind.

I turn to repack my bags, barely hearing Kai's quiet "good luck." Looking back, he's already gone. I sigh and call forth my own portal.As it shimmer into place, a picture of grassy fields dotted with small flowers takes shape in the center. I step through, leaving Wildewell and my life as I've known it, behind.

Stepping out of the portal, I find myself in chest high grass, rolling in the wind that is gently winding its way through the fields having passed through the mountains, traveling from one coast to the other. I'm lost in my thoughts as I search for any sign of her.

She's of the Old Ways. She must know of the prophecy. Right?

I move further into the field, scanning the horizon on either side for a girlish figure cutting a haphazard path in the distance. Behind me is Eternis, but from this distance it's easily mistaken for a small mountain range rather than the ruined city it truly is. To my right are the Hilwe Wildes, an expansive forest covering most of the horizon. Beyond them lie the Dartneau Hills, and the Aceolevia.

Turning to check the skyline, I frown. The day has passed quickly. The solaris are already descending, and it won't be too long before nightfall. While the fields are beautiful in the daylight, the darkness is another thing altogether.

Continuing to survey the horizon and fanning my arms through the tall grass, I'm becoming more desperate to find her and more worried she has gone missing with every passing moment. A shadow passes in the taller grass toward the edge of the field. Taking a few steps back, I reach for my dagger.

I laugh softly to myself. "Training in the temple my entire life, and I'm hiding from a girl."

Chuckling again, I continue to scan the grass surrounding me, my mind traveling back in time. Since birth, Kai and I have been bonded to one another, a promise sealed in our blood and bound onto our souls as a way to connect us to the Aceolevia, our only allegiance.

Kai is my Morei, and I have been training side by side with him and our master for many years. In successful Morei bonds, the efforts of the pair are seamless, and indistinguishable. Balancing our strong personalities and skills made matters difficult for our master since the first day.

We spent much of our childhood on forced bonding outings, being sent on small hunting parties, scouting missions, and errands across the years in 'service to the temple.' It was on one such mission that we encountered a *severn*–a short haired, spotted red beast with wild yellow eyes, fangs as thick as a thumb, and stronger than the mightiest guardian. They were known as the most fearsome creature in the Hilwe Wildes, before the dark beasts began to roam.

Cut off from the rest of our hunting party, we were forced to work together to survive. In the end, our battle against the beast left both of us close to death, and had it not been for the two of us finally working as one, we would have surely been killed.

My gut clenches. While not a perfect partnership, from that day on we have always trusted each other's instincts. The pain of Kai turning his back on me hurts far worse than a deep cut, but I know I've made the right choice. I can't expect him to abandon everything we've been taught so easily.

My attention snaps back to the present, as the sound grows closer. I crouch lower, ready to spring out of the way or onto the beast, depending on what steps through the grass and into my space. My legs buckle from shock as the mountain girl towers over me, resting on the back of a *rabbeon*.

"Thank the stars you're alive."

I tuck my dagger away and push myself up. Even standing, she's several shoulders higher than me, perched on the *rabbeon*. The beast snarls, irritated at my outburst but makes no move to back away.

Stars, she looks beautiful.

Her hair is wild, the wind pulling at the loose tendrils that fell out of her braid, tickling her face in the breeze. Her eyes are momentarily surprised but turn cold within a blink.

A guttural shriek pierces the air and the lithe girl springs from the *rabbeon*'s back, attacking me. In a flash, she has a dagger to my throat and my arms pinned uselessly under her knees. "Monster," she yells in my face.

I did not see this coming.

"Where are they?" The girl is shaking but her grip on the dagger against my throat has not let up. "What did you do?"

The *rabbeon* has not stopped pacing, the agitation apparent in the curled lips, spit and foam dripping down its jaw. I stare at the bear as it draws closer, forgetting momentarily the blade at my neck. She follows my gaze, and the dagger bites a little deeper.

"Don't you even think about hurting her." And then quieter, "You've taken everything from me. You can't have her, too."

Her voice is strangled, and past the anger flushing her face red, is the pain and anguish she's masking. Her hair sticks to her tear stained cheeks, knuckles still tight around the dagger at my throat. The desperation will force her hand, I am sure of it.

"You have my word," I rasp out.

She laughs in my face.

"Worthless," she growls.

The dagger knicks my neck, and I hiss.

"You gave me your word before, and a lot of good it did. She's still gone. They're all gone. And I–" she chokes. "I let it happen."

She shifts her weight, and that's all it takes for me to get an arm free, wrenching the dagger from her hand and throwing it into the tall grass.

I take both of her hands in my own. She overcomes the shock of being bested and struggles against me, trying to wrench her arms free. I punch her injured leg, a low but effective blow, and she screams in agony.

"No, let go of me you monster." Her voice is frantic. Searching wildly, she strains against me to reach the *rabbeon*. She is mumbling something, but I can't make out the words. The *rabbeon* has shifted its focus to me.

The beast shuffles toward us, a low growl echoing in the depths of its throat. I stare into its massive face, locking eyes with it. It curls its lips, massive canines the length of my fingers jutting from the four corners of its mouth, saliva dripping from its large jowls as it shakes its head and continues stalking me.

"Call it off." I turn back to the girl, my grip on her wrists tightening. "Call it off now, I don't want to hurt it."

She snorts, sounding much like the *rabbeon*. "As if you could."

"Why is it listening to you? How is that possible?" My wonderment at her control of the beast momentarily replaces my fear of being eaten.

She shrugs her shoulders and continues to strain against me, throwing her weight around to force me off balance. She kicks me in the shin, and when I grunt in pain, her mouth quirks up with satisfaction. I step a fraction closer to her to maintain my hold on her wrists and that is when her boot connects with my knee with a sickening 'pop.'

Annoyed at her for being unreasonable, and tired of fighting her, I resort to using the little bit of magic I've been granted. I let go of one of her wrists, bringing my hand to her open wound, swiping a finger through her blood. She squirms, trying to claw my hands and pry my fingers off her wrist. I stare into her panicked blue eyes, as she realizes the danger she is now in. I whisper "*Lunka.*" Her body goes slack in my hands, her eyes taking on a far away expression. I check and see, to my relief, the *rabbeon* also slows, eventually settling to the ground in a dream-like trance.

I reach to the back of my belt and pull free a short strip of soft leather. The guilt of using magic on her weighs on me, scrambling my guts like a dagger to the stomach. I gently slip one loop of the leather around her wrist, tightening it just enough that she won't be able to slip them, but not so much that they will hurt.

The spell wears off quickly with so little blood to fuel it, and my meager gifts to boot. But, it was long enough for me to get her under control and hopefully get the chance to apologize and explain myself.

Her crystal blue eyes glare back at me.

"You are not as frightening as you seem to believe you are."
My comment earns another glare from her as she struggles
against the leather bindings.

She scoffs and laughs softly under her breath. "*Ruffira*," she
mutters. The insult stings, but I won't let her know just how
much it gets under my skin.

"You know, that was a favorite dagger of mine."

I chuckle softly. "Yes, I remember it from before." My
comment seems to bring her some satisfaction because she
smirks. A heat creeps up my neck.

"Are you going to kill me?" she asks, very matter of
fact. There is no trace of fear on her face, just grim
determination–like back in the village.

I shake my head, "No. But there are others out there that
will without hesitation. You need to trust me. Please, let me
explain." Off to the side, the *rabbeon* snort and grunt, as if she
is laughing at me.

"Vendeekta." The *rabbeon*'s eyes shift to the girl. "Vendeekta,
rest." The *rabbeon* settles down with a huff, her brown eyes
watching me.

How strange I still do not know her name.

I touched her leg where her wound is continuing to soak her
clothes in blood. "You're rather brave for someone bleeding in
the presence of a Haematite."

Her face pales with understanding before she collects herself
and reschools her features into a scowl. "I'm not afraid of you,
sanguinar."

I don't correct her, she doesn't need to know that I am not considered one. Among the gifted of the Haematites I am as good as giftless. My "talent" is used in other, more sinister ways.

"We got off on the wrong foot. Can we start over?" I pause, taking a breath. "What's your name?" I ask, unable to stop myself and desperate to change the topic.

She hesitates. "It's Eliana. Yours?"

"I'm Cire."

With her wrists secured, she sits with her knees pulled tight to her chest. Where moments before as she threatened to kill me she appeared so strong, she now looks young and afraid.

Eliana.

"My mother–" her voice cracks. "My mother is the chieftess of our clan." There's a weighted pause. "Was the chieftess," she corrects herself.

"I'm sorry for your loss." She flinches at the confirmation of her mother's death. She finally glances at me, tears glistening in her eyes. The weight of her mother's loss, the loss of her clan, weighs heavily on her, that much is easy to see.

"I didn't know temple guardians knew how to apologize. I didn't think they had emotions."

It's my turn to chuckle. "No, they don't. We're mannerless monsters."

She nods, her tone light and teasing. "That's what I thought."

She reaches out a boot and nudges me. "Thank you for not killing me just now." She brings her hand to her throat, pointing to the spot where she nicked mine. "Sorry about your neck."

Reflexively I touch my neck, the knick now scabbed over and dried. Even that little bit of blood in the presence of Kai would have been enough to drop the *rabbeon* and ensure she never stood again. "Want my advice? Don't make a habit of cutting Haematites, it could get you into a lot of trouble. And, you're welcome. I'm sorry I couldn't –" I stop myself, unable to voice my failure, to relive the guilt.

"How did I get here? Why am I here? I need to know why. It's eating at me. I'll be on my way after that." Her eyes scan my face, searching for any sort of clue.

I keep my features plain, unreadable. She's baiting me to see whether I will let her go.

"I can't let you go. Kai knows you've escaped. You're in danger."

"I don't care about the danger, I was in danger in the village too but that didn't stop you or the other Haematites from attacking. I asked you to explain yourself."

"It's not that simple. You don't understand what that means, for him to know about your escape. There's a target on your back now. You shouldn't so easily dismiss him."

A twig snaps somewhere off in the high grass, causing us both to jump at the sound. Her bound hands darted to her boot on reflex.

"I will tell you when you remove that dagger from your boot, and any others hidden on you."

She glares at me in contempt. I smile thinly back at her, hiding the relief that I managed to catch her deceit.

She grunts in frustration as she reaches into her boot and pulls out a beautiful dagger, the hilt engraved with an old prayer. A second comes from within her coat, a third from the belt on her hip. "Fine, that's all of them. I swear it."

I kicked them all away from her, hesitant to throw them into the tall grass as I had before. She watches my every move, her eyes locked onto the ornate dagger from her boot–it must hold special significance for her.

"That's better." I settle down across from her, our legs practically touching. I know it's stupid to sit so close, she's proven many times today that she can take me on and has no qualms about doing so, and even still I know what I am about to say may be shocking, and I selfishly wish that my presence can be of some comfort to her.

"I will explain everything. Just, try to keep an open mind."

She leans in conspiratorially, a glint in her eyes. "This better be worth not killing you over."

Eliana

MY HANDS ARE TANGLED in Vendeekta's fur, combing out the small knots from the bramble she must have stuck her head into, stretching to reach the prized berries. After Cire finished telling me his tale, he moved away from me. I think he's still nervous of Vendeekta.

I glance toward him, and his eyes are focused on the swaying grass, lost in his own thoughts and leaving me to my own musings. My satchel with my daggers and my mother's parting gift is at his feet, out of reach. My wrists ache from the leather binds, even if Cire was surprisingly gentle with them.

That smug ruffira. The leech.

My mother would have blushed at the use of such a nasty word. He used magic on me. My body feels violated with the wrongness of it. I was a fool for drawing his blood. He could have killed me in a blink of an eye.

So, why didn't he?

I study him from where I sit. Cire's blonde hair and soft green eyes make him seem younger than he is. If I had to guess he's only a few years older than me. He's clever to have caught me reaching for my dagger. I curse myself for being so careless.

Why did I hesitate? I owe him nothing but a swift death. Which is generous for the Haematite's crimes against my people, and that of all of Hevastia.

Cire's story is absurd, but his conviction was evident. He claims I am the lost princess of Hevastia, the mythical queen of a forgotten time long-past. As a child, she was one of my favorite characters from the stories my mother would tell to help me fall asleep.

Our clan is of the 'old faith.' We practice incantations, recite old prayers and continue to worship Lady Hevastia, the patron saintess and goddess of our land. Even giftless, we continue the Old Ways in case magic returns when Lady Hevastia delivers us from the evil that devours Her land.

The last princess, Atrya, is a legend, one of many stories told in our clan. Elders like to weave stories for the children of her final stand against the darkness that invaded our land, how she stood for Lady Hevastia's Light. How after, she vanished without a trace.

Mythica especially would spin tales of her fateful return to save us from the evil blight that pervades the land, the evil machinations of the Haematites and the Morei guardians.

Cire is a Haematite, of the 'True Faith' as they call it. The Haematites are monsters, their magic is unnatural. When everyone lost their connection to Lady Hevastia and the wellspring of magic dried up, those that remained with power took control of the land for themselves and formed the formidable Council. They use *blood* to source their magic—it's perverse and disgusting.

A betraying thought whispers across my mind. *At least they have magic.*

Natural magic died 100 years ago, vanished without a trace–it was that very magic that elders in my village and my ancestors, the ancestors of all in Hevastia, were able to harness.

What could it mean that one of the Haematite's most trusted guardians is discussing this openly?

I told him he was absurd, and I threatened to turn him over to the Haematitian Council. I remember how he flinched at the mention of the Council.

If it could save my clan I would venture to the Temple to turn him over. It would be a lot easier on my conscience than killing him myself.

I shudder at the idea of approaching the Grand Temple of my own free will. The merchant, Jasath's, warning circles in my head. The Haematites are not to be trusted. This could be a trick, a way to lure me to the Grand Temple and kill me just as easily as if I had been successfully captured in the village alongside my people.

The loss of my clan is still fresh, and my heart clutches at the thought of my people left alone in the mountains, of those left rotting in the village, lost to us. It feels like a betrayal to admit I hesitated to kill this monster when I first had the chance.

Even now, it would be easy enough to overtake him, and yet I cannot bring myself to do it.

You're a coward, Eliana Bellamere.

Knowing why he saved me seems hardly worth my chance at vengeance. If I ever have the chance to explain myself to the elders, I know they will be ashamed of my actions.

But what if this was the goddess's doing all along?

My mother's final words haunt me. *It is time for you to walk a new journey, you will never be far from this land or our people.*

I think back to all the times an elder spun the tale for us as children. The princess was never spoken of in past-tense, always present, always with reverence. Our clan was of the Old Ways. Our customs are reflective of a time long past. It is all I have ever known.

Very few ever ventured into our mountain valley, the only word of the outside world came from the traveling merchants. They brought with them strange new inventions, confusing tales of the world far beyond our borders. I used to gape at them like they held all the answers in the world, and I realize now they treated at us with a similar curiosity—with the air of *otherness.*

Could what Cire's telling me be true?

The True Faith claims the princess died in the siege 100 years ago like all the rest. No one from the royal family or nobility survived. The Haematitian Council came into power shortly after the siege, claiming divine right, as the only gifted mages remaining. Cire said that in the time since then, the Council has destroyed everything relating to the Old Ways and killed anyone in their way.

My mind wanders to the gift from my mother and her words as she handed it to me just this morning. *"This holds some of the answers to the questions brimming in your eyes, my star, I am sorry we do not have more time."*

What secret was so important she would defend it with her life? And what would she think of me, to know it still ended up in the Haematites' hands?

The crunch of a snapped twig pulls me from my thoughts. Cire stands not too far off, his green eyes glowing in the setting solari's light.

"I thought you might want this back." His outstretched hand holds a familiar worn leather journal. My sketchbook. I snatch it away from him, hungry for the comfort of its soft pages. I flip through the pages, and the smell of fresh mountain breeze mixed with my mother's cooking wafts from the pages.

"Thank you. How did you find this?"

"I retraced your steps on the mountain after slaying the beast. That's... how I found you." He takes the sketchbook back and expertly flips to the back page.

"You opened it?" The irritation is plain in my voice, and he winces.

"It's not like it was hidden. And, it's not a diary."

"You couldn't have known that." I snarl, glaring.

"Call it my lack of manners," he says with an annoying wink. He taps the drawing on the last page. "What is this?"

I shrug my shoulders. "How am I supposed to know? It's just a scribble. It appears in my dreams sometimes." I don't tell him that it has haunted my dreams every night for a year. I blink during the day, and it flashes across my eyelids, branded to them.

"That's not possible–no one has seen this outside of the most trusted Haematites in almost 100 years. It's heavily guarded, and besides you've never left the mountain."

"You don't know for sure that I've never left." I snatched my sketchbook back from him. "I still don't know what it is. I just thought it was pretty." Leaving out the part about the blood and violence that accompany this particular dream.

"This is Hevastia's Heart–the historical source of all magic in Hevastia. It is forbidden knowledge. The only way you would know of it would be to have seen it yourself. And since that could not possibly have been done in this lifetime, perhaps it is possible that you are, in fact, who I claim you to be."

I find myself at a loss for words, not even a witty response on my tongue. My fight is draining from my body, replaced by a spreading dread.

I cannot be who he claims. I'm just me, Eliana.

"I don't want to hurt you. And, I won't turn you over to the Council. But, you have to trust me." Cire peers into my eyes, searching. His green eyes are bright in comparison to the darkening sky above us, small pools reflecting back at me. I am the first to turn away.

"And if I trust you, what then?" I say to the dirt.

"I will take you somewhere safe, to someone who might have more answers." Cire's voice is hopeful, a soft smile on his lips.

"You're not the only one with a target on your back now." Cire says quietly. "I went against the Temple, there's no place for me there anymore. I'm a dead man walking, when the Haematites find me, I face a fate worse than death. I want to help you understand the prophecy and stop the Council.... If you'll let me."

"If I say yes, will you untie my hands?"

Cire laughs, shaking his head. "Not at the risk of a dagger to the face or back." I smile back at him.

I'll let him believe I only had those three daggers. A small, thin blade sits secure in my braid.

"We have to start trusting one another," I say, coyly.

He bends down, taking my wrists gently in his hands, untying the binds. "You're right, let's start here." He drops the leather band to the dirt, not bothering to pick it up. I rub my wrists, sore from the leather wraps, silently grateful he let me go. He leans toward me, extending his arm to help me stand.

As he leans, the package from my mother falls out of the bag, the bundle partially unwrapped. A necklace chain lies in the dirt, the pendant obscured by the cloth it's wrapped in.

My hands shake and I hesitate to touch the chain, but curiosity always gets the better of me. I pinch the chain, and gingerly pull it toward me, revealing a small metal pendant.

I gasp.

"Unbelievable." Cire whispers. "I've found you."

The pendant has the same intricate knot design as my sketch, the familiar loops that haunt me every night. Hevastia's Heart.

Kai

I LEAVE CIRE BEHIND, returning to the mountain village now lying in smoking ruins. The stench of burnt flesh, drying blood, and death hang heavily in the air. I walk slowly, searching for signs of life among the scattered bodies of my fellow Morei guardians, and the clever, wicked villagers.

This battle was the worst my regiment has ever faced, the first time we've received any casualties from a village raid. My gut twists with the knowledge that I will have to explain this disastrous mission to the High Priest and Priestess. They will not be pleased to know they lost twelve good men to 'simple mountain folk.'

I nudge the body of a villager with my boot, and cringe with disgust as its head disconnects from its body and rolls.

How is it possible we cut them down so brutally and yet still lost?

Without the captured 'mage,' and any other survivors, the acolytes will not be able to perform the cleansing ritual, and I may stand to face even worse dangers in the wild forests and plains of Hevastia. If I am permitted to live after this mess.

After wandering the ruins of the battle field and finding no survivors among my men, I begin the gruesome task of dragging their broken bodies out from the rubble.

First, I find Borlius, an ax in his back, his preferred weapon and method, the very instrument of his own ruin. I struggle to pull him from the wreckage, settling for leaving him where he lies. I find five more of my men buried under the wall of the village—a clever defense mechanism.

The magic that swelled within me in the throng of battle has long left me, and dry blood and stale bodies will not aid me in finding renewed strength in my gifts. I kneel to roll another large stone out of my way when movement catches my eye.

I stand slowly, listening, and the faint sound of boots on crushed rock alerts me to someone stalking me from my left.

I draw my swords and turn, shocked to see the same black haired girl I fought before brandishing a large sword, pointed at my chest. Her dark blue eyes are burning, chest heaving as she barely holds the massive weapon out in front of her. Blood crusts her arms, face and braided hair—standing in stark contrast to her cool brown skin, and sapphire blue eyes.

She probably can't even swing that, and her only plan was to catch me unaware.

I sheath my swords, Virtue and Faith, not interested in fighting her even if her death would aid me in restoring my gifts. Cire's accusations of my blood lust and the disgust that twisted his features as he tore me apart nags the back of my mind. The sword falters, but she continues to hold it out, maintaining her distance from me.

"What are you doing with the bodies?" she stutters out, breathing heavily. "Why?" She nods her head toward the pile of bodies stacked on Borlius.

"They have to be cleansed." I grab the sword in my gloved hands and pull it easily out of her own as she stumbles to the ground, landing at my feet. I chuck the great sword away. "It would be wise for you to do the same for your own people, or far worse fates await them than death."

Her shoulders are shaking as tears stream down her face. "Why won't you kill me?"

"Two sets of hands will make for easier work. These bodies must be burned before the black beasts arrive." I bend down so we are eye level.

"I won't do this work alone, so either you help me willingly and keep your life, or I will use your blood to strengthen myself so I may do it alone. Either way, you will help me."

She flinches at my nearness and my threat. Impressively, she pulls herself to her feet, grim determination on her face. "I'm not afraid to die, but I won't let your monstrous hands touch my people another time."

She stalks away from me, bending down near the body of her first clansperson, dragging it out from the rubble and lying it several yards from my own pile. Satisfied with her assistance, I turn my back on her and continue to search for Virstar and Kristir's bodies.

I find Kristir first, his body lying on top of a mound of rubble, not far from where he felled the chieftess of the village clan. After Borlius's ax disarmed her, he made quick work of her and must have found himself swarmed by the remaining villagers who mobbed him in their rage and grief.

Several other bodies lie nearby, deep gashes in them from his great sword. I realize now his sword was the one the girl held against me just moments ago.

I remember tackling Cire before he could take down Kristir, and my body floods with shame. I abandoned my men for him, and yet he still turned his back on me, on our oath.

The sound of footsteps pulls me back to the present, and the smell of smoke and singed metal attack my senses.

"Get out of my way." She growls at me.

I turn and step aside as she pulls a cart up behind me, stopping it just short of the chieftess's body. I can see she has continued to cry, the tear tracks clean through the soot thick on her forehead and cheeks, deep blue eyes bright against the dark stain.

Wanting to give her privacy, I gather Kristir's body on my shoulder and haul him to the pile of my fallen comrades. It takes me another hour before I find Virstar, buried under the body of a young woman donned in old, dented armor.

When I bend down to move her and collect my friend, the village girl is back and she chokes back a sob. "No, no, not Brynne." She bends down, sweeping the blonde girl's hair back from her face, gingerly touching her cheeks.

"Why did you have to be the one to topple the temple? Why were we so foolish? And where is Eliana? I saw the two of you together running from the temple. You would have never left her alone, you were so stupidly in love with her."

I step back, giving her time and space. She carefully, lovingly picks up her friend's body, the last she needed to collect, and places her at the top of the pyre.

I place Virstar at the top of my pile, his heavy body landing with a loud thud.

"I can't believe they're all gone. How could this happen?" she whispers, in shock, standing close to me, momentarily forgetting we are enemies, as she voices my own inner thoughts.

At this moment, I find myself at a crossroads–duty demands I capture her, force her to accompany me to the Temple as the sacrifice to complete the cleansing ritual, but my heart whispers that I should let her go. She's proven herself strong, a fighting spirit, and it feels wrong to cut her down so close to her prime.

Is this guilt I'm feeling?

I shake my head, pressing my fingers to my temple. I can't let this feeling stand, I can't let Cire's words affect me, it will assuredly mean my death, or worse.

She glances at me, and my heart pinches. Fresh tears glisten in her eyes as she hands me a torch. I tear my eyes away from her face, lighting my regiment on fire, the smell of burning flesh stinging my nostrils. I hand her the torch, and her hands shake as she touches the torch to the first body before throwing it onto the pile of her fallen brethren.

Together, we stand and watch the pyres ignite, her cheeks glistening with tears, my own also grow wet–*from the smoke.* We stand in silence, and somehow her presence is comforting. I still have not decided what to do with her when I hear a gurgled choke. I turn to see her choking up blood, a dagger in her gut.

Shocked, I catch her as she falls and she clutches the dagger in place. "Why did you do this?" I whisper, a tear falling down my cheek.

"I won't let you take me like you have the others. I know what you are—" her words are cut off by a choking spasm, blood spurting from her mouth all over my face, her blood coating my hands.

Panic sets in, *I don't know how to save her.*

I wish desperately to ease her pain, she must sense my inner struggle because her blood soaked hand touches mine.

"Thank you for putting them to rest." she whispers, her breath leaving her body as her hand falls limply to the ground.

A sob racks my body, and suddenly, I feel very alone. I hold her to my chest before laying her body between the pyres, and watch the flames lick across her, setting her ablaze with the rest.

It didn't have to end this way.

I stand there alone for some time before stepping through a portal back to the Aceolevia, leaving the hidden village and my own betraying thoughts behind.

Eliana

"Vendeekta has to come with." I argue with Cire, standing next to the *rabbeon*, stroking her fur.

"You can't honestly suggest I sneak a giant bear into the village? Are you insane?" He throws up his hands. "Absolutely not."

I sigh in resignation and tucked my head into Vendeekta's neck, whispering goodbye to her. She nuzzles my shoulder, and I give her one final scratch behind the ear. "We will meet again," I whisper to her. "I promise."

Cire stands to the side, a shimmering orb floating in front of him. He glances back one more time before stepping through. I hesitate, but swallow my fears and follow after him.

Stepping out of the portal, I plow straight into Cire's back. I sidestep to avoid touching him again, and I get my first glimpse at their village.

Huts lay crumbling along the perimeter of the village, moss and wildflowers climb the broken stone and brick, reclaiming them to the wild. Charred beams twist from the rubble like broken bones jutting from a wound, tattered sheets catching in the wind.

Beyond the broken edge of the village, lie newer tiled roofs and chimneys lazily puffing smoke. My stomach growls at the thought of a warm meal.

"What happened here?" Something about it tugs at the back of my mind, unease settles in my gut.

"Wildewell was the first village to be 'saved' by the Temple." Cire's hand forms a fist at his side. "We rebuilt what we could many years ago, but with the recent increased attack from dark beasts or night dwellers, it's hard to keep up with maintaining everything."

Crucias. They attacked their own people? They saw this done to their home and still chose to burn down everyone else's.

I follow behind him as we wind through the village, and I take note of the thick, colorful fabric hung on every home's door. The *rashiki*, tapestry, is very beautiful in its simplicity.

In my village such tapestries are meant to tie you to your family, the colors are bloodline specific with unique imagery interwoven for each member. When a new child is born, the eldest child of the family has the honor of praying over the tapestry and working the needle and thread to add their new member to the family crest. Before magic left, the prayers were meant to divine whether the child was born blessed, gifted.

Somehow I get the feeling they don't mean the same thing here.

We pause in front of a large hut, and I can't help but think the walls of the hut are mesmerizing. The stitching in the tapestry is a deep red with black accents. The pictures are beautiful, with a small fox-like creature chasing a large, imposing bird.

My boots crush the dried grass in front of the doorstep, as I move to enter the hut. Cire flinches at the sound, and places a tentative hand on my shoulder, pulling me away from the door.

"Not this hut."

Soft voices resound behind the doorway, two women deep in a game of clever wordsmithing. Their laughter is light as they trade nonsensical combinations, and again my heart aches knowing I will never laugh like that with my friends again. I back slowly away from the hut, and Cire's relief is evident in his posture. Something about this hut or the people inside makes him tense. Odd then that he chose to walk past it, when from what I've gathered of the village lanes, it would have been easy enough to avoid.

"Why did you stay? After the attack, I mean." I ask the air around me, musing out loud as I peek inside the doorway of another colorful hut just to the side of the red and black one.

"The villagers are resilient, Wildewell was their home, they refused to abandon it. The Aceolevia, Temple of Clarity, lies just north of the village, in the Dartneau Hills. Kai and I would venture down here as children to sneak treats from the market square and to fish with the elders." Cire's voice is wistful, his memory transporting him to a simpler time, a different version of the broken village we now stand in.

We continue walking, and I quicken my pace to match his longer strides, urgency or annoyance carrying him far from the red and black hut and into the far side of the village.

My nose scrunches at the hut we stop in front of as Cire disappears into the darkness beyond the doorway. I step in, pulling back a plain, unadorned cloth at the entrance. All the other huts are so colorful and lively, this one appears forgotten, practically abandoned.

He offers me a seat around the fire pit, bending down to get started on relighting the logs, half burnt from his last visit to this place. Before sitting down I scan the small hut, it is bare except for the fire pit and a few mismatched dishes. There are no sleeping quarters or decorations in sight.

"You don't live here, do you?"

Cire shakes his head, continuing to focus on his fire building. "No, this place is mine in use but not in name, or title. We are not permitted to own anything."

"You can't own anything when you do not own yourself."

He flinches at my words, but doesn't disagree.

"As Morei, we have no need for wants or dreams. Our existence, our sole purpose is to fulfill the Temple's Will." Cire's words ring with regret, and not an edge of malice.

"Why did you become Morei?"

"As children we are trained to be warriors, duty before all else. When selected, you are paired with another guardian, like Kai and me." Cire hands me a cup of water from a small pump in the corner.

I'm annoyed that he did not answer my question directly.

"You mean you are lap dogs for the Council."

He scoffs. I may have been too weak-willed to kill him, but that does not mean I am unable to hurt him in other ways. Words carry meaning, and can cut deeper than any sword. My mother taught me that.

"Don't speak as if you know us, or our circumstances." Cire's response is as sharp as my daggers.

"We have done terrible, unspeakable things in order to survive. Morei have nothing of their own, to go against the Council would be to lose the one thing you possess, a beating heart," he growls.

"Our thoughts, actions, choices, and the clothes on our backs are all granted to us by the Council in exchange for the chance to stay standing to fight one more day. Serve or die. There is no other way."

His eyes bore into my own, down into my gut, my very soul. "We may have ruined your life, but at least you had one in the first place. And if you're who I believe you to be, then your life is no longer your own, and you will learn very quickly what it feels like to put duty before self."

"That was a very moving speech." I sneer at him. "You can't burn down my village and cut down my people like stalks of grain and expect me to pity you. How dare you assume I don't know sacrifice?"

Cire opens his mouth to interrupt me, but I silence him with a glare.

"I went back after my mother sent me away to lead our people to safety. I was supposed to protect them, and I thought I knew better so I went back to turn myself over to you as a prisoner, to spare the bloodshed. It was foolish of me to think it would make a difference." My voice dies out with my confession, tears threaten to build in my eyes.

"My mother sacrificed everything, twenty-nine other souls followed her to their deaths because they believed me when I said we had a fighting chance. My mistake cost my clan so much, their deaths may as well have been by my own hands."

His voice is soft, exhausted. "There is nothing I can do to erase the pain we have caused you, the hurt we inflicted on your people. Me most of all. I want to do better, and I believe that other Morei will want to be better as well. To follow a new order."

"They're not worthy of redemption." I say the words but I don't believe them, I remember my prayer to Lady Hevastia for the lost souls in my village's siege. Tears threaten to spill over onto my cheeks and I avert my eyes. "And, even if I am who you say, I'm not worthy of being followed."

Cire tries to sit down next to me, but I shift closer to the flames. I chanced a glance at him, and the fire cast shadows across his eyes. He reaches a hesitant hand out to me before letting it drop at his side.

"You and I, we want the same outcome–to see the Council on its knees, destroyed." He sighs. "We could be powerful allies, we don't have to be enemies. You are Lady Hevastia's chosen, the lost princess, it's your destiny to restore Hevastia's Light. Let me help you."

I stare into the fire, pretending not to hear his offer. The pain of my people's loss is still too fresh, I can't imagine aligning myself with their murderer.

"I need to collect more firewood."

He leaves the hut, the thick cloth hung in the doorway falls softly closed behind him, catching slightly in the soft breeze whipping through the village.

In the corner sits a stack of logs, and I realize he meant to give me privacy. This small mercy is too much after this awful, horrific day, and I drop my head into my hands and weep.

Kai

T HE CREAK AND GROAN of someone moving on their cot
pulls me from a fitful dream. Sighing, I sit up, swinging my
legs over the side of my uncomfortable bed. I rub the sleep from
my eyes, dragging my hands down my face.

Today, I will have to face the Haematitian Council to answer
for the disaster in the mountains. A 'simple' mission gone horribly
wrong, and as one of the few who survived, it is my duty to account
for the failure of those that were slain.

High Priest Marius is gifted in torture. My skin crawls and
prickles with the dreaded anticipation of it crawling across my skin,
a cold, wet feeling. He's a *sanguinar*, one of the strongest, and
gifted in water magic. It's disgusting what he's learned to do with
it.

They must not find out that Cire is alive, or what he's doing.

I picture him by a fire, the auburn haired girl from the
mountains wrapped in a blanket beside him. Her hair glowing in
the firelight. The flash of the black haired girl from the village,
her blood soaked body burns across my mind. The images flashing
make my stomach turn. The anger at Cire's betrayal quickly climbs

to the surface, finding a home in my gut and warming me as no fire can.

I strap on my boots and shove my arms into my coat. Thoughts of Cire's betrayal and the accompanying anger have fully awakened me, there's no sense trying to fall back asleep. I quietly close the barrack door behind me, cautious to not wake up the other Morei, before sneaking down the hallway and to the gardens outside the Aceolevia.

The light of the lunei shines bright as it descends from the sky, ushering in the three solari that warm the land and bring about the start of a new day.

My first day without my Morei.

"Kai," a soft, surprised voice rises from the darkness over my right shoulder. High Priestess Tallulah strides toward me, her long white robe swishing softly over the stone walkway in the garden.

"High Priestess." I bow my head. "It's always a pleasure to see you."

She smiles, and it lights up her face.

I've never seen her look so normal before.

Her smile almost makes me forget that she is one of the most dangerous council members.

"I was not expecting to see another soul out so late." She eyes me questioningly.

"Or so early, if you ask me." I flash an easy, comfortable smile. The unease of standing so close to her, speaking so informally toward her has a chill rising across my arms and back. I take a step to the side of the path, offering to let her pass me.

She surprises me by offering her arm, a snake-like smile now on her face. It's almost a relief to see the familiar expression, rather than the kind and genuine smile just moments ago. "Walk with me?"

I nod my head, taking her arm in mine as we walk deeper into the gardens that meet the forest and hills which surround the Aceolevia. Her arm is heavy on mine, the thick robes and long trailing sleeves adding tremendous weight to her small frame.

I don't know what kind of *sanguinar* she is. She rarely uses her magic as it is very powerful, and rumored to be quite destructive. The High Priestess oversees the day to day activities of the temple, the High Priest's right hand, and mine and Cire's master.

"I heard from the other Morei that guardians are being dispatched to Sandovell." I say casually. The path she chooses leads us toward the large fountain in the center of the garden.

"Yes, there has been word of a sighting of the *alte vie,* the Old Ways, and it must be crushed." Her words are spoken with finality, it makes my skin crawl. I mask my concern as she turns to face me. "Word has spread that it was spotted in the hidden village?"

"No, it was a false lead." The lie rolls easily off my tongue, and I silently dare her to question me. "We were unable to collect the tithe. An unfortunate loss."

"Without your efforts the plague would have certainly spread. Your conquering of the village's blight is not a loss. We will find the cure in Sandovell, Sefrina is leading that mission."

My body stiffens.

Sefrina is alive? Then this is all a trap, she must have already told the Council everything.

We pass the fountain, the soft light of the lunei casting a beautiful glow across the water as it falls and splashes. My steps falter in my distraction, and I accidentally step on the High Prietess's robes.

"My apologies, your grace." I dip my head in a show of remorse and respect. "I misstepped. Are you alright?"

She clucks her tongue, reminding me of an old friend, but the chiding noise sounds wrong coming from her. "Captain, you seem distracted. Perhaps the meeting with the Council weighs heavily on you?"

"If I may speak freely." She nods her head, approving. "The loss of my men weighs heavily on me. It's as though I failed them."

"I was sorry to hear about Cire." She peeks at me from the corner of her eye, careful over where she places her steps as we leave the well marked path and venture into the lesser maintained corner of the garden. I turn away to keep from showing my unease at being so far from the temple.

"Thank you, High Priestess, it's a shame that he was lost to us. He had so much potential." I keep my tone soft, remorseful.

She chuckles quietly to herself. "It is quite a shame."

Her grip on my arm tightens, my fingers growing numb from her hold on me. She pulls me in front of her, impressive for her small build–I stand a foot taller than her. She gazes at me coldly, her eyes boring into mine.

"That is why you are going to bring him back to us, and the girl, too." She smiles again. "Is that understood?"

I open my mouth to object, to lie once more, but a new sensation washes over my body, it is a coldness like death. *Is this her gift?*

"Are you worried about missing your meeting with the High Council?" She smirks, knowing I am caught in her snare.

"Yes, High Priestess." I swallow. "I am expected to meet with them to debrief the events of the attack on Bellamere, the hidden village."

"I will let High Priest Marius know that we have already spoken. Besides, Sefrina was able to provide a very informative debrief in your absence, Captain." She smiles cruelly. "You won't be missed for a day or so."

The chill has spread to my bones and deep within my chest. I lock eyes with the High Priestess, but she shows no sign of recognizing my pain. "Bring back Cire and the tithe, do not disappoint me."

Do I truly wish to stand beside someone who asks me to deliver my best friend, and Morei partner, to his death? How is it possible I've turned such a blind eye to the cruelty I am party to?

She lets me go, and the darkness and chilling cold recede from my body. I bow at the waist and quickly exit the garden, not looking back.

Cire leaves the hut in the village. I have not been back to Wildewell since I was a young boy, not since I was selected. He walks with his back rigid—he's frustrated.

I rub my arm. The High Priestess's grasp left a bruise that continues to bloom as more time passes. I wish I had more time to explain, but I must be quick. If she discovers that I warned him, there's no telling what punishment might await us both.

"You're still terrible at hiding." Cire glances back at me, a smirk on his face.

"I've gotten better," I mutter.

He snorts and continues walking through the narrow lanes of the village, dark except for a few open windows that spill out light from fires tucked safely within. With the distance between us, and the girl left alone by the fire, Cire is tight and ready to snap.

"High Priestess Tallulah knows you're alive." Cire flinches at the mention of her name, but he keeps walking, not looking back at me. "And she knows about the girl."

"Did she send you?" His voice is casual, but his hand tensed at his side, dangerously near a concealed dagger.

I know where all of them lie hidden on his body having watched him prepare for battle more times than I can count. I know his movements as if they're my own. I understand what he means.

Shame heats my face realizing that Cire thinks so lowly of me, that I would force him to be fed to the wolves.

I did threaten to tell the Haematitian Council about the mountain village massacre, I suppose I've earned his distrust. How could I be so blind to all of these changes in him?

Cire walks to the edge of the village, the ruins giving way to the soft grasses of the outer forest. He squats next to a dried patch of grass, scorched by the fires long past, but never regrown.

"I'll find some firewood for us." I leave Cire to his thoughts, and me to mine.

Late into the night, it's not safe to wander into the forest too far, for dark beasts are rampant in these parts, and other monsters stalk these woods. My boots sink into the soft ground. So soon after a rain it may be hard to find dry logs. I pick up a few that crumble in my hands, the moss and forest reclaiming them.

A haunting melody echoes in the canopy of the trees, the song of a *crost* bird. Its shrill echo ringing through the trees. They're supposed to be a good omen, if you believe the Old Ways's superstitions. It brings a smile to my lips, and my mind travels back to the image of the mountain girl sitting by the fire, wrapped in a blanket. She could probably tell me more about the *crost* bird's legend.

Getting too close to her would be a bad idea.

I finish collecting a few logs dry enough to make a decent fire. When I return, he is standing right where I left him, flipping his dagger in his hand. I drop the bundle in my arms, stacking them. I strike the flint and watch sparks jump across the damp logs several times more, and the sparks finally catch.

"Cire, I think we need to talk." I stand up, staring down at him.

He shifts and places his head in his hands. "You shouldn't have come."

"I couldn't leave you unaware. They will come for you, Cire, you deserved to know that."

"I can't do this alone, Kai. But, you can't continue toeing the line." He looks at me, eyes boring into mine. "So, have you made your choice?"

My stomach turns at the thought of being involved in this madness. The weight of walking away from the only life I've known—no matter how bleak it may be—into the unknown feels like too large a chasm to see across. Its depths promise nothing, no hint of a certain future, and the fear sucks me down into the blackness.

I shake my head, trying to brush away those thoughts. Only one thing is for certain, Cire is my Morei, he's been loyal and fair to me when many other Morei would not have been. He's done everything asked of him, and now he's asking me a simple, weighted question.

"Kai." His voice pulls me back to the present. "Please."

I extend my arm across the fire, the low flames climb just high enough to lick the hairs on my arm. The memory of the village girl with blue eyes and black hair flits across my mind, it's as if I can feel her standing there beside me, a comforting presence. *I'm not alone.* The heat builds, slightly burning, but I don't lower my arm. "Without fail."

Cire's relief is evident on his face, his shoulders relax. He grips my arm in his, holding us in place over the fire, repeating after me. "Without fail."

We shook on our most sacred promise. If Cire is that certain of Eliana and the prophecy, I won't let myself regret my decision. Cire can be trusted.

I pull my arm away. "Did you find her?"

Cire snorts. "I know you have been watching us. It wasn't a coincidence that you happened to arrive at the village as I left for firewood."

I laugh, he's always been able to call my bluffs. "Then let's not pretend there wasn't a large stack of firewood already dry in the hut."

"She needs time, it's been very hard for her." I swallow the lump in my throat at the memory of her slain villagers burning in the pyre. I can't bring myself to tell Cire about the village aftermath, or the girl. Not yet.

I clear my throat, swallowing down the thick emotions that rose in my body at the girl's death. I still see her blood staining my hands. "What is your plan?"

He hesitates to answer, taking a deep breath. "There are few in the village who can be trusted with such knowledge, even fewer who are undeniably loyal to Hevastia and her people and not to the will of the Council. I plan to find Alana and Hama."

"Are you sure that's wise?" I chuckle. "Alana still hasn't forgiven us .. you shouldn't go alone."

Cire frowns and shakes his head. "Kai, you must return to the Aceolevia, tell the High Priestess where to find me. Perhaps we can persuade them to show us both mercy, if not, I have no doubt they will send other Morei to hunt us down. We can't risk someone finding us and exposing the girl."

"That's suicide." I forcibly grab his shoulder, giving it a firm shake. "You can't just hand yourself over. They'll kill you for your defection."

He shakes his head. "No, they won't. You're one of the most powerful *sanguinars* they've seen in years. The thought of keeping you at full power, at their disposal is too good a deal to kill me over, no matter my crime.

"It would take too much time for you to bond with another Morei, it's only because of you that I get to keep my head."

I flinch at the bitterness of his words, the resentment sitting so plainly on his face. It's hard to argue with his logic, but the thought of handing him back over makes me uneasy. "I thought the whole idea was to leave the Council behind?"

"Eliana thinks there's more happening than what the Council has let anyone speak of. I think we need to stay close to them for now, until we can learn what they're up to."

Eliana. So that's her name. It's pretty.

"What about the girl?" I can't bring myself to say her name just yet.

"She has to stay behind. She can't –" He stops himself short.

There's no need to voice the horrors of the prison, the cruel end so many have met at our own blades. Cire must try to block it out of his mind just as I do. Anything to sleep at night.

"She's not ready to face Morei. She believes she is, but I think her grief is blinding her to the very real dangers."

I smother the remnants of our fire and trail Cire back into the village, splitting ways a few lanes from the hut he's taken shelter in. I recognize it as the cabin we used to stay in as children before we became Morei. Even after, Cire had more freedom than I did, less expectations.

I step in, seeing Eliana curled tightly in a ball by the fire, fast asleep. I shake out a thick blanket from a chest along the wall and drape it gently over her.

We can't risk her waking up. And selfishly, I am not ready to face her accusations. No matter how justified they may be.

I search cabinets, and sigh with relief when I find some dried nala petals. Crushing them in my palm, I rub my thumb across my palm smudging the powder. I kneel down in front of her and gingerly reach out a hand to smear the crushed petals across her soft lips. *There, now she won't wake up for several more hours.*

I remember Hama making this paste for Cire as a child when he had trouble falling asleep. Hopefully I didn't use too much. A half hour passes, and the curtain over the entrance is pulled back, revealing two hooded figures entering before Cire. I take a deep breath preparing for the worst.

"It's been too long." I close my eyes and brace myself for a sharp tongue to punish me for my stupidity, for our absence. But I am surprised when I feel their strong arms embracing me, Hama's small frame shaking with the force of their silent tears.

"You are a fool for being gone so long, but I am so happy to see you both." Alana says, still holding me tight. "Do not ever disobey me again, I mean it this time."

Relieving me from their arms, I make eye contact with Cire across the room, and he joins me around the fire as I motion for Alana and Hama to sit.

Many hours pass, well into when the first solaris has begun to rise, when Cire and I finish telling Alana and Hama of our travels across Hevastia, the secret village hidden in the mountains, and the secret Cire brought back with him to Wildewell.

When Cire and I explain the horrific things we witnessed and took part in, Hama silently weeps into their hands, murmuring prayers under their breath. I flinch away, the fresh shame of our actions urging me to close off and hide. Cire's strong hand lands on my shoulder, letting me know he also carries that burden.

Alana and Hama's disbelief was so thick you could slice it with a dagger. Alana insisted on seeing the pendant for herself. Cire and her quietly argued over touching Eliana for fear she would wake up, even with the nala petals. Eliana lay asleep beside the fire unaware of the eyes assessing her intently.

"What do you want us to do?" Alana asks, her eyes never leaving Eliana.

"Keep her safe. Train her if you can." Cire says. "She is wicked good with a throwing dagger, but she will need more than that to aid her in whatever is to come."

Alana chuckles. "Are you preparing her for battle? Against the Haematites?"

"If it comes to that, then yes." Cire sighs heavily. "We have no idea what we all may face on this path, preparation is the only way."

Eliana is still just a girl of eighteen, hardly a warrior.

"It's wise to do everything we can to ensure she can protect herself. But, we also need to educate her, and ourselves. None of us truly knows what is happening, what to expect. We need to know more about her and the prophecy."

"I think I may have something that can be of assistance." Hama offers meekly, their eyes cast at our boots, unable to meet our eyes after hearing the atrocities we took part in.

"When the Temple came to Wildewell, I hid something away in the forest. When the solari rise in the sky, I will retrieve it."

"It may hold some of the answers to our questions." Alana takes Hama's hand. "We'll return in the morning." Alana and Hama gather their cloaks and step outside the hut, off to retrieve the artifact Hama has hidden away.

As we watch them wind down the path leading to their own hut, I ask Cire, "Do you think they can be trusted?"

"Yes, there is no doubt in my mind. Alana and Hama are faithful servants of the Old Ways and to Lady Hevastia. They will serve well as Eliana's guardians in our absence."

Eliana

S OME TIME LATER, I wake to see the fire has died to a small,
pulsing heat instead of the high flames it was before. I stretch
closer, warming my hands. Small carvings glimmer in the wood
licked by the dying flames. My fingers trace over the familiar
symbols, a prayer from the old teachings, one I am familiar with.

There is promise in the Light.

I recite the prayer again.

Cire has not returned, and I am alone. My eyes feel heavy and
soon I drift off back to sleep.

When I awake next, the fire has fresh logs, and Cire is asleep, his
head peeking out from under thick blankets like the one draped
over me. I touch the cloth gingerly, grateful for the kind gesture.

My boots scrape the ground as I stand, and Cire shifts in
his sleep. I step closer to the fire, drawing the blanket over my
shoulders and stare into the dancing flames. My reflection stares
back at me from the embers, and I freeze, panic surging through
my body.

No, not my reflection, someone else.

The face in the flames has the same facial structure as me, but
her eyes are bigger, her mouth less full. I blink rapidly and glance
back, relieved to no longer see anything in the embers.

Sleep is hard to come by afterwards, flashes of the familiar symbol of Hevastia's Heart disturb all my dreams. The last dream was the most vivid, and even now with the morning light warming my face I am chilled to the bone.

I was in a village, or what remained of one. At my feet there was an old woman, much like the elders of my clan, though I could not place her face.

Her body was broken, her forehead crying blood as she clasped my hand in hers, the rags on her body turning redder. She gazed up to me pleading with her eyes to see her and to listen. She insisted that I run, escape, that someone or something would come for me if I did not run.

"Vaiccar" was coming for me, and in my nightmare my body turned to ice in fear.

I ran from the dying woman, my heart hurting for her and my lungs burning from the smell of sulfur and copper in the air. The streets were littered with building debris-wooden beams splintered on the ground or hanging from half fallen walls, colorful fabric flapping solemnly in the chilling breeze.

I run fast, faster, refusing to focus on the other forms collapsed on the street. I cannot think of them. There are just too many.

I never told my mother of these night terrors, and now I long for nothing more than to be curled in her arms, comforted by her strength.

I wake once more, and pull the blanket tighter around my shoulders and wait.

Cire sleeps, his own dreams fitful and disturbing. He sleeps with his dagger clutched to his chest. At one point in the night he cries out for someone named Kai, sounding more desperate than I knew a man could be.

I recite the prayer from last night, silently begging Lady Hevastia for a sign. With every minute I awake into the second day without my mother, my will to live shrivels up, warring with my desire for vengeance against her murderer. I see only these two paths, and neither feels right. I'm unwhole, my entire world off balance.

Closing my eyes I envision my mother, and the clan elders.

They are smiling at me, it is a memory of my naming ceremony five years ago. My mother is wearing the ceremonial headdress and robes, the elders each wearing a different stoll for the elements–red for fire, green for earth, blue for water, yellow for air, and purple for soul. The ceremonial robes are like a rainbow, celebrating all of Lady Hevastia's gifts to us, and the gifts with which we bestow upon Her in our humble service.

My white shift catches in the breeze, which pulls at my loose braid, auburn hair whipping across my face. The goosebumps of excitement rush over my arms all over again, the anticipation growing in my heart.

My mother turns to face me, her smile wide and her eyes alight with excitement and pride. She reaches for my hands, and they seem so small in hers, I can feel the rough calluses from her sword training and years of hard work on the land. I smile up at her, and bow my head to receive my blessing.

"Lady Hevastia, bless this favored child that she may walk in the path of your evershining Light. Born of your blood and forged from fire, arisen from the ashes of the past, guide her to deliver our cursed land from shadow and restore your glorious Light to the Heart."

"I now declare in front of our people, and Lady Hevastia, herself, that henceforth you shall be known as Eliana, Guardian of Fate."

I open my eyes to the solari's warmth against my skin, my thoughts spiraling.

Cire stands in the entrance, watching me, his eyes mixed with sadness and something like hope.

Memories of the day before come to me like arrows hitting me in the chest with the fresh pain of loss, and the guilt of abandoning my people.

Just as he turns to walk toward me, there's a loud pounding on the wall of the hut. His shoulders tense, and he reaches quickly for the sword strapped to his side. His unease fills my stomach with dread.

My boots slip on easily despite my shaky fingers. I have to tie my right boot tighter, the absence of my daggers more painfully obvious than before.

Is it worth asking for them back? I want him dead, I think, but at my own hands, and being defenseless is not good for me either.

"I'm more helpful to you armed." I whisper, my voice nearly a hiss. "I can help."

The breeze shifts the cloth obscuring the window, I can make out the large shapes of two men, standing side by side. Another bang disturbs the settled dust in the rafters of the hut, and it rains down on us.

Fearfully I whisper, "Cire, what is going on? Who are those guys?"

"I would presume they are the Council's messengers, someone must have seen us enter the village and reported us to the Council." I jump, at the sound of a second man's voice from behind me. The stranger's voice has an uneasy edge to it. He emerges from the shadows of the hut, dressed in all black.

A sanguinar.

If I thought Cire was a *sanguinar* before, I was wrong. The man standing in front of me, head to toe in black, with the same fierceness of a *laseron*, is clearly powerful with dark magic.

I stare open mouthed with shock at the monster that strode into the morning light. The stranger's face is sharp angles and creased brows, the face of someone not akin to smiling often–or ever. His dark hair hangs in unruly curls that fall into his dark brown, cold eyes.

The reality that I am less than a day's hike from the Grand High Temple and the Council sends chills down my spine. The faceless demons that have destroyed Hevastia are dangerously close, leaving me feeling trapped.

I will continue to play along with Cire's misbegotten beliefs that I am the lost princess. Anything that will get me closer to the Temple, closer to making those responsible pay for the deaths of my family.

As the figures turn to leave, the stranger strides past me without a second glance, slips his head out the door and plucks a letter nailed into the door frame. Turning back to me and Cire, he reads it out loud: "Brothers Kai and Cire, your presence is requested immediately at the Aceolevia, Temple of Clarity. Signed, High Priestess Tallulah."

So he's Kai, the one from Cire's dream—he's not what I expected.

"Eliana, this is Kai. He's my Morei partner." Cire says stiffly. "Kai, this is the lost heir of Lady Hevastia, the prophesied princess, Eliana."

Kai gazes unabashedly into my eyes, not blinking. I feel too seen, like I am staring into the eyes of a deadly predator, and I suppose that is what he is. I will myself to stare back, to not break first.

Cire clears his throat, pulling Kai's attention away from me. I sigh inwardly with relief, my chest swelling with a small bit of pride for standing before this monster, unflinching.

My fingers itch for my daggers, but they're still tucked away, out of my reach. To face the *sanguinar* head on is too much of a risk, I have no idea what he may be capable of.

I remember Cire dropping me to the ground momentarily with a single drop of my blood. I suddenly become more aware of my injuries, how weak I am from blood loss and poor sleep.

Cire motions for us to sit by the fire. "Eliana, do you believe me? That you're the lost princess?"

I start to lie, but my tongue is suddenly dry, the lie no longer forming easily on my tongue after my nightmare last night. I opt for a nod of the head, which seems to satisfy them both.

I shiver.

It was only a dream, you're still Eliana. Uncover the truth of the 'prophecy,' live another day, decide what to do after you know more.

I recite the mantra in my head, wanting to believe it is as simple as that. But, I fear it is becoming far more complicated. I settle closer to the fire, hugging myself for warmth against the morning chill as much as for comfort.

"I explained to Kai your depictions of Hevastia's Heart, it's still a mystery why you know what it is but not about your part in the prophecy. Or your past as the princess, Atrya."

"So, what happened to her?" Kai asks. "Why is Atrya important?"

"You really don't know?" I can't hide the disbelief in my voice. Kai's face is awash with shame for asking, but underneath I sense he is eager to understand.

"I'll admit that I never thought to question what we were told. I chose to believe the True Faith's teachings, and that we were doing what was best for our people, that the loss of a few meant the strength and safety of the many." Kai's eyes are heavy with regret. "I realize now how naive that was."

I scrutinize Cire, daring him to explain his own ignorance. "The Temple has a library full of old texts, some of them about the Great War, others about the Old Ways. All of it is forbidden to be read. I used to sneak into the library to escape from sparring with the other Morei. I read a few of the books, they're the reason I began to question the True Faith."

Kai's surprised by Cire's confession, and even more ashamed of his own actions. The urge to pity them sneaks up on me, but I swallow it down and lock it away. They deserve none of my kindness, even if I do need their help.

"Mother said that when the corruption within the Temple was discovered, they attacked the king and queen, and decimated the royal court. No one survived. Magic was said to have died that day.

"The elders of my clan that remember magic, remember the rightness, the wholeness of it, used to whisper that they could feel the wall keeping it from their grasp. They believed there's something blocking our connection to Lady Hevastia."

I wait for Kai or Cire to react. Their faces give away nothing, and I worry I said too much. I dare to say the final accusation that has been burned into my very being. The reason for all the hatred and fear.

"You fight to maintain a system that is purposefully broken—you protect murderers. Worse yet, you participate in them under the guise of 'protection.'" I spit out the word, fury building in my gut.

"The Haematitian Council was formed to restore Hevastia after the Great War. Somehow, they must have found a way to break our connection. Or they simply chose to never repair it. And now without magic, the darkness and the corruption have not been kept at bay, it will consume all of Hevastia without our Ladyship's Light to fight it."

"All this time, we thought we were fighting to restore our strength and rid Hevastia of the dark plague. The Haematites said the cure to the plague was hidden in one of the villages, that was the reason for the tithes–the sacrifices. They were just using us to keep everyone in line." Kai's voice breaks, utterly defeated.

Cire nods his head in agreement with Kai.

They may not know much about the Council's true intentions or inner workings, but they know about their own life there. Anything they can share may help me later.

"How did you end up with the Haematites? What made you choose this life?"

Kai shakes his head. "It was chosen for us. Our parents gave us to the Council as infants. We were raised by priestesses in the orphanage alongside other Morei."

"I just can't believe someone would give away their baby like that. Were they able to visit you?" I ask, hopeful. I lean forward searching their faces through the fire's glow, my heart aching for a loss they don't even feel.

"We are not permitted to have any knowledge of our parentage. We were raised to be one with the Temple and outside distractions at such crucial years in our lives would have risked our unfettered loyalty."

"They manipulated you into becoming what you are," I say, remorseful.

Kai flinches, and Cire's eye twitches. They may understand that they've been lied to their whole life, but listening to me, they are fighting every instinct in order not to defend the Council and fight me.

Kai gives Cire a look, and shakes off the jab. He's much more easy going than I expected, but Cire seems stiff and distant in his presence.

"We should really go, Kai. The Haematitian Council will not accept being kept waiting for much longer. This delay is only going to urge them to probe further into our unexplained absence."

"You're leaving?" I ask, incredulous. "Just like that?"

"We have no choice, we've been summoned. They know we're here and they know about you escaping." Cire says. Tension coils in his neck, a muscle in his jaw ticking with the growing frustration at having to explain himself to me. "You have to stay hidden, here, where it's safe. I can't let you fall into the Council's hands."

I don't want to, but I ask, "What happens if they find me?"

"Like Cire said, it's better if they don't. Just ... try to keep a low profile." Kai gazes apologetically at me.

I smirk at him. "Easy, I'll just sit right here until you get back." I pat the log I am perched on, the picture of innocence.

This time Kai smiles for real. "You're going to be trouble, I can tell." He steps forward, holding something in his hand. He flips the dagger in his palm and extends it to me. "I believe this is yours."

Sure enough my dagger is resting in his hand, the inscribed hilt glinting in the firelight.

"Thank you, Kai." I take my dagger and tuck it safely back in my boot. "Can I have my satchel and other daggers back?"

Kai tosses me my satchel. I immediately opened it to check for my other daggers and my sketchbook, all of it nestled safely inside. I slip it over my shoulder and feel myself relax into its familiar weight.

"Let's go, Kai." Cire growls out, yanking Kai's arm toward the door. He glances back at me. "Stay here, please."

I smile sweetly at them both. "I wouldn't dream of leaving."

Cire frowns, and Kai smirks at my joke.

"Good bye, Eliana." Cire's jaw is tight, the muscle sticking out.

Going back to the Temple has him on edge, and for a brief moment I worry whether they will truly come back.

I shake off the concern, with or without them I will get the answers I seek or I will force them straight from the High Priest's mouth. I remind myself that I only need Kai and Cire to make it easier, that it's not impossible without them.

I close my sketch book, my new drawing of Vendeekta's soft, warm eyes staring back at me. I miss the silly bear, her presence would be a real comfort right now.

Three hours, as best as I can guess, have passed since they left for the Temple. I have paced the doorway of their hut, straining my ears for any sign of someone coming down the path.

In an effort to distract myself from the growing unease in my gut, I explore the hut. As I open the pantry drawers in the kitchen area, I find a variety of dried or rotten vegetables I can't identify, and some wicked daggers. Further exploration in the hours that follow uncover hidden weapons all over their hut.

After spending the greater part of the day poking through their things, I have a count of thirteen daggers of varying size and style, six swords, two of which have matching blades and hilts, and two sets of bow and quiver. What I can't seem to find is any sort of keepsakes, they have nothing of any emotional value, everything is practical and serves one purpose, to inflict pain. Surveying the pile in front of me, pity swells in my chest at seeing how empty and lonely their lives must be. No one to come back to or fight for, nothing to call their own.

Peeking out the crack between the entrance to the hut and the post, I can see it is getting dark outside again, and I wonder when Kai and Cire will return. I find myself annoyed that I kept my word and did not immediately leave. Even greater shame washes over me with the knowledge that the reason I remained in the hut all day was out of fear of leaving and facing potential dangers alone.

Have I trained for nothing? How can I be so strong of body and yet so weak of soul?

A chill settles over my skin as the three solari of Odora sink below the horizon. I turn my back to the entrance and settle on trying to get the fire going.

I think back to when it was me and my mother in the valley, her trying to teach me basic survival skills, how she showed me to strike stones to create sparks. I was seven years old, and we spent the night under the stars making up silly stories, whittling small figurines out of the spare logs. I settle down by the fire, my hands tucked under my head and my thoughts drifting back to a better time.

I reach into my satchel and pull out my sketchbook. The wrapping from the medallion now hanging around my neck falls out, nearly landing in the fire. The glow of the flames dances over the parchment and in the light faint writing appears on the inner lining of the parchment wrapping. I would recognize that handwriting anywhere. My heart squeezes tightly.

With shaky fingers, I gingerly pick at the seal of the parchment, careful not to tear the paper. The wrapping unfolds easily in my hands, and reveals it is actually pages of letters held together by the wax.

Tears spring to my eyes, my vision swimming with my mother's purposeful script, each letter lined up in precise rows like the fence posts around our village, the bricks of our hut. Everything had an organized place in her life, even her words were carefully chosen.

I set the stack of papers aside, holding just the top letter in my hands and shifting closer to the fire, the light illuminating the letter and making the words seem to jump right off the page.

Eliana,

My star, if you are reading this it can only mean that I am not able to tell you these things myself. For that, please know I am deeply sorry. These letters hold great purpose, the responsibility I pass on to you is not light, but I am confident you will carry it with dignity and strength. You have always been braver than I.

This is the only letter I leave you, the rest are from our previous chieftess, your grandmother, Sarlaine. What is detailed in those letters is the reason our people lived in isolation, a question I know has burned in your heart your whole life.

I gave you the best life I could, I only wish I could have filled it with adventure, or joined you on the one you're on now. I imagine it will be epic, my star.

Our people were tasked with an incredible responsibility by Lady Hevastia. Our village was chosen as the guardians of the next reincarnation of her ladyships' essence. This may not mean anything to you, or as I imagine, you may have already begun to put together the pieces.

The legends are true, Lady Hevastia will return, just not as we imagine her to be.

A seer of a Keladoneon clan predicted her next reincarnation would be a girl born into our village. That was when your great grandmother was a girl not much younger than you.

We have been waiting for a sign that Lady Hevastia was walking among us for three generations. I have begun to fear it is a lost hope. The seer could have been wrong, maybe she sold our ancestor what she wanted to hear.

Your grandmother's letters contain a more detailed account of the prophecy and the reincarnation's role in restoring balance.

I fear too much time has passed since the last reincarnation, princess Atrya, was on Hevastia. The magic has grown too weak. You were right to question everything beyond our valley, to fear the Temple and their influence.

I protected you for selfish reasons, because I love you and because of this burden I now pass on to you.

Perhaps if you are reading this, all is not lost, and if luck is on our side, then maybe you're not alone and someone can help you carry this knowledge. Seek out answers pertaining to her ladyship's reincarnation, and what is required to fulfill the prophecy and restore balance to Hevastia.

I believe in you, my guiding light, my star. I only wish I could be there with you. Be brave, sweet girl.

With love,

Mother

Tears prick the corner of my eyes and I am powerless to stop them from falling freely. Careful not to let my tears ruin the letter, I fold it carefully and tuck it between the pages of my sketchbook. The other letters from my grandmother, the third chieftess of our clan, sit on top of my satchel, beckoning.

Mother knew all along. I run through the names of the other girls in the village around my age and I can only think of my friends, Naomi and Brynne. The pain of losing them rushes into my heart, leaving my body feeling heavy.

Who else in the village knew our true purpose for being secluded? Could one of the elders help explain this all to me? Do I risk returning home?

So many questions swirl in my brain, with no clear path to getting answers and understanding what or who I am. But, there is a sense of relief knowing I am still myself, Cire and Kai are wrong–I am not literally the princess. She must have been a reincarnation as well.

Am I only receiving these visions because I possess the knowledge of Lady Hevastia's reincarnations, or is it because I am the next vessel?

It hurts to think deeply on these thoughts, my mind's eye continues to flash horrific images of my friends slaughtered in front of me, while I am powerless to help them. The guilt creeps back in, weighing on my tired body and soul.

I fold my legs to my chest and hug myself tightly, trying to press out the bad thoughts and self doubt. Their weight digs under my skin and settles into my bones.

I have been a burden on our village, on my mother, and now potentially all of Hevastia. My people were wrong to keep this knowledge hidden, what if in doing so we severed any chance of connecting to Hevastia's Heart and the magic necessary to bring about her next reincarnation?

What if now it will never happen because too much time has passed? What if I am not strong enough? What if I am only meant to be the guide and protector, and the reincarnation died in the village fire? What if it was Brynne or Naomi? Or someone lost in the mountains after I abandoned them?

I squeeze my eyes shut, bringing my fists to either side of my head, applying pressure to stop the swelling wave of what ifs and fear that threatens to overtake me. Those thoughts are not helpful, they will not serve me, only bring me down. I rock back and forth, muttering an old prayer my mother would whisper to me late at night when the night terrors became too much, or a storm threatened to blow the roof off of our home.

"There is promise in the Light. A new day springs forth a well of new opportunities if only one is brave enough to see themselves through the darkness. Hold fast to your light, it is the fire that will cleanse and deliver us from the darkness." I repeat it several times to myself, taking calming breaths with each iteration.

Did mother say my light or Lady Hevastia's Light? I strain to recall the wording my mother used, her voice is a whisper across my mind that is too faint to hear.

The fire has died down low again, and the chill of the evening air pulls me from my thoughts. A quick glance outside confirms that the day has passed, and potentially my opportunity to escape.

Staying may mean the death of me, if I am discovered, but a night alone in unfamiliar wilderness with the beasts of the forest and the dark monsters that now prowl everywhere feels most certainly like a death sentence.

I pull my grandmother's letters from my satchel, the crackle and pop of the logs in the fire causes me to jump, my body humming with frantic energy as I unfold the first letter and settle into the fire's warmth and glow.

Journal,

The Keladoneon clan elder visited again today. My mother continues to meet with her privately in the new temple. Today is the fourth meeting in as many days.

I grow agitated that mother is shutting me out from these discussions. Affairs that impact our clan are part of my responsibilities as future chieftess, but I am also our recorder, I should be there to record. As is my duty and my right.

Mother caught me spying on her yesterday from outside the temple window. I have been banned from the village center and confined to my room at home. How undignified.

Mother's voice is in my head, I am being prideful, again. Well, if pride is a trait undeserving of a leader then maybe I am not fit to lead. Though I desperately want to. How I long to improve our people's lives through my ideas. We could expand our great claim on this mountain valley, making the whole of the range our domain.

Noellia thinks I am being rash. She also thinks I am too prideful, too headstrong. But I know that she secretly delights in my ideas, they excite her too. There is so much promise in what we can accomplish together, for our people.

This planting season has been bleak, poor weather and mysterious blights cause many issues. We struggle to harvest enough grain to prepare for the colder season that will soon be upon us. The Keladoneon clan's presence puts an even further strain on our dwindling resources.

The elders and mother believe that the new temple to Lady Hevastia will please her Ladyship, and she will grant us a bountiful fall harvest.

Noellia and I have our own ideas on how we can improve our harvests, among other needs. Our blacksmith is currently helping me to create a tool to aid in the planting and harvesting of grains and vegetables.

Noellia is writing a guide on mountain plants so that our people can safely venture into the wilderness and find new hunting grounds and fruits or plants for us to use. She is currently gone on another long trek through the mountainside.

I miss her when she leaves, soon I will have my naming ceremony and I can publicly announce our union. We can participate in the Envocia Amorei rite and then be tied together forevermore. How thrilling to be in love!

Mother has left the temple with the clan elders, I must corner her for answers. I promise to write again and share all that I know.

Respectfully,

Sarlaine, Future Chieftessof the Bellamere Clan

In frustration, I set down the first letter from my grandmother, Sarlaine. I sigh. She reminds me of myself, just a short week ago. Shame for my own ignorance and pride blooms on my cheeks. The fire has dwindled while I read. Adding a fresh log, I stoked the red embers and coaxed the flame to grow again, returning heat to my chilled fingers.

I refold the first letter, placing it with my mother's letter in my satchel. I unfold the next letter, and read.

Journal,

It has been several months since I have been able to write. Much has changed in our village. Mother finally shared with me the purpose of the Keladonean clan's journey to our remote home, and of the burden they have placed upon our shoulders.

Nearly thirty years ago, shortly before my mother was born, news traveled from the "mainland" as the last merchants of the year ventured into our valley.

The Helesatra royal line had been eliminated. The king, queen, royal court, and Princess Atrya perished in an unspeakable tragedy. The Haematitian Temple Council resumed power of Hevastia and Hevastia's Heart.

The Keladonean clan claimed they had been searching for us for these few decades because we are destined to bear the next reincarnation of Lady Hevastia, as prophesied. Our clan is the last of the wild mages, we did not bow to the power of the crown.

Though, out of respect, we did hold a soul rite ceremony, praying for their souls to return safely to the hearth of Lady Hevastia's home in the Beyond, that they find peace and rest.

Mother and I have argued over this absurd claim. We are far removed from the whole of Hevastia, why would her Ladyship choose us to usher in the Light meant to save us all? The Keladonean seer gave us a scroll with the prophecy, my mother has it locked away for safekeeping.

The new temple did not aid in improving our harvest, it was meager. We now rely on Noellia's guidance on treks into the wilderness to collect the measly berries, mushrooms, and wild game that can be caught within the confines of the edge of our valley.

How could I forget to mention the reason for my delay? I have worked alongside our blacksmith, and men in the village to construct a wall. Yes, a wall. Our village has been walled off, marking a small boundary for our lands. My mother ceased claim to the mountain valley and range, content to claim our small corner of the world, and to fortify it.

We have had many arguments over her decision. She believes it is best, that it will ensure Lady Hevastia's protection and our safety as we carry the burden placed on us by her Ladyship. Noellia's trip into the mountainside today is to be the last one before the cold season. I fear we may lose many of our people to starvation with such few supplies.

Mother's only concern has been focused on ensuring that the prophecy comes true. Our temple has been expanded, now an entire building and shrine in the village center. Every family has a painting of her Ladyship's likeness hanging in their home. Mother has decreed daily prayers and soul cleansings for every clan member.

Now that the wall and temple are complete, I spend my days praying to her Ladyship for health and strength, and stealing away small moments with Noellia. Though it becomes incredibly difficult to find time together. I miss her desperately, it is as if she is gone all the time.

Mother's paranoia of the "prophecy" worries me. She swears the clan elders and the Keladonean seer told her we will bring about the next goddess-touched soul. She whispers of the promised one over and over to herself, a never ending hum of noise from her chapped lips.

"A girl will be born to this line, the last of the goddess-touched. Forged in fire, bound in blood, she will be the Light embodied, and cleanse Hevastia of the darkness."

I do not understand the darkness my mother warns of. We had a bad planting season, which happen, but there is no curse, no plague coming for us. I worry my mother will lose all touch with reality.

Respectfully,

Sarlaine, Future Chieftess of the Bellamere Clan

My frustration resurfaces. I am no closer to receiving any answers. My mother was wrong, these letters contain nothing but the ravings of an immature girl who thought only of herself.

The final letter sits in my lap. I tear it open, reading it furiously. But after the first few lines I slow down, letting the words on the page sink in. It's a series of short notes, written at different times, all scratched hurriedly onto the parchment.

Journal,

The winter was harsh. The soul rite is burned into my tongue from reciting it for the forty clanspeople we have lost these last few months. I was right that a bad harvest would be our downfall.

I sit now, writing from Noellia's grave, the flowers I picked in the meadow right outside our village wilting in the spring sun. She was lost to us, there was nothing I could do.

My new partner, selected by the clan elders, Julian, stands not too far off, also mourning those he has lost. I touch my belly, it has started to swell with the pregnancy.

The clan elders whisper hopes that the prophecy will come true with this birth and we will be delivered from the darkness and pain that has befallen our people.

Secretly I, too, wish for this all to end. Mother was right, the burden is not light. Our magic is gone, there is no explanation for it.

The soul rite is little more than a prayer without our gifts to usher the dead to their final resting place. I try not to think of what that means for those we have lost.

Hunting parties come back with less meat. This planting season promises to be worse than the last. I say more prayers to Lady Hevastia for her protection, joining my people in the temple now three times daily.

I can see from our vantage point on the hill that another group is departing. Their meager belongings are strapped to their backs.

I would go down to wish them safe travels, but that seems fruitless. We all know of the horrors and beasts that lurk in the dark shadows of the mountains waiting for the chance to feast.

If they believe they will have better luck on their own outside our lands, then good riddance. It is callous of me, but less mouths to feed gives those that remain a fighting chance against the worsening conditions of our homeland.

There has been very little news from the "mainland" since the final merchants passed through last fall. I can only hope that the problems we face here are not widespread. For if they are, Hevastia, help us.

Respectfully,

Sarlaine, Chieftess of the Bellamere Clan

Journal,
It saddens me to write that my birth was not a girl, but a healthy, happy baby boy. I know the elders are disappointed in me.

They say fervent prayers in the temple five times daily now. I have been seeing one of the elders for herbs to help with another pregnancy, supposedly these will help ensure a girl. Julian tries to comfort me. He assures me he is not upset.

I miss Noellia. Sometimes, in the dark when I'm most lonely, I even miss my mother. What has my life become?

Rollan is a young toddler now, I have given him to the blacksmith's wife for care. My responsibilities in patrolling the lands and leading hunting parties alongside Julian keep me from being a proper mother to a boy. Only a girl matters to the prophecy.

Beasts threaten our sanctuary weekly now. We no longer eat their meat for it smells wrong and tastes rotten. There have been no merchants this spring, no news of what fairs beyond our mountain range. I fear we have been forgotten.

Respectfully,
Sarlaine, Chieftess of the Bellamere Clan

Journal,
Rollan is a boy of twelve now, he grows strong and bold. Julian has been teaching him to fight alongside the other children of the village. What has become of our people that our children must fight for survival?

The herbs, the prayers, the various other treatments the clan elders have given me over the years have not worked. I have lost many to sickness, early pains, and poor diet.

I fear I may never have a girl, and what will become of our people, or Hevastia if I cannot make the prophecy come true?

We have finally successfully fortified our village against the outside world. Beasts are nearly gone from our village, the stragglers are picked off by our hunting parties with ever improving skill and efficiency.

Our harvests have improved with the help of the blacksmith and my ideas.

It is bittersweet to see them used. I am reminded of Noellia every time the meadow flowers and crops wave in the breeze.

Respectfully,
Sarlaine, Chieftess of the Bellamere Clan

Journal,
It finally happened, I have had a baby girl. She is strong, and beautiful. Julian insists that I stay home now, to protect the baby and to keep my strength.

This last pregnancy has left me very weak and I worry I am not long for this world.

Rollan is a young man now, apprenticing with the blacksmith. Julian and I are so proud. He does not know of his heritage, that I am his mother. I fear I will never have the chance to tell him the truth.

The elders fuss over me and the baby constantly. I can hear their prayers from behind the bedroom door. They worship Lady Hevastia night and day now.

I have decided to name my baby Bellaema, after our people, for she will be their deliverer.

Respectfully,

Sarlaine, Chieftess of the Bellamere Clan

My mother's name jumps out on the page, and tears sting my eyes. There is not another letter, I can only imagine that Sarlaine must have passed shortly after my mother was born.

I am sad for my ancestor, she suffered greatly under the burden of producing the goddess-touched savior.

What happened in my mother's childhood that made the elders give up those practices? I have no memory of being fussed over by them, they hardly gave me any attention. They avoided my mother except when clan business needed to be discussed.

These letters have left me with nothing but questions that swirl in my head, over and over as my eyes close and sleep finally claims me.

I sleep fitfully.

Kai

SEVERAL HOURS HAVE PASSED since we left Wildewell, and Eliana. Cire has been stalling our return to the Aceolevia. "We can't hide here forever, you know."

Cire continues walking, blazing a trail deeper into the hillside. By miracle or dumb luck, we haven't encountered a single monster or beast since we began traveling to the Temple.

Walking ahead of me, his boots crunching the fallen leaves, the first sign of the cold season, Cire works to clear the path of overhanging limbs and thick brush.

"High Priestess Tallulah knows of our failure. She sent me to find you, my failure to return could spell a lot of trouble for us." I say, my voice falling silent as I think of the destruction we left behind in Eliana's village just yesterday.

My mind wanders away from that memory, still painful to think of, and instead to Eliana, likely gone, having slipped away before Alana or Hama could stop by and introduce themselves.

My argument with Cire over his refusal to tell Eliana about our friends still annoys me. He claimed that he knew her best, and telling her about Alana or Hama would only all but ensure she left Wildewell immediately.

She doesn't trust us, there's nothing truly stopping her from leaving.

A foolish hope creeps into my chest that she will break through the dense brush to my left, hellbent on getting to the Temple. Guilt claws at me for not telling her about her clan's fate. The dark haired girl still haunts my every breath.

When I snap out of my thoughts, Cire has been watching me keenly, and I can tell he sensed my thoughts. He nodded his head in agreement.

"Kai, we cannot dwell on that, you didn't know. I should have told you. We were misled, and I should have trusted you then."

He turns away from me, and continues to carefully pick his path up the side of the hill. The forest is extremely dense around the Temple, almost like a natural barrier, but it's not difficult if you know where you're going.

Cire stops, his gaze meeting mine. "I want to bring the Council to its knees. They're hiding something, their intentions with finding the 'cure' are not clear.

"They've wronged the people of Hevastia in the past and continue to do so. Whatever they've done, it's spreading and infecting all of Hevastia. Soon there won't be anything left. I want to be the one to stop them."

"It's just as Eliana said last night, they know more than they have ever shared with us. Something is happening that must be stopped." I breathe deeply, a sense of calm purpose washing over me. It feels far more pure than the frenzy my mind enters before a battle. It's almost a pleasant feeling.

"By the time the Haematitian Council discovers they've been played for fools, it will be them that is standing in fear." Cire says, extending his hand out to me. "The power will no longer be in their hands."

I hesitate for only a moment, Cire's vow ringing in my ears. We lock our forearms in a tight grip and shake on the deal. "Without fail," we say in unison.

As we round the last corner of the path, our view opens up to a beautiful grassy glade in the middle of the forest, and at its center sits a large, crystal and white marble temple. Native flowers in vibrant yellows and pinks spring up from the ground surrounding the temple.

"I almost missed the place," says Cire.

"It has always been the hidden gem of Hevastia herself," I say, sorrowfully.

Down the path to the entrance of the temple, stands a woman clad in a suit of chainmail armor. Her impatience is evident from the frown creasing her brow. The most formidable woman in all of Hevastia, High Priestess Tallulah.

"High Priestess Tallulah." Cire extends his arm in greeting. "I have returned home, a humble servant of the True Faith." Cire bows deeply, eyes cast to the ground, but I see the smirk on his lips.

"Hello, High Priestess Tallulah, I apologize for keeping you waiting. I've delivered Cire, just as you commanded." I say with practiced sincerity. I have not forgotten my walk with her in the garden just a day ago. How time moves differently when you are not under her constant watchful eye.

Tallulah crosses her arms, and gazes disapprovingly down her nose at us. "Cire I expected more of you."

Flinching at the ice in her words, I steal a glance at Cire, who is hanging his head.

He's playing the repetent role very well. But, Cire and I are not so blind now. Gone are the days of taking orders.

"Yes, High Priestess Tallulah, you are correct," Cire says with sadness. "These last several days have not been spent in great service to our Temple and to you, and I humbly ask that I be given the opportunity to make up for my transgressions."

She turns her cold gaze to me. "Captain, where is the tithe?"

"Gone, slain by a beast in the Thessimis Fields." I tell the lie with relative ease, Eliana's face passing through my mind, and a sense of calm at the notion of protecting her helps me relax into the lie even more. "Cire found her remains."

"How unfortunate." She frowns, her eyes boring into mine. "You've been summoned by the High Priest. Marius is expecting you in the inner gardens."

The High Priestess bows, eyeing me as she walks away. The faint clicking of her armor fades as she walks farther away. When she disappears down the next hallway, I grab Cire's arm and pull him into a window alcove.

"A private audience?" I whisper, peering past Cire and down an adjacent corridor that leads to the inner gardens. "This cannot be good."

Leading the way down the corridor, I run my hand along its smooth, cold walls as I did frequently as a child, running and laughing, winding my way to the Temple gardens.

The inner gardens were mine and Cire's favorite place in all of the Haematitian Temple. Our spare time between literature lessons, strength conditioning, and agility and battle training was spent hidden among the plants grown in the garden.

That is before Cire began hiding his trips to the library from me.

Entering the garden, I am surprised by the stillness. The air is normally boisterous with the noises of native birds, but instead it feels charged with powerful, sinister energy.

As we venture further into the gardens, High Priest Marius's oversized hat pokes out from the greenery. He's seated at a small table with two empty chairs, sipping herbal tea.

"High Priest Marius," says Cire, with a deep bow mirroring mine next to him. "What summons us to your council?"

He waves his hands at us, beckoning us to sit across from him. With a snap of his fingers a young priestess sets cups in front of me and Cire. Her hands shake ever so slightly as she lifts the tea pot to serve us.

"Thank you, Oleanna, you can return to your studies now." The High Priest takes her hands in his own, giving them a light squeeze before ushering her away.

She bows one final time before darting away, disappearing behind a large fern, her footsteps echoing softly as she leaves.

When High Priest Marius turns back, gone are his soft eyes and laid back demeanor.

"I see no reason to start with pleasantries. These are unpleasant circumstances." His voice is quiet, cold.

"Sefrina told me of the circumstances surrounding our loss in the Village of Bellamere. Most unfortunate." He folds his hands in front of him, tucking them into the deep recesses of his oversized sleeves.

"Cire, you forsake your duty to the True Faith. You've been found guilty before the Haematitian Council. Due to the staggering allegations and evidence against your case–you will not be permitted to live."

And, pausing for dramatic effect, High Priest Marius simply asks, "How do you plead?"

Setting my undrunk tea down, I swallow the fear rising in my gut as Cire says, "Guilty, High Priest Marius. I plead guilty, and humbly ask for your forgiveness and a final opportunity to show my devotion to the Haematitian Council and the True Faith."

High Priest Marius blinks slowly, lost in deep thought, and when he peers back into each of our faces in turn, he says, "What gives you the right to question the Council's decision?"

"My service to the True Faith is not yet complete. Respectfully, sir, I only ask for a chance to redeem myself. I know I abandoned our sacred duty." Cire bows his head as he repeats his request for forgiveness.

"It's true, High Priest Marius. Cire is repentant of his actions, he deserves a second chance. Without him, I will be weakened, the opportunity to leverage Cire's talents is too great a cost for this transgression.

"Please, sir, I want to serve the Council at full capacity, I need Cire for that."

High Priest Marius sits, listening. He gives no hint of his thoughts.

I plead once more for my closest friend. "He's my Morei, his actions are a reflection of my own. If the Council sees fit, I will execute the appropriate punishment myself."

At the mention of punishment, High Priest Marius leans forward, intrigued.

"Interesting indeed." The High Priest stands up and tucks his hands into the deep sleeves of his robes.

"Very well, I will allow you one final test to show your unquestionable oath of servitude to our great Temple and to the True Faith. Have either of you heard of the *Krothesu*?"

I flinch.

Cire visibly shudders. "Yes, we have."

"Good, then you know it is the punishment inflicted on prisoners charged with treason." He smiles at us, showing all of his teeth. It brings a chill down my spine.

"A prisoner who does not successfully pass one of the trials is vanquished."

I swallow, my mouth suddenly dry. Cire tenses next to me. "Is this the punishment you have found for me, master?"

"You are correct, Cire." He stops smiling, but it remains in the humorous glint in his eyes.

He's taking sick pleasure in knowing that the Krothesu spells near certain death for Cire.

"You will both enter the *Krothesu*, fighting alongside each other. If you can prove to me that you are ready, and if you survive the trials, I will allow you to remain in service to the Haematitian Council, and we will continue on as if your disgraceful behavior never occurred."

A sweat builds on the back of my neck. High Priest Marius suspects me though he has no evidence to prove my deceit. It's the only reason he would punish us both.

An anger boils in my gut, even innocent I would have been punished. He cannot possibly know my allegiance has strayed.

"Thank you, Master. We will not let you down," I say. I clench my hand into a fist at my side to keep from lashing out in frustration.

"So, do we have a deal?" asks High Priest Marius.

"Yes, sir, we have a deal. When shall we run the *Krothesu* for you?" asks Cire.

"Since I can only assume you are fully rested and prepared for battle after such a long vacation from your duties, the *Krothesu* begins tonight."

Eliana

T HE MORNING CHILL WAKES me from my sleep, as I realize the fire must have died in the middle of the night.

I woke up this morning with one all consuming thought–I need to get to the Temple to get the answers I still seek. My grandmother's letters haunt me.

She experienced so much loss and pain – and it is all their fault. My ancestors' lives were destroyed by the prophecy, the need to drive the darkness of the Haematitian Council out of Hevastia. I will not let their sacrifices be in vain.

I check that all of my daggers are secure and slip out of the hut, letting the cloth flap close behind me. I take three deep breaths.

"There is promise in the Light," I whisper to myself.

To the right is the center of the village, so I turn left and walk silently, careful to avoid the light that pours from the open windows and doors of other huts in the lane.

It does not take long before I have left the glow of the village behind and I am surrounded by the same decimated huts and deteriorating wood that greeted us when we arrived.

My gut clenches at the thought of my village still smoldering, sharing this same fate.

Glancing back my vision fills with the soft light of the homes.

Be faithful, your people will rebuild, just like they did. I tell myself this several times to help calm my nerves and distract from the eerie silence of the open fields outside the village.

The tall grass that was soft and inviting yesterday is now sinister and bleak in the sliver of light on the horizon as the solari rise and the day creeps in.

I pull the sword I stole from Kai and Cire's hut off my back, holding it out to help part the grass ahead of me. *Kai and Cire said the Temple of Clarity lies in the Dartneau Hills just outside the village.*

The grass rustles in the wind, tickling my face and sending a chill down my spine. I continue walking, breaking stalks of grass every few steps to mark a trail should I get turned around.

I tighten my grip on the sword, nerves wash over me at the thought of encountering a beast of the night or one of the monsters like I saw on the mountain back home.

While trading in the village market, merchants would whisper of deadly encounters with corrupted beasts along the trade routes. So few merchants travel nowadays, the journey far too treacherous a price for even the promise of riches. Without their essential goods, my village was beginning to suffer.

Anger pools in my gut.

If the Haematitian Council truly cared for the people, this black plague and the unnecessary death and destruction would already be over. Instead they pluck up their people like one picks wildflowers, blatantly disregarding their existence or the worth they provide where they're planted.

A shadow passes through the grass to my right, and I crouch low. Peering through a small gap in the grass a hunched figure in tattered, dirty clothes shuffles past me, oblivious. I shake my head, letting out the breath I was holding with a soft huff.

"You're paranoid," I whisper to myself.

I stand, and part the grass with my blade, stepping towards the lost villager.

"Excuse me,' I say, reaching my hand out to tap them on the shoulder.

They twitch, their body convulsing unnaturally and I stagger backwards, dread growing in my gut.

The villager pivots to face me, suddenly moving far faster than its slow shamble. It rushes at me, black blood and yellow pus spewing from its open mouth, rotting teeth sticking out in every direction.

I scream, bringing the sword up and thrusting it forward. The disgusting monster doesn't have a chance to slow down, impaling itself on my outstretched blade, all the way to the crossguard.

Black blood oozes down the blade, and my hands. The monster wheezes, its nasty, crusted yellow eyes fading to a dull, lifeless color.

I brace my boot against its scarred leg and yank my sword out of its soft, deteriorating chest. It slumps the ground in a crumpled heap.

Tears of relief cascade down my cheeks. I laugh softly to myself, surveying the area in case there are more.

A corrupted soul. All this time, Jasath was telling the truth, the dead do walk the land.

The black blood is difficult to wipe off the blade. It takes me several handfuls of grass to get the blade even partially clean of the sticky, foul-smelling goo.

Disappointed, I wipe my hands on my pants and use a pant leg to wipe the blade clean.

If my mother saw me now– I stop myself from continuing the thought. I can't think of her right now, if I do I might never stop.

I wipe my cheeks, suck in three deep breaths and continue on my way. Even further resigned to make the Haematitian Council answer for their crimes against its citizens.

My sword cuts through air, and the field falls away to the start of the forest towering above me. Just several rows of trees beyond the edge of the forest, all light is gone, blocked by the canopy overhead. It makes me feel even smaller and alone. I plan each step, careful to avoid dried twigs or leaves. Up ahead is a sharp hill, and beyond the hill I hope is the Temple.

I grab a hold of a large root sticking out from the loose dirt, pulling on it to make sure it's secure.

"This will have to do, I suppose." I mutter to myself.

Hesitant, I slip the sword onto my back. I need both hands to climb. I grit my teeth and pull myself up, finding small foot holds.

Halfway up my boot slips on a smooth rock and my head smacks into the dirt wall, sending stars across my vision. I bite down a yell, and find a new foot hold. My arms scream in pain from holding myself up, and I can feel a headache forming.

"Come on El, you can do it." I breathe through clenched teeth and coach myself to continue up the hill.

Making it to the top, I pull myself over the edge, rolling onto my back and taking big gulping breaths.

"Hah, I did it." I thrust my hand in the air over my head and smile to myself.

A twig snaps to my right, and my muscles tense. I freeze in place, and wait for the next sound. There's nothing at first, so I listen harder, slowing my breaths.

There. I can hear it breathing.

Just a few yards away the sound of slow, heavy panting. It's muffled, but unmistakable. A cold sweat runs down my back and the hairs on my arm stand at attention.

I could play dead, maybe it will just move on. I think to myself. *How fast can I grab my sword, or a dagger?*

The breathing grows quieter, another twig snaps further to my right. I sag in relief, the beast did not notice me, but I'm not in the clear yet. I need to get off my back and get away from here.

Three ... two ... one. I roll over onto my knees and jump up, pulling the sword off my back as I crouch.

My eyes strain to see anything in the growing darkness, there's not enough light to show the glow of eyes or cast a shadow. My unease grows at the idea of being so vulnerable.

Stupid, stupid, stupid. I'm going to get myself killed.

I crouch for what feels like forever, but whatever was nearby must have moved on. There are no other sounds except the shrill call of a *crost* bird echoing through the canopy.

I stand tall, and see that the top of the hill only leads to more dense forest, no sign of the Temple or anything else in sight. I sheath my sword.

"Where to go from here?"

A blur comes at me from my right, and I'm knocked sideways by a young *severn*, a spotted, ruthless beast of the forest with yellow eyes and unparalleled hunting skill. My knees hit the dirt as I slide in the soft mud.

I calm my breathing as I stare down one of the most fearsome creatures in all of Hevastia. Its yellow eyes stare back at me, crusted, dried blood on its muzzle and paws.

I reach behind me to grab my sword and the *severn* growls and swats at me.

The *severn* strikes and I dance backward, narrowly avoiding getting raked across the chest by its massive paw. The *severn* paces in front of me, growling. I'm reminded of the monster from the mountains–could it have been a *severn* sick with disease? Was it one of the black beasts Cire mentioned?

The *severn* leaps at me, knocking me to the ground, sending me tumbling several yards. Pain shoots through my head and shoulder. I scramble to my feet, leaning on my sword and pull myself up on my feet, squinting against the blood pooling on my eyelashes from a gash on my forehead. My leg and hip are still healing from the last beast's attack–a dull, throbbing pain from just days old injuries.

When it lunges next, I pull the sword up in a long arc and sidestep, slicing the severon's flank. It growls and hisses in pain, bringing a satisfied smirk to my lips.

My leg is stained with fresh blood, my injuries have reopened, and my shoulder is bleeding from where its claws raked me when it knocked me down. I touch my leg with shaking fingers, my hand coming away covered in fresh blood. I clench my jaw and set my feet, ready to attack when it strikes next.

Blood loss is making my mind foggy, and I am finding it hard to concentrate. I flex my hand around the sword and hold it in front of me, but it feels so heavy.

I drop the sword, grappling for the daggers on my hip. The *severn* growls low and deep, the leaves crunching under its paws as it paces, watching me, deciding its next move. My only hope now is to draw it closer to me, I won't risk throwing my daggers and missing. My vision blurs with the blood running down my face from the gash on my forehead.

It snarls, charging at me, and I let it come. Just as it lunges to swipe at me, I sidestep its massive paw, stabbing one dagger into its neck, taking us both to the ground. The beast is on top of me, my body pinned. It yowls, whipping its head to tear my arm off for stabbing it, and with my other arm, I bring another dagger up and plunge it right into its heart.

I fall back, the *severn* bleeding out on top of me, and I pant, exhausted. When I've collected my breath, I shove the beast off of me, and stand, my body swaying as I struggle to walk to my sword left discarded several feet away.

My last thought as my knees hit the ground is that I'm going to die, and staring at me from behind my closed eyelids is the intricate knot of Hevastia's Heart.

There's smoke all around me, the bitter smell of burnt hair and flesh fills my nostrils. Choking, I pull my sleeve to cover my mouth and calm my breathing.

My vision is tinted red. I touch my forehead, pulling my fingers back and finding no blood on them.

The scene in front of me is familiar, I have seen hundreds of variations of it in my nightmares for nearly a year now. My nights are plagued with images of mangled huts, their bones sticking out, smoldering after being chewed and spit out by the flames that continue to race through the village, cutting down everything in their hunger. I peek down to my right, expecting to see the same dying woman from before, but she's not there.

My boots crunch on the loose gravel of the lane. Crumbled bricks and stones are scattered as I jump down from a collapsed wall into a pit that was once a home. The tapestry of the family that died here is singed by the flames, flapping in the soft breeze that fans the fire and urges it on.

I continue walking into the destruction, chasing the fire. It's not long before I catch up, the glowing embers cast an eerie shadow in the dense smoke as I travel closer to the flames. The heat pushes me back, but I urge myself forward. I've never made it this far before, and I can't turn back. Everything ahead of me is red and orange, pulsing, alive.

The smoke clears, and roaring before me is a wall of flames that threatens to consume all of Hevastia. The wildfire has slowed, as if it's waiting for me. My boots kick up soot, and the air is thick with ash that coats my hair and shoulders as I near the edge of the blaze. I gaze deep into the fire, and I see myself, again. This time it's my entire reflection, not just my face.

My steps falter, and I hesitate. The fiery reflection smiles back at me, beckoning me closer.

When I don't move, the flames part, burning brighter and causing me to squint against their bright light.

Through the curtain of the fire, emerges a girl not much older than I am. Her auburn hair falls like a curtain around her lithe silhouette.

It's her eyes that draw me in—they're twin pools calling to me, I could fall into them and never stop.

She's god-touched.

"Hello, Eliana." Her voice is melodic, light. She smiles warmly.
"I'm Atrya."

"You're the last reincarnation."

Atrya nods her head, smiling, and steps fully out of the flames.
"Yes, and I've come to warn you."

Her hands are ice cold to the touch as she takes my arms in her firm grip.

"You are the last daughter of Hevastia, our only hope. But without access to your magic, you will fail. You must reopen the connection to the Heart before He is able to return."

"That doesn't make any sense. Who? What does this have to do with the Haematitian Council?"

Her lips are soft as she kisses me on the forehead.

"You are weak now, but there is a strength within you, greater than you can fathom. Find your clan's elders, seek your answers from their writings."

She steps back, letting my hands go. "Your connection to the Amorei, what you refer to as Hevastia's Heart, must be re-established."

She holds her arms out, shooting sparks. "Fate's Guardian, embrace your destiny. Only then will you have the power to free Hevastia from the darkness."

"What if I can't? What if you're wrong, and I am not strong enough?"

"There is promise in the Light. You, Eliana, are the Light."

"Wait," I shout, reaching out to stop her from leaving.

"I can't stay, I must conserve my energy for when you need me most. I will find you again."

The flames come rushing back, consuming us both. Atrya steps into the blaze, fading away. The heat climbs up my body, burning me to my core.

I scream and run, tripping. I fall into Atrya's black eyes, surrounded by the red hot flames before I disappear into total, cold, darkness.

Cire

WE HAVE BEEN SILENT since leaving the gardens, I cannot find the right words to help calm Kai. Nothing I say is going to soothe this kind of anger.

I know he's angry to be standing here with me. Even knowing he is betraying the Council, their decision to punish him alongside me is a different kind of betrayal.

It has been a long time since I have sensed this kind of fervor in Kai, it's different from the bloodlust he used to get before a battle. It feels more pure, more like his old self.

He tightens the leather straps of his gauntlets and fastens on the feeble chest guard provided by the Temple. Stripped of our Morei blades, and armed only with small daggers, I will be practically defenseless against whatever horrors await us in the test.

Kai will have more fortuitous options. He draws back to walk beside me as we near the entrance to the arena beyond the high walls of the boundary lines.

"I understand your anger." My comment must surprise him because his steps falter, breath hitching before he recovers his composure.

Kai sighs. "You said so yourself, we have to prove ourselves to the Council, convince them. If I denied the Gauntlet, then they would suspect us both. Better to die by my brother's side than choose the coward's way out."

"Somber words before we march to our potential deaths. You couldn't think of a more rousing speech? You've said so many better ones before."

We both chuckle. Kai was always the more congenial one between the two of us – which is saying a lot when he was also the more brutal in battle.

"Cire, if anything should happen in there, promise to continue on without me. Hevastia needs you." Kai says soberly, slowing his pace to stop me, his arm clasped tightly on my shoulder.

"You understand the prophecy. Eliana will need that guidance."

I nod, and gaze upward to the stars, making a sign of thanks and asking for protection from Lady Hevastia, kissing my fingers and turning them inward to my heart.

"Where did you learn that prayer?"

I smile softly, lost in a pleasant memory. "I heard Eliana recite it to herself. It feels right for the occasion."

"What was it again?" he asks.

"There is promise in the Light." I reply softly, confidently.

"We will both make it out of this, now is not the time to lose spirit." I grip his shoulder, giving him a soft shake.

Kai squeezes back. "Without fail, remember?" He smirks.

He adds a jauntiness to his step, his brown curls bobbing with each footfall. At this moment he appears younger, years of battle and death aren't weighing down his shoulders and aging his face.

Maybe he will find his way back from the dark place he made for himself under the Council's shadow.

Perhaps in this new reality we can be equals, and I can step out from behind his shadow.

The outer walls of the arena are crumbling from the weight of thick, flowering vines weaving colorful trails across its stern face. The delicate beauty of the vines cannot mask the cold chill of death that dances across the skin from just staring up at the colossal, overwhelming size and ferocity of the arena.

We stop just short of the entrance, our breath catching in our throats.

A priestess emerges from the shadows, a small silver tray in hand. The tray wobbles as she draws closer, on it are two small cups of a dark liquid.

"What is this?" Kai asks.

"A toast in honor of your health." She swallows. "High Priestess Tallulah sent for it as a token of good luck."

She extends the tray to us, the dark liquid sloshing in the small crystal goblets. Bowing her head she holds the tray higher, beckoning us to take the goblets.

Kai frowns. "It would be rude to refuse such a nice gesture from the High Priestess." He grips a goblet, handing it to me before taking the other for himself.

"To our health." He raises the goblet toward me before tipping the drink to his lips and finishing it in one large gulp. I raise the goblet to my lips and swallow the contents, wincing at the bitterness.

"Thank you." We place the goblets back on the tray and the young priestess scurries away, back into the shadows.

"Every choice we make is going to be scrutinized. We can't have any missteps–they will cost us our lives."

"Then let's give them one hell of a show." Kai says as he steps through the doorway and into the arena.

With a ground shaking force, the stone doorway slams shut just feet behind us, and we are immersed in sudden, impenetrable darkness.

The air around us moves slowly. Leaving behind the chill of ice like a kiss of death across my skin.

The loss of my senses is immediate and terrifying.

"Cire, do you hear that?"

"Hear what?" I ask. My eyes are not adjusting to the darkness, and I stumble blindly forward. There's a low hum vibrating against my chest, disorienting me.

"Something just flew right by me. Fast, too." There's an uneasy edge to Kai's voice.

Taking a few steps past the doorway, the room seems to buzz more loudly, like a hive of angry bees.

"Something's not right." Kai's arm stops me from stepping forward. "What is that moving in the darkness?" He pauses, his arm still holding me back. "Make that quite a few things." Kai says.

"What is it?" I hiss, resorting to whispering as fear snakes its way up my body.

"I'm not sure." Kai's hand lingers on my arm, holding me back from moving forward. "We need to be patient."

Irritation rises in my gut. "We don't have time for this, we need to keep pressing forward, this is merely an introduction to the hellscape ahead of us."

I shrug off his arm, and step past him. If we take too long, who knows what awful tricks they have up their sleeve to flush us out and make us suffer.

I've heard rumors of the *Krothesu*—that the bodies pulled from the arena are so twisted they are unrecognizable, that the screams can be heard through all the hills. A young acolyte once told me his brother had to reassemble a prisoner after a monster in the gauntlet tore him to pieces and scattered the parts.

The image is enough to make me want to throw up. I imagine Kai is having similar gruesome thoughts.

"Way to keep the spirit up, Cire." Kai mutters, and his laughter is gruff, cut short.

As we continue on, the whirring sound charging through the air continues. With no end to the darkness in sight, we continued forward, my skin chilled and my vision still swallowed by the void of light. It feels like hours have gone by, and still the darkness consumes us.

As we've continued forward, the room has pressed in on us. The walls on either side are only a few paces away, ushering us toward an unknown horror with the low grumble of stone grinding against itself as the walls slowly press inward, trapping us.

A soft ping of metal hitting stone rings through the darkness. As we turn to the wall beside us, another ping sounds from a different corner of the room. Soon the humming sound is punctuated by the steady staccato of metal on stone all around us.

"It's hard to hear anything through the drowning buzzing. It's making finding my way very difficult to concentrate on," I shout to Kai, trying to overcome the rising noise around us.

A sharp pain stabs into my shoulder out of nowhere, and I double over onto the ground. My cry of pain echoes through the dark cavern, slicing through the din of the buzzing.

Kai's feet shuffle, scraping against the stone, as he tries to find me in the darkness. "Cire, what happened?"

I growl out through gritted teeth, "Whatever has been stalking us through this void has finally made its presence known."

"It cut you?"

"More like a quick stab, I never even sensed it coming."

As Kai moves, his boot connects with a small object on the ground, and we both hear the sound of it ringing as it slides across the rocky floor. Reaching to pick it up, he holds it close to his face and runs his fingers gently along it.

"They're blades Cire. We are getting attacked by small blades."

Kai presses his hands into my wound, and my blood stops running down my chest but back up my shoulder and onto his hands. Kai mutters to himself as he draws power from me, gathering my blood to use for his magic.

Kai is a *sanguinar*, one of the strongest. He's mastered several of the elements, something that is almost unheard of, but it takes tremendous amounts of tithing to be done.

And, that's where I come in. I'm his Morei, his *tithe*. When we were younger Kai displayed potential *talent* and was pulled from the orphanage to train with the other "blessed" children. He made such a scene at being taken away from me that the priestesses decided to see if I had talent as well.

When I fell short of making the cut, my meager gifts were seen by the Council as an opportunity to *experiment* – could a *sanguinar* draw greater power from someone of weaker gift?

The answer is yes.

A bitter thought seeps into my head, and irritation rises alongside the pain throbbing in my shoulder.

Even now, when we've sworn to forsake the Haematitian teachings, he falls back to old behaviors, sucking me dry of my energy to further his own.

Kai draws my blood away from my wound, I can sense his restraint at trying not to draw too much–there's always a balance. Draw too much and I will tire too quickly, but if he draws too little then he can't get the job done.

Over the years we've nearly perfected this dance, and the Council has run many tests with me to see if there are ways to extend my stamina, undergo more blood loss while remaining conscious, et cetera.

My stomach pinches and he pulls back, relief flooding my body.

Kai's boots scrape on the ground as he stands. There's a slight change in air pressure as Kai uses the blood he siphoned from me to draw air around his fingers, weaving them in front of him to form a vortex.

Even unable to see, I know Kai's every move having witnessed it many times in training and in battle. Kai continues to weave the air, drawing the knives that were once targeted at us into the air pocket he's formed.

The air comes alive, the humming and buzzing louder than ever. It is a deafening roar, there's no mistaking it now, as my sense of direction and the way to our escape are halted by the sudden onslaught of noise.

Kai yells in frustration as he lowers his hands, bringing with them all of the knives. The noise lessens as the knives fall quietly to the ground, first one by one and then suddenly all at once like a large glass bowl shattering.

As we shuffle along our boots continue to kick fallen blades. Kai supports me as we leave the shrinking room. We hurry forward, the sense of urgency overcoming our need for caution. So much so that Kai almost plunges off the edge of the floor as it comes to an abrupt end.

The knives echo as they fly at us continuously, bouncing off the walls of the cavern in front of us before landing on the floor with a muffled thud. It's a deep hole.

"This is a dead end."

"What?"

"The floor ends, Cire. We have to turn back."

"Well, how deep is the hole?" I ask, exasperated. My breathing is turning ragged from blood loss, from Kai siphoning me.

"How deep do you think it is? If I had to guess, it's probably deep enough to kill us." Kai's voice is even, my blood feeding him strength.

"The first trap would not be fatal, think Kai. This is merely a game to the council, a cruel way to punish criminals. What kind of entertainment would it be if we were to die at the first sign of trouble?"

I cry out again and drop back onto my knees in pain next to Kai, clutching at a second blade lodged into the same shoulder. I drag myself to the side of the cavern, out from the open. Kai follows close behind me.

"You missed one." I hissed.

"That's not possible." He tries to examine the torn flesh of my shoulder, gently poking around the blade. "How bad is it?"

My jaw is clenched with pain. "Bad."

I grind my teeth and breathe out through them sharply as Kai pokes the wound. "You need to wrap this to slow the bleeding."

Kai pulls at the hem of his own shirt, and tears a long strip free. Apologizing for the pain, he grips the razor edge in his wrapped hand and pulls it free quickly.

My scream of pain echoes in the small chamber. When it cuts off, there's the skittering of nails on the stone floor, accompanied by the sound of a blade trailing the rock that sends shivers up my back and arms.

"Kai, something is out there."

"It's just the blade traps, we got caught in one, remember?" He pulls my face to his. In the darkness I can faintly see the whites of his eyes. "Stay with me, okay?"

He wraps my shoulder tightly, and pulls me to my feet. A blade flies from nowhere, narrowly missing Kai's head. He ducks just in time, a small gust of wind pushing the blade off its original path.

"That was close," he growls out. Another blade flies dangerously close to the wall we are braced tightly against.

"We need to make a run for it." I say through clenched teeth.

Kai suddenly vanishes from my view, a blur of teeth and matted fur tackling him to the ground. A large, man-like beast wrestles with him.

The glow of its red eyes and the glint of his yellow, razor sharp teeth flash in the near-darkness. Kai punches the monster square in the jaw, knocking it away before its vicious fangs bite into his neck.

"Cire, knife," Kai gasps for air under the crushing weight of the beast, punching it again and struggling to kick it off of him.

I grab a knife off the floor and leap on the beast's back, sinking the dagger in between its shoulder blades along the spine. When I rip the blade out, it's coated in thick, black blood that smells like death and rot.

The smell is disgusting and I struggle to stay on its back while I gag on the stench. I sink my blade in again, and it screeches, the noise a piercing howl.

Kai wriggles out from under the beast, now coated in the putrid blood. The monster rears on its hind legs, trying to throw me off its back. I hold tight to the dagger, punching it in the neck.

Kai stabs another dagger into its cheek as it lets out another ear splitting screech. Claws as long as our fingers threaten to rake clean through Kai, but he dances out of the way, pulling his dagger free and using it to slice open the monster's neck, lodging the dagger deep into its throat.

The beast drops to the ground. I step away from its rotten corpse, wiping my dagger on my pants.

"I told you we weren't alone."

Kai's lip curls with disgust. "What do you think it is?"

"Does it matter? I'm sure there are more of them. Let's go."

We stand facing the pit once again. Kai gives me a devilish grin that suggests 'here goes nothing,' as he launches himself off of the wall and into the hungry darkness.

Within seconds Kai's form is swallowed whole as he descends into the pit and out of my limited view.

"Kai," I shout as I drag myself up, feeling light-headed from the blood-loss.

Grunting in pain and frustration, I follow Kai's lead and launch myself off the edge, praying to the stars for guidance out of this hellscape.

The pit is not deep. We land easily on our feet. As we move to walk out of the pit, we quickly sink into the sandy mixture surrounding us.

"Kai, don't struggle, it will suck you down faster. We need to let it pull us under."

"Are you crazy?" He gazes wildly at me as panic consumes his thoughts.

"I'm serious, Kai. It's a quicksand hole. We need to let it pull us under and through—this is the challenge. Panic and we get suffocated by the sand as it tightens around us and drags us under faster. Stay calm and it stays loose around us, slowly letting us sink through the quicksand."

The sand is now past my hips and approaching Kai's chest, continuing its slow advance up our bodies. As it reaches my chest, my breaths shorten, and Kai struggles against it. "Don't," I rasp out.

The sand makes it past my chest and to my shoulders as it loosens again, and I am able to breathe.

"Just as the sand is about to reach your mouth suck in a deep breath and close your eyes." I instruct.

Doing as he is told, Kai disappears underneath the sand, just seconds before I am sucked in myself. As I travel through the gritty pit, I can hear the sand shifting around us, and soon the roar of rushing water vibrates around me. A blast of cold air surrounds me, and suddenly Kai and I find ourselves free falling through the sky, plummeting to the roaring rapids rushing below.

Kai braces for the water, tucking himself into a ball, and I follow his lead.

We hit the water so fast our bodies strike against the bottom, forcing me to scream out, losing air and sucking in water as it rushes into my lungs. I choke. Hands grab me by the elbow and pushing off the river bed, I fight hard against the current to pull myself to the surface.

When we break the surface, I cough up water, and blood.

Peering around frantically, I'm dismayed to find we are surrounded by waves crashing against the large rocks, the black water trying to suck us under into the rapids.

Kai is struggling to keep afloat, his eyes are wide with panic.

The water continues to dash us against the sharp rocks threatening to slice us in half. Kai's body slams into a rock, and the rushing water crushes him against it. He grips the rock, trying to pull himself up and out of the water, but the fast current continuously sucks him down.

I cry out to him, and use my legs to push off of the rock behind me, propelling my weakening body forward. He finally pulls himself out of the water, and when our eyes lock I see his relief in finding me alive.

"Kai," I yell as I swim toward him.

He extends an arm out to me, trying to pull me to him and out of the riptide that forces me down. My fingers dig into his arm, and I grip tightly as he pulls me to the rock and helps me climb up.

We both lie on our backs, panting. My wound was ripped open wider in the riptide, and my body is quickly getting soaked in my own blood.

"Kai, I don't think I can make it off this rock. You need to go on without me."

He turns sharply to me, wearing a murderous expression. "Like hell."

He holds his hands against my wound, calling my blood to him again. It sickens me how easily my blood responds to his call when it never does anything if I try. I gave up trying long ago.

"I won't take much, I promise." Kai focuses on me, his expression earnest behind his wide, scared eyes.

His hands are red with my blood as he dips them into the water and chants to himself. The water rises around him, rolling up his arms and over his shoulders and chest, covering him like a cloak.

He rips a piece of his shirt and ties it under my arm and over the wound. I suck in a breath when he tightens it, pinching the wound and sending a sharp pain down my entire body.

He rips his shirt again, tying one end around the wrist of my uninjured arm, the other around his own wrist.

"Whatever you do, don't let go of me. Okay?"

Standing, he extends his hand to me. "We need to jump into the water and swim to the shore. I can get us there."

He points to the far right where I can see the faint outline of a rocky shore. The white caps of the waves break against the rocks blocking our path.

We will be lucky if we make it halfway.

"You have a better chance of making it without me. I can catch up."

We both know I am lying. If I go into the water alone I won't be coming back.

Which is why Kai needs to leave me here, but the stubborn set of his shoulders and the scowl on his face tell me I won't be left behind.

"On the count of three." Kai and I face the black water below us. "One ... two ... three"

Kai leaps into the water, and I am pulled in a second after. The icy chill of the water shocks my body once again, but I fight hard to kick to the surface.

The rapid current continues to suck us further downstream, but Kai does not give up. He swims with the current, keeping his eyes on the shore and pulling me with him.

I can feel his magic pulsing in the water as it works to guide him against the current and toward the shore. We pause for a breath at every rock, and Kai checks the bandage on my arm. It's slow progress but we are getting closer to the shoreline with every passing minute.

A strong current sucks me under and I swallow water, struggling to kick back to the surface. Kai's strong hands grab my arm and pull me up.

When he reaches the edge he throws my numb body onto the bank, and then drags himself up. I cough, water spewing from my mouth. Turning me over, he pumps the water from my lungs, and says a prayer to the stars to help us get through this.

I sense Kai's desperation to save me.

I should be touched, but I can only feel annoyed at my own weakness. Kai has brought us through every scenario. I'm annoyed with my shortcomings, my inability to take care of myself, to use his strength to further my own.

After the third try, I cough up small mouthfuls of water, and Kai turns me onto my side and pats my back to get the rest of the water out.

"Thank you, Kai," I say quietly. fighting down my inner turmoil.

"Don't thank me yet," Kai says, looking beyond where I lay to the dark forest ahead of us.

I sit up, and cough some more. "The Hilwe Wildes, home to the beasts of the forest, monsters of children's night terrors." I say it as a joke, but I know the chill down my spine is not from the cold water.

Kai stands, and extends his hand to help pull me to my feet. He unsheathes his dagger and cuts the tie between our hands, letting it drop to the ground.

He leads the way on our walk into the forest, my eyes searching for anything I can fashion into weapons. Armed with only a dagger, we are easy pickings against a monster, should another one cross our path. The forest floor is smooth like a river washed stone, not even a discarded leaf at our disposal.

As we continue into the forest, I move silently, matching my steps where Kai's foot has already stepped. There is no way to know what traps we may encounter. My shirt is soaked in blood, and its scent poses a great threat to our journey.

Without the sound of a snapping twig, or dried leaves to warn us, we are soon overrun by the beasts of the wild. Their shapes are still concealed in the forest shadows, but their glowing eyes flash in the darkness, and their gleaming, sharp teeth flash with the intention of shredding us to pieces.

"Kai..." I say, drawing out his name, the hairs on the back of my neck alerting me to the danger lurking nearby.

"I can sense them, too. It's now or never, Cire."

I nod my head, though he doesn't see it. We go back to back, fists raised, daggers at the ready. All at once they descend on us, snarling and tearing at our clothes, arms, and legs.

With nothing but bare fists, I punch the first beast in the face, and kick it square in the ribs, hearing a satisfying snap as they break. A second beast leaps at me from the side, and sinks its razor sharp teeth into my uninjured arm.

Kai pulls the beast off of me, and throws it against the closest tree, its body now limp. Two advance on Kai at the same time, going for his leg and shoulder.

I pounded my fist into the head of the one tearing into Kai's shoulder, sending my dagger into its skull. Black blood seeps from the wound, useless.

Kai grunts with frustration as he fails to call the beast's blood to our aid. The beast drops dead, and I force open its jaw to release Kai.

Kai's kick broke the neck of the other one. His shoulder is bleeding, but he can still raise his arm and dagger.

Another beast turns its attention to me, snapping its jaws. As it lunges, I grab its face and pull apart its jaws, my fingers sliced open on the serrated, sharp teeth. The beast struggles to get out of my grip, but it cannot escape before its jaw is broken and its face is bleeding.

Kai quickly dispatches a smaller one that's attacking his legs. The remaining beasts retreat into the shadows, their glowing eyes fading away.

I collapse to the ground on my knees, clutching my bleeding hands to my blood soaked shirt. Kai stands above me, his right shoulder torn open, seeping blood slowly.

And as the beasts lay bleeding out, Kai and I are once again surrounded in darkness and silence. My ragged breathing punctuates the silence, I think one of the beasts broke a few of my ribs.

I limp forward, toward the faint glow at the other end of the dark forest. Kai follows close behind, having stopped to wrap the deep wound on his leg from a beast's bite.

We pause, listening. I don't hear any beasts up ahead and any remaining in the woods must no longer want to take their chances against us. Slowly, painstakingly, we make our way forward. Up ahead there is a hill, smoke climbing from the top and into the canopy.

Kai

THERE IS A YOUNG girl sitting at the fire, sharpening a sword, a bow and arrow lying on the ground by the empty log next to her. Her back is to us, as she works the whetstone against the blade, humming to herself.

I hold Cire back, leaning him against a nearby tree to rest. The blood loss is stealing his remaining strength. I sneak closer to the girl and to the bow discarded on the ground near her.

If I can just get to the bow. I reach out, my fingers barely grazing the polished wood when the girl's head snaps up and she screams. I can't explain it, but I recognize her. *It's impossible.*

The sickly girl in front of us is Princess Atrya, but something is off about her. Her skin is gray, and sagging in places, her eyes are hollow and her dark hair has lost its shine, now full of twigs and dead leaves.

Without knowing how, I am certain it's her. It's at this moment that I realize this is the true test.

Everything leading up to this moment was just a game for the Council, but here, now, they are testing how much we know. We can't give anything away. Somehow they've created this hallucination.

"You failed me," she moans to me. "You left me to die, you never came for me. How could you?"

I school my features, pretending with every ounce of my being to suppress the recognition of her face, of who she is. I glance sideways at Cire, his mouth is set in a thin line, annoyed and in immense pain.

"Kai, what's wrong?" he whispers to me, his eyes looking past the ghostly vision in front of us, scanning the forest beyond for more beasts.

"Cire, don't you see the ghost?" I whisper, my eyes darting back to the bow and the girl now standing in front of us, just feet from where I stand.

"Kai, don't be ridiculous. Now, help me stand so we can continue on. We have to be close to the end." Cire says, exasperated.

"Don't even think about it," she says, laughing mercilessly. "There is no death for me, not this time." Her hand reaches out to the bow and quiver, as if by magic they fly into her hands.

Before I can fully process what I've just witnessed, the distinct thud and whipping sound of arrows being notched and released whistles in the air. She fired three shots so fast I didn't even have time to blink.

As if by luck, or maybe on purpose, two of the shots fail to hit their mark, but the third lands firmly and with lethal accuracy just mere centimeters from Cire's heart.

His head slumps forward, and his eyes close.

"No, no, no. Cire." I turn my back on Atrya, ignoring her and her bow. "I will get us out of this."

His body can't take much more blood loss, he will die in the next few minutes. A moan escapes his lips. But there's no blood around the new wound, and the arrow Atrya fired is now missing, no longer sticking out of his chest.

My vision is full of the haunting version of Atrya standing in front of us, her bow aimed for the killing shot. Her eyes are cold and merciless. A wave of nausea washes over me. *How could I have failed Cire?*

Cire's eyes roll back into his head as he loses consciousness. Panic surges in my body at the sight of his body lying there.

"What have you done?" I ask, anger rising in my chest.

Atrya stands in front of me, watching Cire. When his eyes close fully, lying unconscious she lowers her bow. There's a small purple stone in her hand. She extends the hand holding the stone to me, dropping it by my feet.

"Pick it up." Her boot nudges it closer.

"No, not until you tell me what's wrong with Cire. What did you do to him?"

She rolls her eyes. "I put him to sleep, but that's hardly important. Pick up the stone, now."

"What is it?" I ask.

"It's what you've been searching for," she says impatiently.

I shake my head. "I don't understand. What do you mean?"

I stand, facing her fully, ready to fight if that's what it comes to. She frowns and draws her bow, aiming at my heart.

"Don't play games with me, I can only manifest this form for a short time. I already used so much of my energy bringing down your 'brother.'" Her face twists in a grimace.

"Help him." I demand.

"No, this message is for you alone. This is not part of the *Krothesu*. The gauntlet ended when you killed the wild beasts, as it has the last twelve times.

"I invited you here to speak, where the Council will not see. I'm merely a soul projection. Lady Hevastia sent me here to warn you."

"Twelve times—what do you mean?"

She groans with frustration, glaring down at me with annoyance. "You have completed this same trial twelve times before, repeatedly, this is the thirteenth and final time you will enter the arena. I had to visit you, to warn you, before I lost my chance."

My mind swims with the knowledge that we have completed this trial twelve times already, but I have no recollection of it. I almost miss her last words. "Warn us of what?"

She shudders and the bow drops from her hands. "There isn't much time, He will return soon. You must take this rock to ... the girl. She needs it."

"What does it do?" I narrowed my eyes at her, suspicious.

Atrya is on her knees now, her face is sunken in and even grayer. "Take it to her, you will see."

I hesitate, this could be part of the gauntlet. There's no way of knowing what the correct answer is, so I take the rock.

As my fingers close around it a surge of energy erupts from the stone and into my body, and instantly my senses are heightened.

When I turn to Atrya, she is not gray at all, but actually glowing faintly. The glow is fading, and her form is losing shape.

Her gaze meets mine and smiles ruthlessly. Her voice is deeper, older as she says "the Light will not die this time."

Suddenly she disappears, her soft glow fading out. The darkness subsides, and I find myself standing in the forest of the Dartneau Hills, not far from the Aceolevia.

I stuff the small rock into my pocket.

Hoisting Cire onto my shoulders, I start to walk back to the Temple. I grunt under his weight, and feel my body growing heavier with every step. I stumble and fall, my own blood loss weakening me.

After what feels like hours, the white stone of the temple fills my vision and I collapse, dropping Cire next to me at the bottom of the steps. As I gaze into the sky, choking on my own blood, High Priestess Tallulah stands above me.

The world fades to blackness.

I jolt awake, panic rising in my body as I experience the still fresh shock of surviving the *Krothesu*.

How many days have we lost?

I'm in the Temple's sick room, there's nothing here except the bed and a small bedside table. On the table sits a vial of the same dark red liquid we drank before entering the arena.

Touching my shoulder, I find my skin almost completely healed where there had been a nasty bite from the wild beast. Pulling the covers back, I flex my toes and sigh with relief to see they wiggle and the pain is minimal in my bitten leg.

Cire and I have not seen a battle that nasty since our training days when we stumbled upon a beast as equally ferocious as the ones we conquered in the arena.

I think back to the earlier days when Cire and I were so young, just as bullheaded, and always getting into trouble. No matter what heinous scheme I concocted, no matter how assured our punishment would be when we got caught, Cire always stood by me.

He would disagree, refuse to go, and yell at me for being reckless, but he never left my back vulnerable.

We've grown apart over the years. I left my meddling days behind me and stood firmly in my duties. Stepping further into the inner circle of the Temple, joining the elite of the Morei is a dream Cire and I have shared since our boyhood.

Now, so much has changed, including us, and again I find myself worrying if feigning loyalty to the Temple, even for a brief time, will end up costing us our lives. But, leaving the Temple behind means becoming its enemy, and that is not an option if we want to protect Eliana and train her.

I have to find Cire.

Carefully sitting up and swinging my legs to the side of the bed, I set my bare feet on the cool stone. My torn and bloodied clothes are piled in the corner. I slip them back on. Opening the door, I listen in the hallway for anyone else's voice, and decide to turn to the right.

The recovery wing is an area I am quite familiar with from our years of training accidents. One of us was always bound to get hurt or to hurt the other and a trip to the recovery wing even for a minor injury was mandatory as per High Priestess Tallulah's instructions.

The life of a Morei is too precious to be risked accumulating minor injuries and allowing for the opportunity for infections to grow.

Cire's room was always to the right and directly next to mine, the next room over is my first choice in my search for him. The images of Cire bleeding out and the heavy weight of his lifeless body plague my mind as I open the door into the next room. To my dismay, Cire is not there, the room unused.

Backtracking the direction that I came from, I open the door to the room left of my own, and see the healer, Agnus, leaning over Cire's unconscious body.

"Will he be okay?" I ask, stepping into the room.

Agnus startles at the sight of me in the doorway. She tries to recover from her shock quickly, but she is shaking ever so slightly.

"Kai," Agnus sputters. "You're awake. I was not expecting you to be awake so soon."

She points to the arrow and beckons me over. "I could use your assistance."

Atrya's arrow, it's back—but how?

"Agnus, is he going to be alright?"

She shakes her head no, busying herself with prepping the bandages. "Cire is badly injured, it will take several days for him to recover I'm afraid."

I want to object, but arguing would only bring suspicion and so I bite my tongue. "I understand."

She grabs a small saw from the table next to the bed. "I need to remove the arrow head. Push the arrow deeper, the only chance of keeping him alive is to make a clean exit."

I stare dumbfounded at her. She clucks her tongue, motioning for me to roll Cire onto his side. "Push, Kai, you asked if he would be alright, and this is the only way."

The smell of Cire's blood makes me nauseous as I slowly push the shaft of the arrow deeper into his chest, wincing when the arrow's head breaks through the skin of his back. Agnus cuts it off with brutal efficiency.

"Now, pull it back out, please."

I lay Cire back down on the table, and roll up my sleeves, grabbing hold of the arrow. I yank it cleanly out. With the arrow removed, more blood pours out from the hole, soaking his chest and the bed in seconds.

Agnus steps back up to Cire, layering bandages on his chest. "Apply pressure here."

I take over holding the bandages for her.

Brushing her hands together, and with exhaustion evident on her face, she says, "This has been the worst damage you have ever walked away with."

"I am surprised the High Priest risked your lives putting you through that awful gauntlet. You are the first I've treated who have survived. Normally by the time they stumble all the way back from that accursed place, they're as good as dead and beyond my ability to save. But most do not make it out at all."

She gives my arm a small, reassuring squeeze. "He will be okay, just needs his rest."

"Kai, I believe the High Priestess will want to speak to you. Can you please find her and also let her know of Cire's progress in being treated?"

I swallow a lump in my throat. "What update should I give?"

She purses her lips. "Just let the High Priestess know he is recovering as anticipated – given the extent of his injuries." She picks up a small vial from Cire's bedside, drawing the dark contents into a syringe.

"This is a mild sedative to help him stay relaxed while he recovers." Before I can speak, she plunges the syringe into his arm.

"Kai, you're excused now. Please run along."

Cire's eyelids flutter, the sedative taking effect quickly. He moans in his sleep, shifting ever so slightly.

"I will be back for you, Cire."

Cire nearly bled to death, he should not even be alive right now. Something's not right. Agnus is an excellent healer, but she's not a miracle worker.

As I enter the Grand Hall of the Temple, the High Priest and Priestess are approaching at a brisk pace. Bowing deeply, I address each saying, "High Priest, Priestess."

The High Priest smiles at me and says proudly, "I am happy to see you up and moving again, only a few short days later. Most impressive. Congratulations on passing your trial and earning your second chance to show your devotion to the Temple."

"Thank you, High Priest Marius, for your high praise of our efforts." I say politely. My teeth clack together with the force of my clenched jaw.

High Priestess Tallulah smiles at me. "I wonder if you would be willing to join me in the study, Kai?" She extends her arm to me, and I accept it.

The High Priestess leads me away to her private study. I have not been here often since I was a young boy, not much has changed–the room is overcrowded with stacks of books taller than her or I, plants of all kinds draped over bookshelves, hanging down from large pots strung around the room.

She motions for me to sit in an armchair by the unlit fireplace.

"Your test had an anomaly." She stands behind the other chair across from mine, staring down at me with hands folded on the back of the chair.

"I don't understand, what does that mean?"

She answers my question with another of her own. "Did something happen in the arena? Something you want to tell me?"

My skin crawls, but I keep my composure. "Nothing stood out to me, it seemed like pretty cut and dry torture and trials." I smirk.

She frowns at my words, but nods her head. "If you say so, I will take your word for it."

The High Priestess walks around her desk to stand directly in front of me. "Kai, you know you can come to me."

Her smile is sad. "Though, if you have nothing to share, you are dismissed."

Her back turns to me after her dismissal, and she shuffles parchment on her desk.

"High Priestess?"

Her head swivels back quickly, eyes wide with excitement at what I might share. I have never seen her look so ... hopeful.

"Agnus sends her regards and wants to let you know that Cire's health is improving as expected. He's doing well."

"Is that all?" Her disappointment is evident in her voice. "I will let High Priest Marius know, he will be pleased to know of Cire's viability."

I stand and bow low. "Thank you, High Priestess."

"I will send for you and Cire soon for your next assignment. Don't stray too far." She says the last words with a smile that drips of a thinly veiled threat.

I swallow. "We look forward to it, thank you."

I turn away and don't glance back. My hand closes around the small purple rock, the one from the arena. *I need to get this to Eliana.*

Eliana

A PAT ON THE shoulder, and another one that's a bit too forceful jolts me awake. I scream in surprise, peering into the face of a stranger, who is too close for comfort. I back peddle away from them, cursing myself for being caught unaware. My mind flashes back to the forest, to the *severn* and to my certain death.

I search frantically and see I've made it back safely to the hut in the village.

How is that possible?

I spring to my feet, pulling my dagger from my boot and turn my attention to the stranger. "Who are you? How did I get back here?"

"How do you think?" she laughs. "You're not easy to carry, let me tell you."

There's the pull of a bandage on my shoulder and back as I wince in pain, my grip on the dagger lessening with the shooting pain in my arm.

Her hair is so dark it could be mistaken for black if it weren't for the way the dying fire light plays with its color. She's staring at me so intently, I shift my weight onto the balls of my feet.

The sound of my boots scraping the dirt floor pulls her from her stupor. She smiles, her eyes crinkling in the corners–it's an easy going smile of someone who's seeing an old friend. It makes me even more unsettled.

"Well, are you going to tell me who you are, or am I going to have to make you?" I flex my fingers and make a show of flashing my dagger.

It's a feeble attempt at intimidation. It's obvious from my staggered steps and ragged breathing that just standing is causing me a lot of pain. It's taking everything I have to keep from falling over.

As I wait for her to respond, I study her. She's still wearing that eerily friendly smile, her posture is relaxed, natural.

A flowing top hangs low over her hips cinched by a belt around her waist, holding up thick dirt and soot crusted pants. Her boots are made of a supple brown leather with scorch marks criss crossing the top. Her hands are blackened from some kind of grime, and her face is worn from hard labor. She reminds me of the warriors from my village–strong and powerful.

She walks away from me, bending down to add wood to the fire, stoking it back to life. My irritation rises with each passing moment that she continues to ignore me.

Her demeanor reminds me of Kai and Cire's, and I wonder if she is like them–a *sanguinar*.

I match her stare and dare her to make the first move. If she's a *sanguinar*, she made a grave error waking me up before killing me.

"If you're here to kill me, I warn you, I won't go without a fight. You should have killed me in the forest when you had a chance."

She laughs again. I threaten her one more time.

"I think it's best if you leave now." I use my dagger to point toward the door.

"I save you from certain death and this is the thanks I get?" She laughs quietly to herself. "Can you put that thing away, I'm not here to hurt you."

"I didn't know I was so funny," I grumble to myself. Annoyance rises in my gut at how she continues to laugh at my questions, and my–empty–threats.

She stands with her hands on her hips. "I'm not afraid of you, so if you could save us both the hassle, I really wish you would stop. I know your mother taught you to treat elders with more respect than this."

Her words feel like a slap across my face, shame heating my cheeks. I step back, the dagger still in my hand at my side. I won't thank her for saving me, not yet. She knows more than she's saying.

Her eyes dance over the room before landing on me, and my stomach flips from the intense pressure of her stare–like a child, being caught misbehaving by their mother. My palms sweat and my fingers cramp from gripping the dagger too tightly.

"Don't talk about my mother," I growl out. "You don't know her."

"You're right, I don't. However, I do know that you're in no condition to be making threats, you need to rest. Those are nasty wounds you're suffering from." Her words and face soften. "And I don't just mean those scrapes and bruises. You seem lost, child."

"I'm not lost." I'm quick to say, even as the hollowness echoes within me. "Now, if you do not mind, I'd like to get some more rest, alone." I shift away from her, giving her a clear path to the doorway, motioning for her to leave.

"I won't be leaving, not without you. Kai and Cire asked me to protect you."

I knew she was one of them.

"Is that a threat?" I snarl.

She laughs, comfortable. "Hardly. I already saved your life once–like you said, I could have killed you back there."

I sigh, the energy to keep arguing quickly draining away, and I realize how unreasonable I'm being.

"You're right, I'm sorry." I pause, taking a deep breath. "Thank you for saving me."

She waves me off, and sits down by the fire. "Your reputation precedes you, they've told me about your strength and ferocity. I'm not here to hurt you, just to help–should you decide to ask for it."

She smiles. "Or if you find yourself in another scuffle while searching."

She pauses and gazes directly at me. "I know what you seek."

"Being cryptic will not win me over. Tell me what you know or want and be on your way. I won't tolerate any more of this nonsense."

She shrugs, and settles by the fire. "Suit yourself. Like I said, I am here on Cire's request to keep you safe, should you decide to do anything rash or stupid." Her smirk lights up her eyes.

I can't help but laugh.

I like her. She reminds me a lot of Brynne.

"You still haven't given me your name," I say in frustration.

"Alana, Cire and Kai's elder aunt, so to speak. I believe you're aware of their complicated upbringing."

I nod my head. "I'm Eliana."

"Eliana is your given name, but that's not all that is written on your soul. You are also the lost daughter of Hevastia." She motions for me to take a seat across from her, keeping the fire between us.

I settle on the log, laying the dagger across my knees. A small amount of light peeks through the fabric in the window–it must be morning. "I'm sorry, but what time is it right now?"

"It's been several days, if that is what you're asking," she says, matter-of-factly.

"Do you know how long Kai and Cire will be gone for?" I keep my tone even, disinterested even.

I've been asleep for a few days, and she didn't hurt me, that has to count for something.

With a strained smile, she says, "No, but we should make good use of our time together. There is much to be said and learned."

I realize that while we've spoken, the time has passed faster. Her talking will also distract me, so maybe I don't mind her cryptic words, as much.

Maybe I might even learn something useful.

"Do you by chance have anything to eat? Kai and Cire are poor hosts."

She smiles at my joke. Standing, she hands me a blue cloak the color of midnight. "Put this on for the morning chill. We can go to the market for a meal. Let's go now before it becomes overcrowded."

I hesitate.

"Take the cloak, if Cire and Kai learn of your leaving–again–I will take responsibility." She holds it out to me again. "It's a small village, best not to attract unwanted attention."

I reach out and take it, wincing as I lift my right shoulder. I grit my teeth and slip the heavy cloak over both arms, tying it at the neck.

"Follow me closely," she says, turning toward the entrance to the hut.

I may not fully trust her yet, but my gut tells me she knows something I don't, and I trust myself enough to know that I will get the answers I seek one way or another. When she pulls back the flap, the light from the solari shines in, and I gasp at how vibrant the colors of the village are in the daylight.

I follow behind her to the *tehendra*, a marketplace at the center of the village. Alana's back is covered by two blades crossed over her shoulders, and the belt around her waist contains two daggers tucked in along her lower back.

I'm lucky it was her that found me in the woods. I'm still not certain how she could have known where I was. Had she been following me all along?

"We need to keep from drawing attention to you–you'll need a reason to be here unexpectedly. This village is small, everyone here knows each other. After the attack, fear of the Haematite's wrath has driven neighbors to turn on one another if there's any suspicion of treason, any hint of," she lowers her voice, "the Old Ways."

"What should my reason be?" I ask.

"Probably safest to say you're my niece from Sandovell. Mind that you don't mention Kai or Cire, Morei guardians are respected here. Wildewell is very close to the Aceolevia, but they're not allowed friends or family. Connecting you to them would be too suspicious."

I scowl at her back, but continue to follow behind, unable to come up with a compelling argument against her reasoning.

The idea of being 'attached' to my enemy makes me want to throw up in my mouth. I can feel the bitter acid at the back of my throat.

Alana explains to me how the Haematitian Council has been making life in Hevastia a struggle of survival–they pulled their resources from the lesser villages and smaller cities leaving many defenseless against the growing number of beast attacks.

"Wildewell has suffered from several attacks by the black beasts that wander from the depths of the Hilwe Wildes. There used to be more settlements in this part of the valley, but most have joined Wildewell, unable to support themselves. Trading has also greatly suffered, the roads are unsafe to travel and our crops are not as bountiful as they once were."

Alana sighs. "There isn't much left in Hevastia that's untouched by the blight of darkness pervading the land."

Gratefulness and grief wash over me in equal measure as I recall my home village and my life there. Bellamere was strong under my mother's guidance. We had little to fear, plenty to eat, and much to be thankful for.

The mountain hid us away, kept us safe from the Council for nearly 100 years, but it also kept us ignorant. Seeing more of Hevastia has shown me just how little I truly know or understand, it's making me question everything.

"Kai and Cire mentioned the monsters, and I've seen one myself. I almost didn't survive it ... if it hadn't been for Cire, I'd be dead twice over already." Admitting these truths out loud is so shocking I suck in a breath. "So ungrateful." I whisper to myself.

I kiss my fingers and place them over my heart, silently thanking Lady Hevastia for watching over me. I wish I understood why it was through the actions of my enemies.

Are they truly my enemy, though?

"I have so many questions, Alana." She pauses and turns back to face me.

"These past few days have been so confusing ... I'm torn. What is the Council doing if not actively protecting citizens from the beasts? Why are you all suffering so much? Why does Cire think I can do anything about it?"

Her mouth quirks up into a soft smile of relief. "You've been dealt a heavy hand by our goddess. It's natural to have so many questions. But these are questions better answered behind closed doors, so I shall save it for another time. There is a lot happening that doesn't seem reasonable or possible, your existence being top of that list." She turns back around, continuing to walk down the lane.

I scoff. "That's also top of my list."

She flashes a smile over her shoulder. "Then you're in luck, I think I know just the place and person to help get you some answers. But first, let's find you something to eat."

The end of the next street opens into a large plaza with a crumbled, dried-up fountain in the middle. Milling about the plaza are the villagers. They stop and say hello as they pass, comfortable with one another.

I reach out to Alana to stop and ask her more about what to say should someone stop me, but I don't get the chance to before I am swept up into a dance, Alana slipping gracefully out of the way of the festivities, her form retreating into the gathered crowd, not once does she glance back for me.

My partner is a middle-aged man with a thick beard that tickles my cheek as he holds me unnecessarily close. I wince in pain at his large, calloused hands on my back, and I fight the urge to lay him out flat on his back for the misstep. He smells clean, and his clothes are well worn but maintained, so he must be someone of decent stature in the village.

"You're not from around here." His voice is flat, a practiced indifference.

I have to play along. I swallow down the bile in my throat and force a cheerful smile to my face.

"I just arrived, actually. I'm here with," I hesitate, "my aunt ... Alana, visiting from another village."

"Wildewell is a special place, I hope you enjoy your visit with your aunt?" His eyebrow shoots up.

We say no more and finish out the dance. I bow slightly to him as he takes my hand and places one kiss on my palm. A blessing between friends.

"Thank you, sir."

I pull back my hand and turn to slip into the crowd, my eyes scanning for Alana's tall frame and twin blades.

"I didn't catch your name, miss," he calls for me, but I don't turn back to answer, shoving my way through a line of people waiting for a dance partner.

I need to get away from that creep.

My skin crawls from his touch, and his farewell is too intimate for a stranger. It all feels so wrong.

Everything around me seems so surreal, from the music playing across the plaza, to the smells from vendors on the fringes of the market square–all foreign yet vaguely familiar to me.

Three breaths, it's all going to be okay.

I can feel the homesickness clawing at me, everything around me is reminding me so much of home, of what I lost.

The market is scattered with beautiful booths decorated with colorful scraps of fabric waving in the gentle breeze blowing through town. Villagers mill about with large baskets for goods, bartering with the vendors for a better price or a fair exchange.

I can feel myself being swept away in the hum of the *tehendra* and the colors on the wind.

There. I finally spot Alana ahead, her back is to me as she eyes a pastry vendor's limited assortment. I shoulder my way through a small group of people crowding a baker's cart.

"Why did you leave me behind?" I'm breathless from walking quickly, and my whole body aches from the dance.

"That man who pulled you away, Whalen, he is a leader in the village, respected. Not of high birth or rank, but among the village he is looked to for guidance. Interjecting would be rude, besides you seemed capable.

"Did you enjoy the dance? It's a local favorite."

I want to interject, but this village is different from my clan. While it's dressed in a similar fashion and there's a haunting familiarity to its rhythm, the dynamics and the people are all new and strange. Far more complicated than home.

I nod my head. "Yes, but–" I grimace as pain trembles through my body. I worry I've pulled a stitch.

"I know you're in pain, but please attempt to act like you're enjoying yourself." She leans in closer. "Whalen will be keeping an eye on us, he's very suspicious of me and Hama. Here, loop your arm through mine and lean on me if you need to."

I hesitate to grab her arm and she pulls me closer, resting my arm in hers. As we walk up to the first booth, a nice man with beautiful brown hair twisted into buns, face decorated with colorful powders, asks me if I would like anything.

As I reach for the first baked good, a braided bread spotted with fresh berries, Alana stops me with a swat of her hand and a 'don't you dare test me' kind of smile.

She turns a much sweeter smile to the man, and in a honeyed voice says, "I apologize for her ill manners, she forgot to compliment your assortment and offer you a coin. Her stomach gets ahead of her head sometimes, I'm afraid."

She eyes me with the smallest turn of her head, beckoning me to play along. Taking three breaths, I smile and offer an apology.

Definitely not like home.

"My apologies, your samples smell amazing, and I'm sorry for not saying so first." I say through a thin-lipped smile as I peek at Alana for this coin I'm supposed to have.

Sensing my question, she hands the man a small coin, and hands me a small, hard roll, not the soft, braided loaf I was hoping for. I hide my disappointment. With a goodbye and a smile, we are off to the next booth that smells good.

And so we went from one food booth to the next, practicing pleasantries, and collecting a small buffet. Past the last food vendor, there are only a few large, colorful tents similar to the colors and patterns on huts lining the outer edge of the plaza.

"What are in those tents?" I ask Alana as I bite into a crumbly biscuit. My tongue bursts in silent ecstasy with just how delicious it tastes.

"Those are the clothing vendors. The one we seek out is at the other end of the *tehendra*. You can trust Hama to keep your secret and get you a fresh outfit," she says as she eyes my cloak which I have to have pulled tight to hide my ripped clothes and bandaged shoulder underneath. "They're my partner."

"Were they your Morei partner?" I ask through a mouthful of biscuit.

She frowns at my poor manners, or possibly because I figured out her little secret so quickly.

"Yes, they were. We're retired now. Many of the trades people of the village are retired Morei. Hama has taken up dressmaking as their craft. They enjoy the intricacy of sewing and cloth, I still prefer a blade to a needle, and so I work as a blacksmith for the village."

As we continue down the row of tents, the colorful fabrics of the stalls dance in the wind, the huts themselves fat with hidden secrets and wares tucked safely within their walls. The last tent is a vibrant purple color with gemstones sewn into the cloth.

"That's absolutely incredible," I say. Like a prism playing with the light to make rainbows, each small gemstone sewn into the sides of the tent catches and bounces the solari's rays between them as they sway gracefully in the breeze.

The rainbows lie across the sides of the hut to create a pattern like a map of the stars.

Alana laughs quietly to herself. "When we enter, please make sure to tell Hama your thoughts, they would love to hear that someone appreciates their gaudiness. I don't have a taste for it, but they have the greatest gift, so I don't complain."

The inside of the tent is plum full of colorful bolts of fabric piled haphazardly everywhere, unfinished pieces of sewing projects lay strewn about, and the wild chaos of the inside of the tent is beautiful in its own weird way.

"Hama and I were chosen by the first High Priestess to become the second generation of Morei and as we trained together, we couldn't deny the pull that we felt to each other, and on the day of our Rising, we also performed the *Envocia Amorei*. Or, the soul binding ritual. It was a glorious day for us both. We celebrate it every year together."

I blush at the intensity of Alana's words, she speaks so confidently about her feelings.

"That's beautiful," I say, smiling to myself. I've seen other couples of my clan complete the soul rite, but I have always known that was not in my future. The Champion's Rite, a life partner in strategy, but not love, is all I have ever sought for myself. "If you are of the True Faith, how did you complete the *Envocia Amorei*?"

"It was a different time in the Haematitian Council's history, the radical 'True Faith' was early in its formation. Hama and I are part of the second generation of *sanguinars*."

Alana's comment brings so many questions bubbling up inside me, but from my right side, a short person with red hair woven with colorful fabric and a dress of the same rainbow of threads, comes barreling over and almost topples Alana.

"Stars. Where have you been these past few days? I went to the smith earlier to drop off a meal, and you weren't there and no one had seen you."

"Kai and Cire left to answer the summoning from the Council. I was delivering on our promise to watch over their guest."

My gut twists on the way she says guest, as if I had much choice in being brought here.

Standing up taller, and plastering a big smile on my face that I hope appears warm and happy, I rush to introduce myself. Hama cuts me off from making a fool of myself. Taking me by my wrist and Alana by the arm, they drag us to the back of the tent and close a secondary curtain that separates the store front from the small room.

Gazing at me with eyes full of wonderment, they reach out and touch a lock of my hair. "Princess, you've come home to us."

Caught somewhere between shocked at the tenderness and sincerity in Hama's touch, and exasperated with the continued insistence that I am anyone other than myself, I step back, scowling. I stumble, falling onto the dirt floor, kicking up dust. I cough, trying to clear my throat. Hama offers me their hand to pull me to my feet, but I swat it away, coughing harder.

Undeterred, Hama rubs my back reassuringly, giving it two soft pats to help comfort me. My heart aches for my mother and her hugs, but I finally catch my breath and am able to relax. My fingers uncurl from around the small dagger in my belt, and a hot shame climbs up my cheeks at the thought of having almost attacked Hama for comforting me.

Alana stands assessing me again, her gaze focused on my hands. She relaxes as I let go of the dagger, and fold my hands calmly in front of myself. Alana motions at the crate in the corner of the curtained room. "Sit," she orders.

I bite my cheek to keep from arguing as I settle onto the crate, pulling the bunched cloak into my lap. Hama leaves the small room, hurt in their eyes, pretending to attend to something in the front of the shop, leaving Alana standing in front of me.

"I'm sorry. I don't know what came over me."

"You're not a prisoner here, Eliana, you're among people you can trust." Alana says. "Trust is earned, I understand that. But that means we need to be able to trust you, too."

Shame heats my cheeks, and I can't bring myself to meet Alana's eyes. My mother would be so upset at my behavior. Alana was right earlier, I wasn't taught to pull weapons on my elders.

"I brought you here to provide some explanation for everything that's happened, or will potentially happen to you. Hama and I have been secretly studying the lore of the Old Ways for quite some time now, and we believe we stumbled upon a scroll that possesses the key to unlocking the block on your magic and your reincarnation."

I peer up at her, hopeful. "I'm not even sure I'm this foretold princess. Why would you help me?"

"Hevastia has fallen on dark times, and I used to believe that the True Faith of the Haematites was going to deliver our people from the struggle to survive, but I no longer believe that.

"When we were Morei, our duties were about protecting the villages, instilling the True Faith, and bringing everyone together in a time of uncertainty and turmoil. Now, it's all focused on destruction. The atrocities Kai and Cire have been asked to commit, I can't abide by that."

"Cire told me about how they attacked Wildewell."

Alana nods her head, acknowledging the village's rocky history. "I can tell you have more questions about that, but they will have to wait. Do you know much about the reincarnation prophecy?"

I shake my head, no.

"Most of the knowledge Hama and I have comes from the scroll Hama inherited from their family before the Old Ways were outlawed. We hid it during the raid on Wildewell several years ago."

Hama steps back into the room, holding a bundle of colorful fabrics.

"You were last reborn as Atrya Helesatra, Princess of Hevastia, to King Annenon and Queen Xristiana Helesatra," Hama says, busying themself with organizing the clothes they pulled from their storefront.

I interrupted them, earning me a scowl, to ask, "The same King and Queen who formed the first Haematitian Council?"

Alana seems surprised by my question, and returning where Hama left off she says, "Yes, that same King and Queen–may the spirits hold them gently. You were reborn as Atrya during our first centennial of true peace after the Great War. A gift to our new kingdom, from Hevastia herself. But on the eve of Atrya's sixteenth birthday, she was taken from us."

"Everyone knows the royal family was killed," I say.

Alana nods her head. "It was a brutal slaughter of the devout followers of Lady Hevastia chosen to lead our people. Their deaths are what ushered in the belief in the 'True Faith' and the 'New Order' within the Haematitian Council.

"It all began when an attempt to destroy Hevastia's Heart was made. The heinous act was led by a man named Reinauden. He tried to lay waste to the original Aceolevia Temple by preying on the youngest priestess for her power and using her magic to commit atrocities against the other Temple priests and priestesses. The gruesome aftermath lay for everyone to witness. Hearing of the attack, the King and Queen, along with the princess, traveled to the temple ruins and sent out search parties to find Reinauden."

Hama jumps in. "After the manhunt turned up no sign of Reinauden he was presumed dead. The royal family returned to Eternis, the capital city, to celebrate Atrya's naming ceremony, and ascension into society as a third governing head alongside her parents. That's when the attack on the capital took place."

"Eternis was attacked, that seems pretty straightforward. Why is it such a mystery how Princess Atrya died?" I ask, feeling myself sucked into the story.

Hama continues, excitement evident in their voice. "Her body was never found. The mysterious circumstances fueled the prophetic return of the next reincarnation and all magic. Your glorious return to power has been a legend, a myth we tell our children to help them sleep.

"The Haematitian Council may have turned their backs on Lady Hevastia and the myth, but many across Hevastia are still loyal to the Old Ways, my dear. They stay ever patient, hiding, waiting for you to emerge triumphant from the hidden corners of Hevastia. In all our years of searching for answers and waiting, I never dreamed that you would be here in our lifetime."

Alana interjects, taking back control of the story. "The greatest mystery has always been the whereabouts of the prophesied heir. With the royal bloodline terminated, there was no clear sign of who would be chosen as the next line to carry Lady Hevastia's blessing.

"All magic died with the royal family, no living heir stepped forward to claim the throne, and without the god-touched anchor, magic vanished overnight and the Haematitian Council stepped into power unchallenged."

Some part of me knows these things, but another part of me doesn't want to.

How will I know what to believe?

"I don't have anything special about me, no magic to call upon," I sigh, almost disappointed by my normalcy.

"I'm sorry. In my village, we spoke very little of the past. My mother, the chieftess, was adamant about maintaining the practices of the Old Ways and keeping with the devotional practices to Lady Hevastia, but she all but forbade discussion of Hevastia's history or the happenings beyond our small village and clan lands." I swallow down the threat of tears at the mention of my mother and my people.

"I was just as ignorant to part of this story as Cire and Kai. I judged them so harshly."

"No need to apologize dear," Hama says. "The temple has been very selective about the history taught to children born within the Aceolevia's walls. Ignorance is a powerful weapon when wielded as the Haematitian Council has. Many have fallen prey to their deceptive teachings."

"The truth behind the origins of the dark magic Reinauden used to manipulate the young priestess remains a mystery — or the Haematitian Council's best kept secret, if you ask me. Before he could be taken for questioning, he took his own life, or so they say. And so, his answers died with him. The young priestess he threatened into helping him lost her mind after the whole ordeal, and fled the country days later out of fear." Alana explains, continuing her story where it left off.

"With the King and Queen gone, and the princess presumed dead, the power to lead Hevastia's people fell to what remained of the Haematitian Council. And as I'm sure you're aware, they've only made things worse." She clenches her fist.

"If everyone thought the reincarnation was long dead or never returning, how did Cire find me? Why were the Haematites searching for me?"

Hama peeks up from their work and in a soft voice says, "It was my doing. I used to tell them stories at bedtime as children to fill their dreams with adventure, fighting, magic, and heroism. They were so young, I just wanted them to have hope. The Haematites are not searching for you, at least I don't believe they are, as they don't believe in the reincarnation prophecy."

Alana adds, "Before they left for your village, Cire and I fought over the prophecy. He mentioned in passing a thought against the Council, and I panicked and told him to back off before he got himself killed. He didn't take it well, insisting he needed to find you, I've never seen him so determined."

My next thought chills me.

I need to understand more about the reincarnation and uncover what happened to the last one. And what the Council has in store for the next.

"I'm ready, no more of this talk for now," Hama says in a sing-song voice. Laying down an assortment of colorful fabrics, Hama motions for me to stand up and try on the first piece.

My irritation at being dressed like a doll fades the instant I see the assortment of clothes Hama fashioned for me.

I scan the pile, choosing a pair of pants with a matching top, and Hama nods their head in approval.

"This will serve you well, it will be the most comfortable clothes you'll ever have," they say with a kind smile.

The outfit is a basic white tunic, with a black jacket lined in soft fur, blue accents stitched along the arms of the jacket in a vined pattern, paired with black pants, a new leather belt and a pair of sturdy boots. I run my hands over the supple fabrics. I have never owned something so lavish.

"Thank you, both of you."

Hama smiles and folds the matching pants and jacket, tucking the scroll Alana mentioned into the folds of the clothes before tying a ribbon around them and handing the parcel to me.

Alana holds open the tent flap and signals for me to follow her. I smile back at Hama and follow Alana out of the market and back to the hut.

Along the way I fiddle with the ribbon on the package, my thoughts taking me away from Wildewell and back to Bellamere. I've been gone for a week, and I am no closer to having a plan for attacking the Aceolevia and seeking revenge for my people.

More and more I find myself wanting to abandon the quest for revenge in search of answers for my potential role in the reincarnation prophecy, but guilt gnaws at me. Alana assured me that she's told me everything she knows, the only people alive who might be able to help me are hidden away on a mountain range halfway across Hevastia.

How can I face them after all this time away and all I've learned, and better yet, how do I even get home to them?

Cire

A soft, constant noise pulls me from sleep. I lay with my eyes closed, continuing to listen to the drip of water from the ceiling to the small pool forming on the floor. I wiggle my fingers, toes, and slowly work movement back into my stiff muscles.

There's no concept of time in the windowless rooms of the recovery bay, and from the uncomfortable, lumpy mattress I'm lying on, that's where I am. Judging by my body's stiffness and the dryness of my mouth, it has been more than a day.

When I open my eyes, I find myself alone in the healer's bay, a place I am quite familiar with. A cup of water sits on the table beside the bed, and I guzzle it down immediately.

A fuzzy static spreads across my body up to my head, and my eyes grow heavy. My head rests back on the pillow, and I drift back to sleep once again.

Kai's in front of me, the blurred shadows of a battle raging all around us, but Kai stands clearly in my view, brimming with confidence in full regalia. He bends down in front of me, mouthing words I can't hear or understand.

A sharp pain stabs me, and my hands wrap around the hilt of a dagger Kai's shoved into my chest, gutting me like an animal. His hands close around the wound, and the energy leaves my body with a sickening pull. I tell him to stop, that he's taken too much, but I can't find my voice.

My vision fades to black.

I open my eyes, I'm not back in my room, but another battle field, shadows of my comrades running past me, the smell of blood, sulfur, and death in the air.

Kai stands in front of me again, a different dagger in his hand. This time he takes my arm, and I resist, but I can't pull my arm away. He runs the tip of the dagger down my arm, and I scream in pain as blood seeps from the deep cut, so deep the bone lays exposed. His hands cover the wound once more, my energy leaving me as he steals my lifeforce again.

I fight against him, but find myself unable to move, only watching with growing dread as he takes more and more of my blood, until he's taken too much, and I pass out, again.

The horror of Kai, the dagger, my blood, and my life leaving me repeats itself again and again. I am unable to stop him, unable to save myself, and I face my personal failure repeatedly. My mind goes dizzy with the flashing images of Kai from my memories of past battles, these new horrors, and my own weakness, over and over.

I wake, gasping for air.

"Cire, you're awake. Finally." I flinched at the sound of Kai's voice so closeby after enduring my nightmares. Opening my eyes, he's sitting beside the bed. "You've been resting for several days now. How do you feel?"

"Never better." I swallow, suppressing the memory of my nightmare.

That's all it was, a nightmare.

Eliana

A FEW WEEKS HAVE gone by, and Alana, Hama, and I have found a rhythm with one another. It's easy for me to allow their comfortable presence to soothe my aching heart. It helps that the mere sight of their faces does not pain me, or cause fury to build in my stomach in the same way that Kai's or Cire's does.

It would be easy to forget what I've left behind, if I did not remind myself of it often. I have remained in Kai and Cire's hut, as promised. I try not to let myself be annoyed that I kept a promise to my enemies, that I continue to hide from my mission of avenging my people.

How simple it would be to forget, to move on. I could be the princess they are seeking. I could fulfill the prophecy my grandmother and ancestors believed in.

I turn, my boot digging into the well worn groove I have left in the floor as I trace my steps back and forth.

I don't know what to believe.

"If you keep pacing like that you'll dig a new well for the village," says a familiar voice from the doorway.

Alana stands with her hand on her hip, smirking at me, and Hama stops short behind her with an arm full of vegetables and bolts of fabric in bright colors.

"What's all that for?" I point to the assortment of items in Hama's arms as they set it on the makeshift table I helped Alana fashion yesterday. They said they were tired of grumbling about eating on the floor by the fire, and that I "deserved" a proper table and bed.

Now there's even a cozy corner of the hut that I claimed for myself, and it brings a soft smile to my lips.

How strange this place has begun to feel like home.

Alana and Hama have been very kind to me, treating me as an equal and not an outsider. I think back to how we treated merchants who wandered into our valley–they were never met with the same sort of hospitality I've been given here.

"Come." Hama's sweet voice beckons me forward, their head down as they rummage through the different bolts of fabric and thread they carried here.

"I want your opinion."

I share a knowing look with Alana and roll my eyes at her as she snickers quietly into her hand.

What does Hama have in store for me this time?

Hama and I have been doing a dance around each other ever since I commented on how beautiful their store was in the *tehendra* several days ago. They continue to persuade me to wear a gown, and I am running out of clever, yet polite, ways to turn them down.

They peer up at me with hopeful eyes, holding out a midnight blue fabric studded in small rhinestones.

"Oh Hama." I suck in a breath. "You really outdid yourself with this, it's gorgeous. It reminds me of your light catching fabric. Where did you find it?"

Their smile brightens the room. "You wouldn't believe the amount of scrap fabric I have lying around my shop.

"I take it this one is a yes?" They smile once more, pulling the fabric from my fingers.

I bite my lip, trying to hold back a big smile of my own. It feels girlish and naive to be giddy over a dress when there are more important matters at hand, but I've learned there are such rare opportunities as of late to be joyful that I will selfishly hold on to this small moment for myself and Hama.

"Yes." Such a small word.

Hama pulls me in for a tight hug, their arms stronger than I expected. Alana smiles at me over Hama's shoulder and gives me a thumbs up.

I know that this project will help keep Hama's mind off of Cire's and Kai's absence if nothing else.

Alana pushes off the wall. "Now that that's settled, Eliana, would you like to practice magic again?"

And just like that the joy and energy are sucked from the room. My gut twists in on itself, and my mouth runs dry. I want to say no, I would rather eat dirt than try their magic again. But I know Alana's only trying to help, and we don't know where else to start.

I swallow, trying to bring some saliva into my mouth. When that doesn't work, I give up and nod my head, trying to appear enthusiastic. Hama gives me a quick, worried glance before turning back to sorting the vegetables, trying to seem busy. I follow Alana through the door to the dirt lane behind the hut.

Alana sighs. "We both wish there was another way, but we can't stop trying now."

I grit my teeth, making a fist at my side. The tension helps pull the queasiness from my stomach, and I feel more like myself again.

That is, until Alana hands me a dead rabbit outside. The blood drips onto the stone lane outside the house, splashing small droplets on my boot.

"Rabbit blood isn't very strong, but it's the best I could do today." Alana eyes the rabbit with a predatory focus, her eyes fixated on the blood.

Alana is a *sanguinar*, and before they "retired" from the Haematites, Hama was her Morei. When Alana explained to me the relationship between a *sanguinar* and their Morei, I threw up a little in my mouth.

Hama would bleed in battle so Alana didn't have to use her own blood for magic, so she could be stronger.

A shudder runs through my body as I take the rabbit from her, letting the blood drip into my right hand.

I match her concentration, reaching out into the world, feeling for something that is pulling or pushing against me. Alana said it's different for everyone, some feel the wind push lightly against them, to others it's the pull of a storm.

We don't know what my magic will feel like yet, so I put my senses out to all elements in case any of them respond.

There's nothing except this poor rabbit's blood making my fingers slick.

I squeeze my eyes shut tighter, equal parts hoping to feel *something* and hoping nothing happens. Minutes pass with no results, not even a faint whisper of a gift.

Maybe everyone is wrong, and I am just ordinary.

In moments like this, the thought of being normal feels attainable, but in the quiet of the night, when I'm alone, trapped in my nightmares, I'm reminded that while I may not have access to magic, I am not normal.

I sigh in exasperation and open my eyes to Alana. She shifts her focus from the blood on my hands to my face, frowning.

"Nothing?" she asks.

I shake my head no, handing her the rabbit for our dinner.

"I'm going to go clean up." I walk away, leaving her to go inside the house and tell Hama that I failed, yet again. It sickens me how badly I want to perform *sanguinar* magic, how it's an affront to Lady Hevastia, to nature. And yet, there are no other options, no other magic.

"Eliana, wait," Alana says, grabbing my wrist. "I can see the disgust on your face. I know this isn't what you hoped for."

I sigh. "You're only trying to help, please don't take it personally. It just feels so wrong–"

"It doesn't have to be a weapon," Alana cuts me off, trying to hide the hurt behind her eyes. "The way the Morei use it now ... it wasn't always like that. It started with more noble intentions."

"You don't have to defend yourself, Alana."

"Just listen, please."

I nod my head in response, allowing her to continue.

"When Hama and I learned blood magic, it was so that we could help villages struggling to rebuild after the destruction of the Great War. After the royal family's death, and with our natural gifts gone, many who relied on theirs to sustain themselves were barely surviving. Two generations since the loss of our gifts and they couldn't rebuild. It was abysmal. The blood gave me the strength to dig canals, build stronger homes, and work tirelessly for months. We would travel to the villages, teach them of the True Faith and rebuild their homes in exchange for any articles relating to Lady Hevastia."

"What is the True Faith?" I ask. "I still don't understand how the council originally formed around faith in Lady Hevastia would allow itself to fall prey to blasphemy and corruption."

"The simple answer is power. After the deaths of the royal family and the loss of Hevastian magic, the Haematitian Council made a show of waiting for our Lady to make herself known and restore Hevastia. When a generation passed and nothing happened that was all it took for many who were faithful to turn their backs on Lady Hevastia in search of something new and tangible to believe in.

"The True Faith was the belief that the only faith we needed was in our own strength, that the power was within us to restore Hevastia, without her Ladyship's Light."

"And what they meant by the power within you –"

"They meant our blood. That's how *sanguinars* were created. Over time, that mission was twisted, becoming the violence your village fell victim to."

A single tear falls down her cheek. "I'm so sorry for your loss. We've watched the very villages we rebuilt with our blood fall at the hands of our friends and former comrades. It's why Hama and I abandoned the Aceolevia and the Council's teachings and dedicated our remaining years to the study of Lady Hevastia."

I pull Alana in for a hug. Her shoulders shake as she cries, and soon we are both wiping tears and laughing softly together. She gives me another hug before we go back inside.

The smell of roasted vegetables and herbs fills the hut, making my mouth drool. Alana and Hama join me for dinner, and we work in relative silence to finish preparing the meal.

Revenge is seeming less of an option, the Council is too powerful. I would be foolish to travel there alone. That most likely ends with me dying. Dead, I am no use to my people.

But, I can't stay here. The only trouble is, I know very little of Hevastia's geography, and have no idea how to safely travel home with the presence of dark beasts so rampant in these parts.

Hama snaps their fingers, pulling me from my thoughts. "You need to freshen up, and let me inspect that wound." Their lips are pursed, annoyed that I've neglected to take care of myself.

"Hama, I'm fine," I reassure them.

They do not seem convinced.

"Hush." Their hands are around my arm and pulling me to my feet, out the doorway and behind the hut to a makeshift bath. An old steel tub and a moth-eaten cloth sit concealed in the shadow of the hut, tucked behind a small privacy fence.

"It's not much, but it will do." Hama's hands are on their hips as they survey the "bath."

"Let me heat some water over the fire for the bath, and while we wait I can clean your bandage."

I follow them reluctantly back into the hut, sitting down on the dirt floor while they perch on a stool behind me.

Their hands are cold on my bare shoulder, but their touch is gentle as they peel back the blood crusted bandages, dabbing the wound with a damp cloth soaked in an herbal blend pulled from their pocket.

I glance questioningly at the pile of crushed herbs mixed into a poultice.

"It's an old family recipe of medicinal herbs. Before we lost magic, my mother would pray over the blend and ask Lady Hevastia to assist the herbs in sharing their energy with the wounded." They smile at the memory. "Now, it's just good old fashioned medicine."

After Hama helps me to fasten a new bandage on my shoulder, they plait my hair. The feeling of their fingers pulling softly through my hair brings a tear to my eyes. It's as if I am transported back in time, and I am a young girl again, my mother telling me stories in the firelight.

Hama must see my tears because they whisper, "Sweetie, are you okay?"

"My mother, she would comb my hair as a small girl." I suck in a deep breath and say the words I have rarely said out loud in these last few weeks. "She's gone now, and I miss her terribly."

Hama finishes plaiting my hair before moving to sit across from me. They take my hands, giving them a light squeeze. "Cire and Kai told us about your village. I am so sorry you had to witness that. It is a terrible burden."

Their kindness is so unexpected, a sob escapes my lips. They beckon me closer, pulling my head into their soft lap. They continue stroking my hair, and say a familiar prayer. The same one I prayed in the fields as I buried my family.

"Lady Hevastia, I humbly ask that you welcome these warriors into your service. They fought valiantly for your Light and your love. Send them to the Beyond for their hard earned rest that they may revisit our world, once again reborn in your evershining Light."

"Alana said that Wildewell is very devoted to the Haematitian Council. If that's true, why did you stay?"

Hama smiles sadly at me, but their eyes wander over my shoulder and up. Hama stands, their eyes full of worry.

Whipping my head around, Kai and Cire gaze down at me, having stopped to stand in the doorway. I stood so fast the stool Hama was perched on topples over.

The small ornate dagger is in my hands and pointed at their necks, my chest heaving with the adrenaline of being caught off guard. Kai and Cire both look like hell, covered in bandages, and their faces are scraped up.

Taking deep breaths to calm my racing heart, I tuck the dagger back into my belt. I pull my shirt back on, grateful for the bandages across my chest.

Kai steps through the doorway, embracing Hama and then Alana. Cire hangs back, watching us before he steps into Hama's outstretched arms.

The joy is apparent, they love Kai and Cire. Hama fusses over each of them while they stand patiently, familiar with their nursemaid tendencies. Alana stands to the side, drilling them with questions about their time away.

They look every part the loving family, and my heart aches for my mother. After they've finished assessing the injuries, Hama begins a barrage of questions, cornering them by the door.

I settle back down beside the fire, my heart still beating fast.

I'm relieved they're alive. I don't know what Alana or Hama would have done if they never came back.

My knee bounces with nerves and I coach myself to refrain from slipping the dagger out of my belt and throwing it at them.

Their return has sent all the memories of the battle in Bellamere rushing back. A pit forms in my stomach as my righteous anger and desire for vengeance bubble back to the surface.

All the promises I almost let myself forget while staying here in Wildewell rise within me, calling me to take action.

I glance back at Kai and Cire. It almost seems unfair to attack them when it's clear they've seen death multiple times over.

One... two... three.. deep breaths to calm my racing heart.

Finally, Hama seems satisfied with Kai's answers. Their face is ghostly pale with worry. I want to ask if they're okay, but Kai's voice pulls my attention back to him and Cire.

He pulls the lid off the water pot hanging over the fire.

"What are we having for dinner?"

Alana laughs, the sound echoing off the walls of the small hut "Bath water." She says between laughs, sending both Hama and I into a fit of giggles.

Over the last few days with them, I have begun to recognize their ticks, and I can tell when they're forcing something–like laughter. Whatever Kai and Cire went through has them both on edge.

Alana waves the knife in her hand as she talks. "I'm making skewers. I was able to fetch a decent price for fresh game meat in the market." The soft chop of the knife against the block is the only sound as she makes quick work of the vegetables from the marketplace.

"Not many hunters have been willing to leave the village to check their snares." Frowning, she puts down the knife.

"There have been more frequent sightings of dark beasts on the edge of the Hilwe Wildes, and so far as the Thessimis Fields."

Hama pulls the large pot off the fire, and takes my hand to lead me to the tub outside. They give Cire and Kai a stern look.

"The lot of you better stay in here and help Alana."

Kai chuckles, but Cire is not paying Hama any attention. He and Alana have their heads bent toward one another, already deep into a serious discussion about the wild beasts and hunting. Kai turns his back to us to join them.

I grab the new outfit Hama gifted me during our first trip the the *tehendra*, and reluctantly follow Hama.

"It's not much but it does in a pinch." Hama dumps the pot into the tub, sprinkling some of the herbs from the poultice into the bath water. They murmur the prayer quietly to themself, turning to leave me to my bath.

"Hama?" My hand rests gently on their arm but they jump as if I have struck them. "Are you okay?"

Hama's smile does not meet their eyes. "Quite alright. Why do you ask, princess?"

My jaw clenches at the mention of that title. I still don't know what to believe, but I know no matter what, I hate being called that. I school my features, unclenching my jaw and softening my cheeks. I'll get right to the point.

"Kai and Cire, what happened to them?"

Hama frowns, fiddling with their robe.

"They were in the *Krothesu*. It's an especially twisted game the Council created to entertain themselves and punish traitors. It's a miracle they survived."

With that, they turn away and leave me to my thoughts. I step out of my mud crusted pants and torn shirt, discarding them on the ground before sinking into the shallow bath. The hot water burns at first, but as I scoop the water in my hands and let it run down my arms, chest, and back, I relax into the soothing heat. I don't see any soap beside the tub, so I let myself sink into the blissful feeling of the water.

I've already decided that I can't possibly make it to the mountains on my own, that I need to ask Kai or Cire for help.

They are able to travel across long distances in a blink–I wonder how they do that.

I resolved myself to get answers after I finish bathing, and if they refuse to help me, then I will force their hand. The shallow water cools quickly and soon the air prickles my skin.

Hama left a clean scrap of cloth next to my clothes, and I use that to dry off before dressing.

I pull on my boots, tucking my favorite dagger into its place, and the rest in my new belt. I leave my hair plaited as Hama made it, the familiarity of it feeling right.

Back in the hut, the fire is bright and the smell of cooked meat wafts through the open window. Voices carry from inside the hut as I near the door. I stop just outside the doorway, listening to the conversation around the fire.

"They had us complete the trials thirteen times. I don't understand how we survived." Kai's voice is ragged, exhausted.

"It's a miracle." Hama says, somber.

"Or, a trick," Cire growls out. "There are holes in our memory."

I want to continue listening, but the breeze catches the cloth that covers the entrance, and I make eye contact with Cire. I sigh and step into the hut, pretending Cire did not just catch me eavesdropping.

"I saved one for you, Eliana, before Kai ate them all." Alana hands me a skewer, the meat slightly charred.

"Alana says there are still large, wild beasts in the forest," Kai says. "She also tells me that you had a run in with one?" A cocky smile flashes my way.

I swallow down my pride. "It's true, I was hoping to travel to the Aceolevia on my own, to get answers."

"You did what?" Cire says sharply. "Do you have a death wish?" He shoots me a glare.

"No," I shout. "Maybe, I just–I wanted them to answer for destroying my home, my family." I take a deep breath.

"We've been through this before–I want justice for my people."

"You foolish, headstrong girl." Cire says, practically spitting out the words.

"You wouldn't get within shouting distance of the Aceolevia before you were caught and killed on the spot. Or worse, brought in front of the High Council as a sacrifice to the 'cure'."

"Cire, don't be so harsh," Kai interjects.

"I don't need you to defend me. I wouldn't be in this situation if it wasn't for you." My eyes shoot daggers at Kai, and Cire.

Kai's nostrils flare. "You're right. And we've apologized. I will spend the rest of my days atoning for the pain I've caused you and countless others."

"Enough," Alana says, her voice stern. "We are not each other's enemies anymore, Eliana. Kai and Cire, you survived the gauntlet, don't go tearing each other apart now."

"Yes, Alana," we say in unison. She clears her throat and continues. "Eliana, if you are able to fulfill the prophecy, you will avenge more than just your village's loss. Kai and Cire, don't talk about matters you don't understand. Grief is a powerful force, it can make even the strongest fall to their knees, or act recklessly."

I retreat to the corner of the room I've made my own while they were away. My journal is lying open on my cot, so I kick it closed with the toe of my boot as I bend down to grab the sword I "borrowed" from them when I left to find the Aceolevia.

Cire's voice catches me off guard. He must have been watching me from beside the fire.

"That sword is one of ours." He laughs softly. "But it seems you already claimed it for yourself."

"Why that one?" Kai asks. "There are many other swords of similar quality stashed in this hut."

I smirk at the memory of finding them all. I turn back to them, the sword resting across both my palms.

"I'm not sure, it just felt like it was made just for me, a sword like that is the best kind to have."

"Then consider it yours," Cire says.

"You don't need to gift me weapons, I'm more than capable of getting them for myself." I sound like a petulant child, but I don't want him to think I owe him any favors.

Cire chuckles quietly to himself. My hand runs over the blade, and I admire it more closely.

"It's very pretty. Something much nicer than I would have ever owned in my village."

"Was your blacksmith not much of a metalworks artist?" Kai asks.

I wince at the memory of our blacksmith, my mother's close friend, possibly her nephew, being cut down during the battle, his apprentice, one of my best friends dropping at Kai's feet. I shut out the memory, blocking my mind from spiraling to that dark place that beckons me daily.

"In my village, you forged your own weapons when you came of age. It was part of the warrior's rite to be able to pick your weapon, mold it with your own sweat and energy. The true mark of a warrior was the care with which they crafted their weapon, imbued it with their spirit."

"What did you craft?" Cire asks.

"My dagger. It's of the same metal as my mother's, a special vein of rock that grows deep within our mountains. I was only fourteen when I journeyed alone into its depths to retrieve the metal ore for my dagger."

"I would love to hear that story some time," Kai says softly. He's watching me from across the fire, his brown eyes softer in the light. His comment catches me off guard, a blush rising to my cheeks. I want to think of a snarky remark, but all that comes out is a snorting laugh. The noise catches everyone off guard and soon we are all laughing, all of our harsh words soon forgotten and forgiven.

"You're lucky you didn't lose this sword. Fate's Guardian is a powerful weapon, and its care should not be taken lightly," Cire says.

"Fate's Guardian?" I ask, scanning the blade in my hands, searching for an inscription. It's the most beautiful thing I have ever seen.

The blade is tapered, well balanced, and the hilt is wrapped in a soft blue leather, along the pommel and crossguard are small green gemstones. The firelight reveals beautiful swirls and flowers etched into the metal on both sides, and there's an inscription on the bottom, but I cannot quite make it out.

"Your sword." He pats his hip. "Only those destined to do great things are given names. My sword is called Light Breaker, and Kai's twin blades are Virtue and Faith."

"What do you mean?"

"We name our blades. It's a Morei superstition, possibly a belief of the Old Ways that the Council has left alone. Harmless, I suppose."

I sat down beside the fire, my interest piqued. Cire smiles at me, the flames glinting in his green eyes.

"When I picked up my sword for the first time, I felt a connection to it, and it became like an extension of myself. I knew its name in my heart, and out of respect for it, I called it by that name. So, when I picked yours up in the market, it whispered its own. It told me its purpose."

"I've never heard of such a thing. My dagger did not whisper a name to me."

Fate's Guardian has a nice ring to it.... Where have I heard it before?

I return the sword to my corner before settling back on the log across from them.

"I've never thanked you," I pause, "for your hospitality. It is strange to be in my enemy's home, even stranger when they no longer feel like my enemy. And I am thankful for it. For your help in finding answers."

The modest sincerity behind the words is shockingly real, surprising me in the admission. And even still, I feel as though

I have betrayed my people by playing nice with the men whose swords are still stained in my people's blood. I grit my teeth.

"I think I may have something of an answer." Kai's words are cautious. "There was a moment in the gauntlet, Cire, when you passed out, where something unexplainable happened that I haven't told you about."

Cire's head perks up, his scowl giving way to curiosity. "What are you talking about?"

"It's about this."

Kai pulls out a small, jagged purple rock from his pocket. He holds it gingerly in his hand, extending his arm out to me.

"Princess Atrya told me to give this to you, Eliana."

Kai explains what happened after Cire passed out in the gauntlet. I sit impatiently, fidgeting with the small rock Kai handed me. It's a purple crystal, and as I hold it to the flames, the fire light dances off it, making it glint and glow.

Kai said when he touched it, he felt a sting, or a surge of power. But what power he couldn't tell. Having never had connection to magic, I don't know that I could tell what it does or should do.

"And you're sure she didn't tell you what it is?" Cire's voice is growing increasingly agitated. He's asked this same question twice before.

"I already told you, all she said was 'this is what we've been looking for'." Kai's voice is exasperated.

"I don't feel any different." I mumble, not that either of them are paying attention.

As Kai opens his mouth to continue arguing with Cire, Alana and Hama stand. "We're going home for the night."

We take turns hugging them goodbye, and as they leave Alana hands me a small journal. "These notes could prove useful," she says with a wink.

Ignoring Kai and Cire as they continue to argue over the stone, I flip open Alana's journal.

As it turns out, Alana had more information to share that she had been withholding these last few days. Her and Hama have been observing the Aceolevia's activities for quite some time. Recording observations in this journal. As I flip through the pages, my eyes flit over notes on the comings and goings of different acolytes, guardian units sent on "cleansing missions," and the prisoners they bring back.

Unfortunately, we are still no closer to knowing the connection between the Council's actions and this stone.

I sigh in frustration and snap the journal closed.

It's no use, I'm never going to get my answers from sitting around.

I take to pacing the length of the room, kicking a small rock with the toe of my boot as I wear a rut into the floor in my frustration.

"We could jump there and check."

Kai's words pull me from my thoughts, and my pacing slows as I turn to them.

"It won't work, we've never been there before. Hama warned us about this." Cire is hunched over, his face is stern as he whispers furiously to Kai.

"But what if we find something, what if we can learn what these rocks do?" Kai motions to me, talking about the small purple gem in my hand.

"No, you said so yourself. High Priestess Tallulah is watching us, we can't draw more suspicion to ourselves."

Cire takes a smooth rock from his pocket. He absentmindedly runs his thumb over the surface, and the stone's gray swirls move, following the traced path of Cire's fidgeting.

To my astonishment the air next to Cire also ripples, just as it did in the Thessimis Fields.

"Kai, we have to stop using these. We need to lay low."

"That will take too long," Kai growls out.

"We have to be patient," Cire says, holding out his hand. Kai reluctantly pulls a similar stone from his pocket and hands it to Cire. Cire tucks both stones back into his coat pocket.

Traveler magic? I have never heard of it. All I know is–I need one of those stones.

Their conversation now over, Cire turns to me. "Alana mentioned she's been trying to teach you Morei magic?" Cire asks, his voice pulling me from my thoughts. "Have you had any success?"

"No." I stop pacing. "She said you feel the push or pull of the magic, but...there's nothing."

Kai clears his throat. "It's like a rising tide surging within me, building until it unleashes. It's as if it would build so much that I would explode if I didn't respond to it."

I turn to him and shame heats his cheeks. "It's hard for me to ignore the call."

"What is it like for you?"

A scowl darkens Cire's face. "It's not as strong as Kai's. There's a soft push, and I have to reach for it."

"Honestly, I'm relieved. I don't want to be a *sanguinar*."

Kai flinches, and I realize I said the word with so much disgust.

I backtrack. "I–I didn't mean it like that, it just...doesn't feel right. Maybe the 'chosen one' shouldn't use the very magic she's fighting against, you know?"

"You're probably right." Kai smiles, a mischievous light glinting in his eyes. "So, if you're not going to fight with it, you should learn how to fight against it."

"Kai, I don't think that's such a good idea." Cire says, stepping between us. "She's still injured, you could lose control and hurt her."

"I'm in," I say, smiling. "I want to learn to fight you."

Kai claps his hands together, beaming. "Excellent. Training starts tomorrow morning.

Cire

I STARE AT ELIANA *sitting across the fire from me, fidgeting with her hair, twirling it between her fingers absentmindedly.*

She catches me staring and smiles, a blush rising in her cheeks. I stand to come around the fire, sitting next to her, our shoulders brushing.

Her fingers stop moving, and she glances at me with her big blue eyes.

They are like twin pools, beckoning me to swim in their depths. Her cheeks are rosy from the heat of the fire between us, and I lean forward, tipping her chin toward me with my hand, pulling her fingers from her hair with my other and wrapping my fingers in her thick locks.

I pull her close, and our lips almost brush.

The solari are barely above the horizon when a boot nudges me in the ribs. I glance up to see Eliana peering down at me, a look of determination on her face. I turn my face away, a blush rising to my cheeks, the memory of my dream rushing back to me.

When I glance up again, she's gone, sitting next to Kai by the fire, whispering. Her sword, Fate's Guardian, sits across both of their laps, and jealousy churns in my gut.

"What are you doing?" I ask, pulling their attention away from their private conversation and to me.

"Kai was telling me about Alana forging this sword for you." She turns the blade over before sheathing it on her back. A biscuit hits me in the chest. "Eat. I want to start training before the village wakes."

"We won't be training in the village, it's not safe." Kai pulls his stone out of his pocket, and I scowl. He must have taken it back while I was sleeping. "I have a different place in mind."

"Kai, I already told you, we need to lie low," I growled.

"And I told you we would,but we need privacy to practice. We're not supposed to be here, remember? What do you think would happen if someone reported us to the Aceolevia?"

"If we're not practicing here, where do you have in mind?" Eliana asks with poorly concealed excitement. "Are we going to use your traveler's stone?"

Kai and I share a glance. She must have heard us talking about them last night.

She's clever.

"You'll just have to trust me and wait to see." Kai flashes a snarky smile, and Eliana rolls her eyes in response.

I get up, grabbing my sword, Light Breaker, and my bow. As I slip on my jacket, Kai forms a portal in the middle of the room. From where I stand, I can't see where he is taking us.

Eliana hesitates before stepping through the portal, disappearing. I follow, Kai entering last and closing it behind him.

We step into the ruins of a fortress, large chunks of stone strewn everywhere, moss and plants growing from the crevices. A lone pillar stands off to the side, vines climbing it, and the remnants of fallen walls create a broken square around us.

"Where are we?" Eliana's voice echoes off the stone. She turns in a small circle, taking in the ruins around us.

"An old outpost on the main trade route. No one passes through here anymore, and hasn't for decades," Kai says, setting down his bow on a large boulder. "We shouldn't be bothered here."

"How did you find this place?" she asks in awe, her eyes wide as she tilts her head to the sky taking in the solari.

"I found it by chance a long time ago, but I kept returning." His voice is quiet, shy. "It's a good place to think."

Frustration builds in my gut, and annoyance at the easy going nature between Kai and Eliana. Another thing he's taken from me. "You never mentioned this place to me."

"And you never told me of your night trips to the library in the Aceolevia." Kai retorts. "Seems there was a lot we did not share with each other, brother."

I scowl at him. "It seems so."

"Where do we begin?" Her voice cuts through the tension, face set, prepared and focused.

"Cire, can you spar with her? I'm going to hunt for a rabbit, then we can start with some basic combat, and work in some low-level Morei magic."

The ring of her sword, Fate's Guardian, echoes on the stone as she draws it in front of her, smiling devilishly at me.

"Do you think you're ready to fight me again? Record shows me winning two to none."

We laugh and the tension in the air dissipates as I focus on her, forgetting Kai and his closeness to her from earlier. There's only us.

I draw my own sword, Light Breaker, and beckon her to start. She dances close, striking at me with her sword, her movements graceful and quick.

I step out of the way, bringing my sword up to block. We continue this dance for several minutes, the sound of our swords clashing echoing across the ruins.

She hops onto a small boulder and takes a large swing at my head, and I'm barely able to bring my sword to meet hers in time. She laughs with victory, and strikes again, more forcefully. I block it easily this time, shoving against her.

The momentum causes her to slip on the rock and she tumbles to the ground, Fate's Guardian clattering away.

I step close to pull her to her feet, about to declare my victory, when she pulls the dagger from her boot and swipes at my legs. I shuffle back and she smirks at me, danger shining in her eyes.

"I won't give up so easily, Cire," she taunts, pulling a second dagger from her belt.

I smile and step close, striking down at her with Light Breaker. She crosses her daggers and catches my blade, stopping it from swiping across her chest.

Her muscles strain, but she holds firm, dropping her arms and shooting away from me, toward her own sword. She discards her daggers, grabbing Fate's Guardian, and beckoning me toward her.

A portal appears between us, and Kai steps through, a dead rabbit in his hand. Eliana's eyes cloud with sadness. She seems to forget me, her eyes on Kai as he draws his knife from his belt, and guts the rabbit.

Kai

THE RABBIT'S BLOOD IS still warm as it runs down my knife and coats my fingers. Magic surges within me and I grasp onto it, growing the feeling in my gut and spreading it throughout my entire body.

Rabbit blood is weak, but it will be enough for Eliana's first lesson. She looks at me expectantly, but her lips are pinched as though she's queasy at "the sight of a dead animal."

My magic is unnatural to her, and I know she fears and despises it in equal measure.

"Are you ready to fight against me?" I ask her, stepping closer. Cire's irritation is shown plainly on his face, but he steps back, sitting on a boulder on the edge of the makeshift arena formed by the rubble.

"I have access to several elements. We'll start with me using them as defense against you."

Eliana rolls her shoulders, determined. "I won't hold back."

I smile at her. "I'm counting on it."

She comes at me quickly, far faster than I thought she would, and swipes her sword down in a quick arc at my left shoulder.

I draw my magic in and call the earth to my aid, shooting a pillar in front of me, and Fate's Guardian glances off the stone, drawing sparks.

She shuffles back, regrouping. I can see her assessing me, trying to decide how to approach me.

She dances to my right, and I send another pillar to block her path, but this time she's ready, and counting on it. I watch in awe as she steps on the stone rising in front of her, gaining higher ground and leaping in the air, her sword slashing toward my neck.

I panic and thrust a burst of air at her, sending her sprawling on the ground, Fate's Guardian clattering from her hands.

I take a step to help her stand, but she's already grabbing a dagger from her belt, wiping the blood from her jaw on the back of her hand. She throws the dagger at me with a flick of her wrist, and the stone wall I call to block barely stops the dagger in its path. I lower all the earth, feeling the energy of the rabbit's blood leaving my body faster than I planned.

She's regained her sword and is running at me, the tip pointed low. The ground in front of her splits, and she skids to a stop, glaring at me.

I strain to hold the hole open.

Eliana takes a few steps back before running and launching herself over the crevice, landing crouched on her feet, sword in hand. She grins at me, and glides forward, keeping on the balls of her feet, her movements quick and unpredictable.

I summon wind to slow her down, but my magic falters–I've run out.

The cool steel of her sword presses gently against my neck, her blue eyes sparkling with pride. "I win," she says, panting.

"How did you–" I ask.

"Alana and I have been training. She never used her magic, but we talked about it at length." She laughs. "I guess I forgot to mention that."

She smiles mischievously, extending her hand to me. "Good match?"

I take her hand in mine, shaking it. "Excellent match."

"We should head back. Alana and Hama will be arriving for dinner soon," Cire grumbles, snatching his sword and bow from the rock beside him.

Eliana regards him with a mischievous expression. "Good warmup, Cire. That one was a draw–rematch tomorrow?"

Cire smiles to himself, turning his back to her as he summons a portal back to Wildewell.

Several weeks pass as we train at the ruins, and with each passing week, Eliana's strength and skill improves.

Her mother and people would be proud to see the warrior she is becoming, the pride she takes in her effort, and her singular focus.

The solari rise on the twenty-third day, and I wake to find Eliana stoking the fire, her journal open in her lap.

"What are you drawing?" I ask sleepily.

She glances up from her lap and smiles. "You're awake." She closes the journal and sets it on the log next to her.

"I was just drawing the fortress from memory."

"Trying to get a leg up on the competition?" I chuckle.

The words rest on the tip of my tongue–I want to tell her that I am proud of her–but Cire stirs next to me, and the moment passes.

"Why–are you worried, Kai?" Cire laughs to himself, sitting up. "The score is Eliana nine, Kai five."

"Well, today I thought we could go at full power," I say, tossing Cire and Eliana each a biscuit.

She bites into her biscuit, undeterred by the threat of fighting me at full strength.

Cire pulls me aside, our backs to Eliana and the fire. "Kai, I won't bleed for you."

I recoil from his assumption, the words a slap to the face.

"I already told you, Cire, I would never ask that of you again." I whisper fiercely. "Why are you so quick to think the worst of me?"

"I just think it's a bad idea to fight her with that much magic, it's reckless," he whispers, frowning.

"Don't dismiss her skill, she's strong, she can handle it. Besides, if she ever meets another guardian, do you think they won't use everything they have against her?" I growl out.

"She can speak for herself, you know." Eliana says, annoyed.

"I agree with Kai, I need to be prepared for someone's worst. You might not want to kill me, but they will. Kai, what did you have in mind?"

"We go hunting," I say, ignoring the glare from Cire.

Cire

KAI IS BEING RECKLESS, and I tell him that again as we leave Wildewell and step into the wilderness beyond the fortress ruins. He shrugs his shoulders, ignoring me.

Eliana hesitates, apprehensive as we stand under the canopy, the shadows blocking out the early morning light.

"You've brought down a *severn* before, you can do it again," I say to her, trying to be encouraging.

Right now, she seems to have more faith in Kai. I don't know why it bothers me so much, but I feel the need for her to trust me more, to be on my side.

She follows him farther into the forest, her sword drawn and ready. Kai and I both hold our bows, an arrow notched on each bow.

Before we left the hut, Kai gave us explicit instructions to maim the animal and not kill. We need to take it with us to the ruins so he can absorb the blood there, maintaining as much of its strength as possible.

I have so many misgivings about this plan. It puts her life at too much risk to play warrior. She should be kept somewhere safe. Eliana wants to grow stronger so she can face the Morei in the

Aceolevia, and her stubborn desire for vengeance clouds better judgment.

We march forward, listening for any sign of life in the forest around us, but it remains quiet except for the occasional bird song. As we walk, Eliana relaxes, and she hums a tune quietly to herself.

I'm about to ask her what she's singing, when a large animal moves into view. It's not a *severn* but a *rabbeon*.

What is it doing so far from the fields?

Kai draws his arrow back, taking aim. Eliana screams and steps into his path just as he is about to release the arrow. Kai pulls up at the last second, missing Eliana and the *rabbeon* she shields.

"Are you crazy?" He whispers, anger evident in his tone, "I could have killed you."

"You would have hurt Vendeekta. I couldn't let you do that."

"What...what are you talking about?" he yells in frustration. "Do you know how much strength I could get from such a large animal? Nearly as much as from a person."

"I won't let you hurt her." Eliana glares at Kai, arms crossed. The *rabbeon* has shuffled closer in the commotion, stopping right behind Eliana.

Kai's face pales, and he steps toward Eliana slowly, his arm reaching out for her. She swats his hand away. The *rabbeon* huffs as if laughing, and nudges Eliana with its large head. When it steps out of the shadows and into the light breaking through the canopy, I recognize it as the same beast she tamed in the Thessimis Fields.

Eliana turns and hugs its huge head, scratching it behind the ears.

"Hi girl, what are you doing all the way out here?" The *rabbeon* snuffles Eliana's face and hands, searching for something.

"I don't have any berries, you fiend." Eliana laughs.

"Cire, it's Vendeekta," she turns and smiles at me. "Kai, this *rabbeon* is my friend. You won't hurt her."

Kai stares at Eliana with a stunned expression, and nods, pointing his bow at the ground. "I'm sorry, Eliana, I didn't know."

She grabs his wrist and pulls him closer to the *rabbeon*. "It's okay, you didn't know." He hesitates to stand so close to the beast. "What..." he trails off.

"Introduce your scent to her." Eliana instructs, grabbing his hand and holding it out to the *rabbeon*. "If she knows your scent, you won't have trouble with her in the future. Cire's already done this."

He peeks at me for confirmation, and I smirk with satisfaction. "C'mon Kai, just do it."

Kai pets the *rabbeon*, and it huffs again, sending hot, stinky breath into his and Eliana's faces. She laughs and hugs Vendeekta's head close, petting her.

"I don't know how you found us, girl, but you need to go home. You're scaring off the other animals."

Her huff sounds almost annoyed as the *rabbeon* grunts and tosses her head.

"Don't sass me," Eliana says sternly, bopping the *rabbeon* on the nose. Vendeekta grumbles at her. "Please, girl, I'll see you again soon."

Eliana hugs Vendeekta's head one more time, stroking her ears and whispering something to her. The *rabbeon* huffs in acceptance and shuffles away, leaving us behind without a backward glance.

"What just happened?" Kai asks in shock.

"Vendeekta came to me when Cire dropped me into the Thessmis Fields. I befriended her, and she seems to be able to track me, I didn't expect to see her again."

"Strange," Kai mumbles quietly as we wander deeper into the forest. The bird song returns and soon we find a bubbling stream. The solari are high in the sky, it's already midday.

A branch snaps to the left, and we all crouch down. A *severn* comes into view, stopping for a drink at the stream.

Kai raises his bow and pulls back, releasing a precise shot into the beast's neck just above its shoulder. It drops with a roar, the water running red as it bleeds into the stream.

Kai stands and walks quickly toward the beast. It stares up at us with frightened, pained eyes. Eliana gasps, bending down close to its head.

Its breaths come raggedly, slowing down with each passing moment. Kai and I stand back as Eliana comforts the animal in its final moments, not willing to remind her we need to move it.

Kai isn't watching her but the *severn*, his face awash in anguish. I've never seen him look upset over the death of anything. Something about him has changed since the battle at Bellamere.

When the *severn* takes its final breath, Eliana takes her hand and gently closes its eyes, saying a prayer over it.

She stands, turning to us. "I'm ready to fight in honor of this animal's sacrifice."

Kai nods, and together, he and I lift the beast, before he summons a portal, and we step into the fortress ruins.

Kai

WE SET THE *SEVERN* down behind a large rock, and I pull the arrow from its neck, warm blood rushing over my fingers. I take my swords, Virtue and Faith, from my back and let the blood run over the blades, the black obsidian absorbing the blood. The surge of wild strength rushes into my body as the *severn*'s energy becomes mine.

A deep sadness washes over me, the raw pain of Eliana's anguish fresh in my mind as she knelt over the beast, comforting it. She has such a soft heart underneath all of the loss and pain that she wears like armor.

When the *severn* has finally bled out, I almost cannot handle the pressure of my magic as it rages inside me, an uncontrolled storm. Eliana stands in the middle of the arena, waiting for me, her breath ragged from warming up with Cire.

I step forward, drawing my own swords in front of me. I use it to channel a blast of air at her, and she rolls, narrowly dodging it.

She bounces back to her feet, striking at me from the right. I sidestep her blade, shoving air at it, throwing her off balance.

She falls, chest heaving, scrambling back to her feet she runs at me again, and when I thrust air at her this time, she ducks, sliding on the stone, and swiping her sword at my knees. I jump back, and almost lose my footing.

She stands, leaning on Fate's Guardian, knees bleeding.

I throw up a wall of stone to block her from me, and she growls in frustration. I give her a moment to catch her breath as I decide what to do next. When I pull the stone down, she's disappeared, hiding. I turn in a slow circle, searching for her. Cire left the ruins as we began to fight, and now there is no sign of him either.

"Eliana?" I call out, my voice echoing off the stone.

There's no response, just the sound of stones scattering on the ground, and Eliana standing above me on a crumbling wall next to the pillar, Fate's Guardian discarded in favor of her daggers.

She smiles ruthlessly, launching herself off the wall at me. I laugh, forming a wall above me, blocking her from jumping on me. Eliana grunts as she rolls off the stone, landing on the ground behind me.

I spin around, sending a blast of air at her chest, but she ducked low, avoiding it. She tackles me to the ground, and I lose my concentration, the wall of stone I built breaking around us.

She pins me, about to bring her dagger to my throat, knees on my arms, keeping me from using my swords. I close my eyes, focusing on the ground around us as I make it quake, throwing her off of me.

I leave my swords, and grab my knife from my belt. The quake threw her to the side, and I send walls of stone up around her, boxing her in. She bangs her fists against them, trying to tear them down. The banging subsides making way for the soft scrape of her daggers against stone as she carves into the rock.

I drop one wall, making enough space for us both before closing the gap once more. Her smile promises danger and she flashes her daggers at me.

My knife brandished in front of me, I dance close to swipe at her. She dodges effortlessly, her boots shuffling on the stone. I step back, forcing her to come closer and she swings a dagger at me, keeping the other close.

I parry her blow by grabbing her wrist, throwing her against the wall. She hits the wall harder than I intended and drops her daggers. I hold my knife to her neck.

"I win," I say, smiling down at her.

She smiles back, showing her teeth. "Not yet."

Her knee drives into my gut, and I drop to the ground, the air leaving my lungs. She swipes my own knife and holds it at my throat, pinning me to the ground once again.

"I believe that's Eliana with ten wins, Kai with five," she says, her eyes bright with the exhilaration of the fight.

I nod my head, and my knife leaves my throat.

We both laugh. I pull down the stone walls, and she gets up, holding out her hand, to pull me to my feet.

"Why do you like to fight with daggers?" I ask, reclaiming my swords left abandoned a few feet away.

"It's the precision, they're an extension of me. It requires a lot more focus." She flips her dagger in her hand. "Control."

"It's also a lot more intimate." The words sound so smooth, but they catch us both off guard.

She blushes at my boldness.

"It's not like that," she says quickly, her face turning red.

"I–I'm sorry I misread the situation. Does that mean you're interested in–" I ask, my words clumsy and awkward with embarrassment.

"No one," she says confidently.

"I'm not interested in anyone, not like that. Before all of this," she says, waving her arm around, "I would have asked my best friend, Brynne, to be my Champion. It's a place of honor in my clan's 'court' of sorts. Not a partner in all senses of the word, more like a deeply trusted friend."

"So you have no interest in..." My words trail off. I don't know where the interest in knowing about this has come from, and shame heats my cheeks. This is none of my business.

"No, I don't. I think it's beautiful that Alana and Hama evoked the *Envocia Amorei*, but that was never part of my future."

Eliana glances awkwardly at me. "I'm sorry if I gave the wrong impression."

I step toward her, and take her hand. She hesitates for a moment, but lets me keep a hold of it.

"No, I'm sorry for assuming. That crossed a line, and it won't happen again. I respect the hell out of you, I would be honored to be counted among your friends."

She smiles genuinely at me, and relief floods my body, the embarrassment of a moment ago forgotten.

"I'll keep you under consideration," she says with a wink, "for friendship, that is."

She squeezes my hand, and steps back to grab her own sword.

Eliana

I SIT BESIDE THE fire, stretching my sore muscles after the last fight with Kai. Our conversation before Cire returned echoes in my memory. The moment was so awkward, how did I not see the signs? My mother always said I was oblivious to the attraction of others. I just never considered that Kai or Cire would think of me in that way.

I open my journal and continue my sketch of the arena, putting the earlier embarrassment behind us.

Kai sets a third log into the pit, trying to angle it just right, as an enormous roar shakes the hut and the ground beneath us quakes. The roar subsides quickly, but I can still feel the tremors deep in my bones.

Kai and Cire are already grabbing things from their hidden spots around the room and shouting at each other to grab some thing or another. Cire shucks off his coat, trading it for makeshift armor, as Kai pulls gauntlets onto his arms and bracers on his legs.

As they both dash toward the door, they turn to me, and Cire, in a demanding voice, yells, "Under no circumstances do you leave this hut" before ducking out and leaving me alone and fuming.

Like hell will I 'stay'.

I tighten my belt, checking for my daggers. I grab Fate's Guardian. I fasten a second belt across my chest and secure the blade on my back, the hilt resting comfortably between my shoulders, within easy reach.

A perfect fit.

I run to where Cire discarded his coat, rummaging through the pockets to find the traveler's stone. Shaking the coat in frustration the weight of a rock hits the top of my boot, and I hear the soft thud of the stones as they fall to the ground. I pick them both up, shoving them into my pockets.

Cire said you can only travel to where you've previously been. I should be able to make it home.

Leaving the hut behind, I run down the paths, trying to decide which way to go, when I see smoke rising from a burning hut at the center of the village. My heart beats faster, it feels like only a few short weeks ago that I was running to a different burning village, running to my mother.

Screams echo all around me and think I have been sucked back into a memory, but they're coming from the villagers as they run toward me, fleeing something I can't yet see.

It roars again, and the thunderous crash of splintering wood and tumbling bricks comes from further down the lane. The screams of those trapped under the rubble haunt me as I turn to leave.

The urge to run to their aid rises within me, but a nagging thought holds me back.

This is my chance to slip away, I shouldn't waste it. I need to make it back to Bellamere.

As I stand, trying to decide what to do, more villagers run past me, some bumping into me in their panic. I barely feel them, so lost in my own thoughts.

It's not until a familiar, large burgundy shape runs into me, knocking me onto my butt that I am pulled from my inner debate. Vendeekta towers over me breathing heavily, having run from somewhere far off to my aid.

Breathlessly I ask, "How did you find me girl?"

She grunts, shaking her head as if to say "that's not important right now." She nudges my shoulder, prompting me to get on her back.

Another scream reverberates through the lane from the rubble farther down, and I run past Vendeekta toward the trapped villagers. She huffs in frustration as she turns to follow me.

"I can't leave them behind." The smoke starts to choke me, burning my eyes and nose. "Vendeekta, I need your help."

She grunts, pushing against the rubble of the hut, clearing it out of the way with a loud crash. She huffs in triumph. With her help, I am able to lift the last large broken beam in my way.

I yell into the rubble, listening for any sounds of survivors. There is a faint cough in response.

"Vendeekta, stay." I take a deep breath, choking on the smoke as I shimmy my way into the debris, searching for the survivors.

I move a large stone from a collapsed wall and a small hand punches through a gap in the loose stone.

I pull the rocks away as quickly as I can. Under all the rubble there's a small girl, her body folded around a baby wrapped in a cloth. She's crying to herself, trying to comfort the baby despite her own fear and pain.

"I'm here to help, can you crawl to me?" I open my arms to her and she slowly pulls herself up, holding the now wailing baby in her arms.

I almost collapsed with relief at the sound of the baby's screams. "Can I hold the baby?"

She hesitates, but soon the blanketed bundle is passed to me, and she climbs out of the rubble, glancing back one more time, tears glistening on her cheeks before she crawls through the gap. She squeaks when she sees Vendeekta.

"It's okay, she's friendly," I called out to the girl, still clutching her sibling close to my chest. I try to soothe the baby, but he is screaming uncontrollably.

Peering into the crevice where the girl crawled out from, I throw up a little in my mouth to see the bodies of her parents, crushed under the wall.

This poor child.

I turn my back on her parents. There is nothing I can do for them now.

When I crawl through the gap, Vendeekta drops the large beam, dust kicking up around us. I handed the girl her baby brother before lifting her onto Vendeekta's back.

Despite the trauma of losing her parents, the idea of riding a *rabbeon* brings a small smile to her lips.

I climb onto Vendeekta's back, holding the girl tightly, and urge Vendeekta to run. Another wall crashes down besides us, but we keep running away from the smoke and the echoing screams.

Vendeekta runs until her lungs give out, putting as much distance between us and Wildewell as she can.

We caught up to the other refugees, leaving the young girl and her baby brother with a neighbor. Feeling better about having found someone to leave the children with, I left behind the refugees and the injured long ago, escaping deep into the high grass of the fields beyond the village walls.

The solari are low in the sky, putting greater urgency on my escape. I don't want to be caught out here alone. Images of the dangerous beasts that lurk in the shadows flit across my mind.

I unsheath Fate's Guardian and help Vendeekta clear a path as we venture further north. Or, at least what I hope is north. The breeze from the hills sweeps down into the fields, causing the grasses to sway and casting new shadows with every gust. It is eerie, and I don't like the sensation of the grass running along my arms and face.

I hack at another clump of grass, annoyed to find more spanning beyond my eyesight in every direction. It would be very easy to get turned around here. A strong gust of wind sends a thick blade of grass whipping into my face and my cheek throbs with a dull pain. I swipe the grass away from me, and my hand comes away sticky with my own blood.

I wander for what feels like hours, my arm is tiring from the constant strain of lifting my sword. But, I cannot stop. I need to continue moving to make sure I am far enough away that they cannot find me before I figure out how to use their traveler stone.

Vendeekta wandered off some time ago, in search of sweet berries no doubt.

Reaching into my left pocket, I check to make sure I still have the stones and feel relief wash over me when my fingers graze the smooth surface of the stones. I wait to see if the air will ripple like it did for Cire, but nothing happens.

I click a clump of dirt and continue on. The breeze has settled, I must be deep within the fields where the hill and mountain breezes all but die away. The new stillness of the high grass around me is even more unsettling than the shifting and dancing shadows of before.

I raise my sword to hack again at the grass ahead of me, when movement on my right makes me pause. A large shadow passes by me, the grass parting around it like a curtain. Its steps are quiet, I can barely hear it moving over the pounding of my heart.

A warm breeze that smells like rotten fruit ruffles my hair and tickles the back of my neck. I tighten my grip on my sword, ready to stab whatever has approached me.

A familiar brown nose brushes against my cheek, snuffling my ear and hair. I drop Fate's Guardian, wrapping my arms around her big fuzzy head. Vendeekta nuzzles me again, her wet nose leaving sloppy trails along my arms and chest.

"I don't have any berries for you." I scratch behind her ears. "I'm sorry."

She huffs in annoyance. Her big head runs into my chest, and I pull her in for another hug. I sheath Fate's Guardian on my back before climbing onto Vendeekta.

"I could use a break, do you mind?" She huffs. "Do you know where the Ventemere Mountains are?" She huffs again.

I laugh to myself, because of course she doesn't. But she does surprise me by continuing forward, ambling along slowly, sniffing the ground and bushes every once in a while in search of more berries or flowers.

Her ears are so soft in my hand as I stroke them, letting the comforting motion soothe my aching heart and rest my sore muscles. I fidget with the purple gemstone, knotted on a rope, like a necklace.

"Keep watch, girl." I lay my head on top of hers and close my eyes.

When I open them, the world around me is red again, but it's not Wildewell that burns around me but the forests that surround my village and valley back home. I recognize a fallen tree that an ancestor carved into a bench to rest on.

"Hello," I shout, coughing as the smoke rushes into my lungs. "Atrya?"

The smoke burns my eyes. I spin around but Vendeekta is not with me in this vision. I am all alone.

An intense heat spreads across my back, and when I turn around I realize I am in the path of a wildfire that hungrily races toward me, cutting down the forest around me like kindling. I run, trying to keep ahead of the flames that threaten to overtake me.

Ahead, there is a break in the destruction, the green of the valley, and I rush forward pumping my arms and legs with all that I have. My lungs choke on the smoke, and I stumble, cutting my hands on the fallen limbs around me, the ash coating my face and body. I pick myself back up and limp onward, desperate to get away from the fire on my heels.

I just know that if I can make it to the green grass and clear sky, I will be safe. I push myself harder but my body is beginning to fail me.

I'm not strong enough, the fire will devour me.

I reach into my left pocket and my fingers close around one of the traveler's stones.

I pull it from my pocket, placing it in my right palm. I trace my thumb in a circular motion over the rock, but nothing happens.

Think Eliana, think. What did Cire do?

Behind me the fire is closing in. The heat sends rivulets of sweat down my entire body, and soon I will cook alive. I close my eyes and attempt to recall what Cire was doing as he whispered with Kai. I focus on how the air rippled around Cire, his actions–he didn't trace circles, he made swirls.

I take a deep cleansing breath and trace swirls, like ripples, on the stone. I picture the green space ahead of me and breathe deeply again, choking on the smoke. Coughing, I keep my composure.

I picture the grass, the clear blue sky, and I trace another wave on the stone. When I peek open my eyes, the air in front of me ripples like it did for Cire in the Thessimis Fields, and just last night around the fire.

Without hesitation, I jump through the rippling air, and tumble into the soft, green grass of my vision. The solari hover bright in the sky, warming me, and the brutal heat of the flames licking my skin is now gone–the fire stopped at the forest's border.

I'm safe, I did it. I know how to use the stones.

My eyes snap open and to my relief, I am awake on top Vendeekta who continued to amble forward, unaware that I fell asleep on her back or the danger I faced in my vision.

I give her ears a scratch and stretch before squeezing my legs, signaling for her to stop walking. I slid off her back, kicking up a small cloud of dust around my boots. The grass here is dry, unlike the lush grasses from the fields closer to Wildewell.

"Where did you take me, girl?"

She huffs in response and sits down. Idly, I pet her. There is nothing as far as the eye can see, except the very beginnings of a mountain range, the rocky terrain and young trees dotting the terrain.

Home.

I pet Vendeekta again. "Go free, girl. I will see you again soon."

I pull one of the traveler's stones from my pocket and picture the grass field just outside my village, where my mother and I used to lay and gaze up at the stars.

A slight pressure presses on my back and I turn around to see Vendeekta's big head nudging my shoulder. I give her another scratch behind the ears and a big hug around her head.

"You have to go. There's someplace I need to go, too." Her big brown eyes stare sadly into mine. "I'm sorry girl, I promise I will find you again. Or, you'll find me."

She huffs in agreement and turns around, leaving me behind without a backward glance.

I reconcentrate on the field, picturing the flowers that dot it this time of year, and how the breeze from the mountains always sends the dancing in the sun.

I trace my finger along the stone and sigh in relief when the air in front of me ripples. I step through the portal and into the field just beyond my village.

I'm going home.

My heart beats with excitement. I step out the other side, and my boots crunch down on dried grass, and my vision swims with the burnt, twisted remains of my village just on the top of the hill. My legs give out, and I scream until my throat is raw.

Kai

C IRE AND I KEEP pace sprinting together toward the *tehendra*.

As we pass our neighbors' huts, the retired Morei kiss their families goodbye as they grab their blades and sprint toward the village center alongside us. Another roar punctures the air, causing us to stop and cover our ears. Even this far away I can feel the pressure of the sound vibrate through my bones.

This is much bigger than any beast of the wild we've ever encountered.

Cire must be having the same thought I am. He slows his running, holding an arm out to pull me back.

"Any ideas on what it might be?" I shake my head, pulling my gaze away from his fearful eyes.

"I was never the studious one, that was always you." I flash a half-smile. "Did you read anything in the temple archives about large, mythical beasts?"

Cire shakes his head. "No, unfortunately."

I think back to Eliana, left behind in the hut.

Cire underestimates her strength, the inner fire that burns bright within her. She's stronger than all of us, even if she turns out not to be goddess-touched.

"Whatever is ahead, we can take it on together. Without fail." I take Cire's forearm in mine, just as we did before entering the gauntlet. I ignore my healing wounds as we race forward again.

"I'm not sure how it made it to the village center so easily, but we need to take it down before it lays waste to all of Wildewell," Cire yells in frustration.

I pray for the first time to Lady Hevastia that we are able to help those trapped amidst the chaos. I shudder at the thought of the villagers in Bellamere, and others just like it, that we left trapped in the rubble to waste away. I can hear their screams of terror, pleading for help.

I would gladly accept re-entering the gauntlet a thousand times before I pick up my sword against one more innocent soul.

The black stain on my own soul from my choices will never be wiped clean, no matter how many lives I may save with the rest of the life Lady Hevastia grants me.

My blood boils at the thought of some monster having the audacity to attack my home, and I push harder and faster than I thought possible.

Through the thick smoke at the center of the village, stands a large shadow. Far larger than anything I've ever seen before, and I realize in horror it's a *craicabra*, a fire breathing monster.

I thought they were a myth, no one has ever recorded seeing one, or if they did, they did not live to tell the tale.

The beast gets down on all fours and lets out another ear shattering screech as it unleashes a torrent of fire from deep within its gut, engulfing three more huts in thick flames. Wildly swinging its tail lined with spikes as tall as a man, the monster keeps any advancing Morei at a distance.

"Look out," I shout as the monster's tail sweeps the perimeter. Diving, I crash into Cire and knock us out of the tail's path.

"Do you have your bow with you?"

"Yeah, but I don't think my arrows can pierce its scales. We need to find its weak spot."

I nod my head in agreement. Cire rolls up his sleeve, exposing his forearm that is criss crossed with old, faded scars.

"Cire, what are you doing?"

"What does it look like I'm doing?" He bites out, wincing in pain.

My hand rests on his, stopping him from pulling the dagger on his belt. "Cire, I won't ask it of you."

He grimaces and tries to reach for his dagger still. "You don't have to ask. I know what's demanded of me, not by you but by the Haematites."

"Well damn the Haematites, I have enough blood on my hands, I can't keep asking for yours. I am strong enough without it."

He opens his mouth to object, but I push him down, covering his body with my own. Rolling to the side to avoid a burst of flames, we duck behind a collapsed wall.

I stand back up and pull out my twin swords, Virtue and Faith, only glancing back once at Cire as I sprint away, trying to keep to the monster's blind spots as it pivots its head away from us.

From behind the fallen hut, Cire pops up and sets aim, "Let me at least fire a few rounds to cover you as you get closer."

As I run, Cire's arrows whistle past me as he launches them with lethal precision. They find their mark in the fleshy, soft skin of the *craicabra's* face, the perfect distraction as I weave below the beast, searching for the best climbing advantage.

The *craicabra* has large claws to match its imposing spikes, and in its fury at Cire's arrows and those of the other Morei, it's stepping wildly, causing me to dodge its massive feet with every swing of its body and tail.

I tuck and roll out of the way, barely avoiding being flattened into the village square as another half-fallen hut is crushed to dust.

Peering up, I notice the monster's soft underside, no impenetrable scales to protect it.

I sprint for the closest leg, avoiding the massive claws. I sheathe my swords and hook my small dagger into the fold of its scales. It's difficult work climbing its body, I hold on tight with every step it takes as it decimates the village.

My grip slips when it turns violently, and I slice open my hand on its scale trying to pull myself onto its hip. I curse loudly at the blood flowing freely from my palm.

Focus, Kai. Keep climbing.

I hiss in pain, and grit my teeth as I continue to climb the beast. My small dagger slips into the beast's flank, grabbing its attention.

A shadow crosses over me, and its large clawed foot draws close to me, narrowly missing my back as it swats at itself to knock me loose.

Three more of Cire's arrows whistle in the wind, landing in the soft webbing of the monster's toes.

The *craicabra* roars in frustration, its body quaking, and I almost lose my footing. I catch myself with my bloodied hand.

My pained scream draws the attention of the beast again, and a giant claw tears into its own flesh just inches from my face. I clamp my lips to keep from yelling out. It takes a thunderous step, nearly knocking me off, but I hold tight to my dagger, my boots finding purchase on the edge of its jagged scales.

The Morei and villagers cheer for me as they charge in, attacking the *craicabra* from below, keeping it distracted. I can smell the blood as it pours from the fresh cuts on their arms, allowing the *sanguinars* on the ground to harness their magic.

As I continue climbing, their taunts to the beast grow faint. Suddenly their screams echo loudly when its spiked tail connects with their soft bodies.

I wince at the sound and pray Cire was not caught in the fray. I can smell burning huts and flesh as Wildewell bows to the power of the monster's flames.

Determined to make it to the top, I push on. Just as quickly as my spirits are bolstered, I am almost thrown off the beast as it sits back on its rear haunches, leaving me clinging desperately to the scales just below its shoulder.

The sharp edges of the scale cut into my fingers, the blood making the scale slick and difficult to grip. I grunt with frustration as I use all of my strength to pull myself upward. My small dagger slips from the scales I wedged it between and it falls away, leaving me with just my swords.

Bracing my legs underneath me, I set myself up to leap. I call the wind to my aid, using my own blood as the tithe, something I have never done. I'm not even sure if it's possible, but I know without magic I won't make the leap.

Relief floods my senses as the air responds to my call, winding between my fingers. I hold fast to the breeze, and I launch off the beast's shoulder, letting out a guttural yell like an avenging demon.

I reach behind for my blades, unsheathing them as I free fall in front of the beast, my magic guiding me. As its black scales give way to a soft brown stomach, I stab my blades in just below its throat, letting my momentum force them deep. As I continue to fall, I pull the blades with me, ripping down the beast's stomach.

Its black, putrid blood flows hot and fast from the wounds, washing over me and splattering onto the charred ground below.

Halfway down my blades catch and stick on a bony scale.

"C'mon," I say to myself. The jolt of stopping my fall nearly makes me lose my grip on the swords. Dangling from them, I give my body a slight push and wiggle them around the scale.

The monster's sharp claw pierce my shoulder, ripping down my back. Searing pain shoots through my entire body, and I lose grip on my blades.

The *craicabra* roars in truimph as I plummet from its stomach toward the ground.

I hit the dirt hard, tumbling over the broken bricks of the huts. Slamming into a wall, my breath is knocked out of me. Coughing from the impact. My chest hurts and I think I broke a rib.

The *craicabra* shrieks again, and its tail lashing out toward another row of huts.

I pull myself fully behind the wall I slammed into and lay down, taking shallow breaths. I close my eyes.

Cire

K AI IS CLIMBING THE beast.

As the beast turns to swipe at him, I catch a glimpse of its stomach, and realization dawns. The monster's stomach is free of the thick scales that line the rest of its body.

I notch an arrow and fire it at the webbing of its feet, sending two more arrows in quick succession. They find their purchase right on target, and the beast moves its claws away from Kai. Its large, reptilian eyes scan the village square, hunting for me, tongue flicking, tasting the blood in the air.

Reaching behind me and finding my quiver empty, I strap my bow to my back and unsheathe Light Breaker. The flames of the nearby huts glint across the polished blade. I wince at the memory of using this same blade in the attack on Eliana's village.

The guilt of leaving her behind once again, creeps up. But it's for her own good, she has no reason to endanger herself needlessly. An opinion that irks her to her core.

She'll forgive me and Kai eventually. We had no choice in the matter, we're all pawns in some larger game. She needs to stay with us. Where she is safe.

I know Kai has developed a rapport with her, one I don't understand.

He is the reason we marched on her village, he led the charge.

The jealousy climbs into my gut, churning, and I shut it down.

Put those thoughts aside, you need to focus.

I shake the intruding thoughts from my head and check back on Kai's advance against the monster. He's still climbing, successfully dodging another blow from the beast as it tries to shake him off.

I rush forward, only yards away from the villagers and other Morei that have coordinated an attack on the beast, drawing its attention away from Kai.

There's movement out of the left corner of my eye, and I roll out of the way narrowly dodging a swing of the monster's tail.

The men in front of me were not so fortunate, and the spikes tear through their backs, spearing them.

Screams of agony ricochet off the rubble as the tail whips back, sending them through the air, crashing into debris and walls. Their screams fall short on impact, and the air is uncomfortably quiet as the village holds its breath.

I swallow my fear, it's just Kai and I left, it seems.

Keep going Kai, I'm right here with you.

The smell of burning flesh pierces my nose, and I gag. I keep from peeking down as I pass by smoldering heaps on the ground around the beast's feet and crushed under the crumbled, smoking huts.

As I near the beast's rear foot, Kai launches himself from the beast's shoulder and stabs its stomach with his blades. Impressed with his technique, I notice a moment too late the monster's claws swinging at Kai.

Kai's body is knocked by the claw and thrown twenty feet before sprawling to the ground.

The clang of metal on stone resounds as Kai's blades fall from the beast's chest.

Its towering form falls to the ground, shaking the village center and toppling the remains of the fountain. The stone becomes a river of black as the blood pours from the gaping wounds Kai inflicted in its soft underbelly. Its chest rises and falls, slower with each labored breath.

Always go for the merciful kill when possible.

Alana's advice whispers across my memory as I examine the monster.

I sigh and shake my head.

I approach the beast cautiously, its giant yellow eyes watching me. It snarls, but doesn't move, taking another pained breath. Giving its vicious teeth a wide berth, I walk along its belly, hot blood rushing over my boots as it continues to bleed out.

In the center lies the large onyx scale that Kai's blades were stuck on, and I set my stance, thrusting my blade just below the scale, presumably where its heart is.

The beast roars one final time and as its voice weakens and ends, the *craicabra* dies.

I pull Light Breaker free from the mess, and wipe it on my pants before slipping it back into my scabbard. I pick up Kai's and wipe them off as well, walking away, the blood of the beast pooled around me higher than the top of my boot.

Kai is tucked against a fallen wall, his body broken, blood caked to his back and splattered all over the ground around him. Gently shaking his arm, he moans quietly, his eyes flicker.

Thank the stars he's alive.

I pull Kai onto my back and trek home. As I leave the destroyed market center, I ignore the bodies littering the ground. The acrid smell of burnt flesh, smoldering bricks, and charred wood burns my nostrils, following me the entire way home.

As I turn down the once colorful lane to our home, all that remains is destruction, and the embers of dying flames glow in the fading light. And where our home once stood is a pile of broken, burning rubble.

"Eliana?" I drop Kai to the ground, and rush toward the ruins of our hut.

The smoke burns my throat and eyes, it's so thick I cannot see anything. I yell her name again, coughing on the black air that chokes me.

"Cire, get away from there." Strong hands circle around my arm, pulling me away.

Over my shoulder, Alana's frightened eyes meet mine. Turning away from the burning pile, I finally see the true scale of the *craicabra*'s destruction.

All of Wildewell is up in flames.

"She's not here." Kai repeats himself, his voice unsure.

His steady hand rests on my shoulder, trying to pull me back to reality, but I am paralyzed and out of touch.

Alana and Hama left some time ago, in search of other survivors. I have not moved since we found our home in ruins, since I screamed Eliana's name until my throat was raw.

I don't know what to believe. That she stayed and died in the fires that have consumed our entire home, or that she fled and abandoned us after promising to trust us.

She had stayed before, why couldn't she stay now?

A part of myself chips off and falls into the ash coated ground all around me.

My body feels hollowed out, a shell of what it was before ever meeting her, before walking away from everything I had built for myself, and before I took my brother down with me.

Without her, I am surely dead. The Haematites will find out what I did. The Krothesu was just a game for them to make us submit. When they understand the true depths of my betrayal, I will be eliminated.

My mind spirals, and my vision blurs until all that remains is darkness and the glowing red of the dying embers.

She betrayed us. And we will all burn for it.

Kai

CIRE HAS NOT MOVED from his spot in front of our burning home. He sits in shock, mumbling to himself.

I told him I was leaving to find Alana and Hama, to help with rescuing trapped neighbors, and tending to the wounded– he did not even register what I said.

If I make myself busy enough, if I focus on the pain of others and helping them, then I can continue to outrun my own pain.

My body still aches from battling the *craicabra*. Its jagged claws left deep gashes and falling from it hurt me badly when it should have surely killed me. That is another mystery I want to ignore for the time being.

I lift another fallen beam, clearing a pathway from the center of the village, which sustained the worst damage, to the outer edge which still lays in ruin from the Haematite's attack years before.

The scorched wood is hot to the touch, and my hands blister from continuing to lift, pull, and throw still-smoking debris from the lane.

Every step strains my injuries and my body weakens from excessive bloodloss. I got carried away when I first began helping

Alana with recovery efforts, drawing on my own blood for the additional strength granted by my gifts. Now, the bloodloss has caught up to me. Without the aid of my magic, my body tires so easily. My mouth has gone dry with thirst, but our well is damaged, the water black with ash.

Wildewell is silent except for the coughing of other survivors that choke on the ashy air and their shouts throughout the village as they call out the names of missing loved ones.

Cire believes Eliana to be among the bodies yet to be pulled from the wreckage. He will not accept that she would leave us, but I have other thoughts.

Though it pains me to think she would desert us, I know in her place, I would have done the same.

She may be the lost princess, the key to saving Hevastia, but she owes Cire and I nothing. After all, we took everything from her, and brought nothing but death and pain into her life.

She saw an opportunity to run, and she did. I hope she made it far away from the flames and the destruction. I hope she lives.

Cire

*S*HE'S NOT HERE.

I strain against the weight of a large beam that collapsed when our roof caved in, lifting it out of the way in order to unearth the crushed walls of the hut that lay beneath. I roll away stone after stone, tossing the burnt, mangled remnants of our home aside as I search for Eliana, and find nothing.

Her weapons, her satchel–everything is gone.

I yell in frustration and kick a half standing wall. The trunk where Kai and I store most of our weapons sits open, as we left it. My coat is singed and Kai's bow lay broken beside it, eaten by the flames.

I pull my tattered coat from the wreckage, checking for the stones I left behind in our haste to get to the monster, both pockets are empty. I claw through the dirt and ash, but all I find is the remains of scorched weapons and pieces of our tapestry, burned and ruined.

"Where are they?" I shout, searching again.

"Cire?" Kai asks. "What's going on?"

I growl in frustration, ignoring him. He pulls me away from the wreckage, taking both my shoulders and shaking me.

"Cire," he peers frantically into my eyes. "Snap out of it."

I shove him off of me, tackling him to the ground. My vision is red like the embers, fury coursing through my body.

They're gone. And, Eliana with them. She got away.

"We're dead," I yell, spit flying from my mouth and landing on Kai's face as he flinches away from me. "She betrayed us."

"Cire, you have to settle down." Kai's words are measured, calm despite the fear in his eyes. "You're in shock, you need help."

I grab him by the shoulders and bash him into the ground. He cries out in pain, but continues fighting me.

I grab him again, raising him higher to try again, when I spot movement from my left and the world goes dark.

Kai

B LOOD COATS MY HANDS as I cough again. Cire lay unconscious at my feet.

Hama's hands are shaking. Alana holds them to her chest whispering softly to Hama.

Hama was the one to stop Cire, they hit him in the back of the head with a large rock, knocking him out. I can see the guilt of hurting him is torturing them, but I owe them my life.

Cire was going to kill me.

I've never seen him fly into such a delusional rage before. In battle, he was always the calm, strategic one. He never let himself be carried by the frenzy of battle and the bloodlust. That was always me. My gut twists with the memories of being bathed in my enemies blood, innocent blood.

What could have possibly gotten into him?

It is not the first time in the last few weeks that I have worried about him. Ever since Eliana was discovered, he has been acting strangely. He found her in that mountain village, protected her from harm in the battle, only to threaten her and scare her afterward.

It never sat right with me why he would do those things, and I've been too ashamed of my own actions to confront him. Seeing him like this today, I know I need to get to the bottom of whatever is happening.

If Eliana has the traveler's stones, she could be anywhere. I can only hope she is far away from here.

Eliana

THE SOLARI HAVE FULLY set, casting the valley into darkness and obscuring the destruction all around me. I have wandered aimlessly through the ruins of my village for many hours now, quietly sobbing.

I sink to my knees in front of the charred remains of my home, now crumbled in on itself, burying with it all that I had left of my family. Reciting the warrior's rite, I pray again for my mother, my neighbors and clans people. How I would give anything to see them again.

The battle destroyed everything in the village. I think of all the brave people who stood on the front line, lighting their own homes and possessions on fire for the chance to thin out the guardian ranks. How, in the end, it must not have mattered if everything now lies in ruin.

But where are all of the bodies? The dead guardians' bodies should be here.

My people sat hidden in the mountains waiting to honor our lost, to return home.

Surely they buried our dead, did they also bury the others? Where are the survivors? They should be here.

I leave the village and walk to our resting grounds, a place of honor for our ancestors. The ground is packed solid, there are no new graves.

That's impossible. As chieftess, my mother would be buried here. It was her birth right.

A sickening thought crosses my mind.

What if the guardians stole my people's bodies for some sick ritual? What if they captured the survivors?

Anguish washes over me at the thought of my people tortured at the hands of the Haematites, giving way to fiery anger at the thought of Kai or Cire knowing and never telling me.

For their sakes, I hope that is not true.

I was supposed to be here to protect them, lead them, but I failed. I sent them to their deaths. Tears spring to my eyes, and I wish to sink deeper into my grief, to bury myself here and never wake again.

The sound of a boot crushing the burnt remnants of my home pulls me from my thoughts, bringing me back to the present. The hairs on my arms and neck raise, an uneasy feeling settling into my gut.

What if there are guardians still nearby? It's been several weeks since the attack, perhaps they lingered to hunt down any survivors.

I duck behind a half-collapsed wall, tucking my body against the jagged bricks. The footsteps get closer. I swallow the fear building in my chest, a cool sweat beading on my lower back.

I reach behind to pull Fate's Guardian free, ready to make a run for it into the forest at the edge of the valley. I know those woods better than anyone. If I can outrun them then I can disappear and hide—they'll never find me.

The crunching stops, a heavy panting sound echoes through the ruins. Their breaths sound labored, as if they're sick or injured. I take that as a good sign that I can easily outrun them. I tighten my grip on my sword, rolling onto the balls of my feet.

I jump from my hiding spot, sprinting for the forest, dodging fallen huts, jumping large beams that lay twisted and snapped blocking my path. I round the corner of a wall that still stands tall, glancing back over my shoulder to make sure I haven't been followed. There's no one behind me. I turn the corner, and I run into the back of a person.

My momentum knocks me back onto my butt, Fate's Guardian clattering away from me.

The bright light of the lunei overhead illuminates the silhouette of a monster. I scream.

Naomi's face stares down at me, but everything about her is all wrong. Her once bright, glowing brown skin is now a sickly gray falling off her bones, and her face is bloated, pus oozing from sores on her cheeks, hands, and exposed skin.

She's a walking corpse, just like in the Thessimis Fields. This isn't possible. This isn't real.

I scream again, backpedaling away from her as she shuffles forward and lunges. I kick at her legs, knocking her to the ground, but she continues to pursue me, unaffected by her now broken kneecap.

Fate's Guardian lies just a few feet away, I turn on my knees and scramble frantically for it as she crawls toward me, her limbs twisting unnaturally as if she feels no pain at all. My fingers graze the hilt of my sword when her hands wrap around my ankle, pulling me toward her.

She snarls, black blood and foam spewing from her mouth. I kick at her face, hearing her howl in pain as I finally break free. She lunges at me again and I scream. Scrambling to my feet, I grab my sword and sprint away, looking back only once to confirm that I'm not being followed.

I run to the forest, past the stream that trails lazily from the hidden mountain stream, and deep into the thicket where it's easy to lose yourself if you don't know where you're going.

I don't stop until I am sure I have put a mile between myself and the ruined remains of my village, and any other monsters potentially lurking in the dark.

It's too risky to start a fire, so I find a sturdy tree and climb high into its branches, letting the leaves obscure me from any lurking eyes below. I secure myself to the branch with a bit of loose rope I stole from Kai and Cire, and I sit still, listening to the sounds of the forest around me.

The soft chirping of bugs and small animals rustling in the dead leaves as they scurry from their dens in search of nuts and berries permeates the night air. I hold my breath, waiting for the sound of heavy footsteps but none ever come.

My dreams were fitful, full of black blood and the face of my dead best friend as she tried to kill me.

The warmth of the solari barely breaks through the dense canopy of the forest, waking me slowly from my nightmares. My throat burns from screaming, my mouth dry from lack of food or water for over a day. I untie myself from the branch, lower myself to the ground, and trace my steps back to the creek I crossed the night before.

Cupping my hands into the cool water, I bring them to my face and gulp down handfuls. I splash my face and neck with the chilly water, bringing goosebumps to my skin as I scrub off the ash and blood from yesterday.

Farther up the stream three rocks sit stacked on top of one another. Something about them nags at the back of my mind, but I ignore the feeling and take one final sip of water before walking away from the tree I camped in last night, scouring the forest floor for berry bushes.

Wandering deeper into the forest, the light from the sky shines through in little bursts, creating spotlights that illuminate the forest floor in a soft glow. Up ahead is another stack of three rocks sitting on a stump, haloed by the light breaking through the canopy.

I walk past the stump, giving the pile of rocks a sideways glance.

What a strange coincidence.

Just ahead sits a bush plump with small, dark berries. I go to pick them and moan in frustration.

"Belladonna." I mutter. "Poison berries."

I drop the dark berries to the ground and continue searching for edible food. To the left rests another stack of three rocks.

"Okay ... so not a coincidence."

I stand on my tiptoes and search for another pile of rocks, spotting one ten feet away, tucked near a fallen tree. I march over the stack, searching for the next. I continue to follow the path marked by the rocks, leading myself deeper into the forest, toward the base of the mountains.

The fallen leaves give way to pebbles and then large rocks, trees to bushes, and then the hardy shrubs that cling to the side of the mountain.

Up ahead, there is another pile of rocks sitting atop a large boulder. I scramble up the steep incline, careful with my footing.

A small rock bounces past me from above, and my vision swims with ghosts. I've been surrounded by people painted in the colors of the mountain–muted grays and browns that blend into the surroundings.

Stupid, I should have been more careful. I just walked myself right into a trap.

I hold my hands low and out in front of me, a symbol of peace in my clan–hoping these people will understand me.

"I mean you no harm. Please, I am only searching for food." I say, kneeling.

A shorter, stout woman steps forward from the circle that surrounds me. She leans on a large stick carved into a walking staff. "I'm disappointed to hear you did not come for us."

The voice is so familiar, and I squint to see past the clever disguise. Standing around me are my people, the woman who spoke is the last remaining clan elder, Mythica.

Tears spring to my eyes as I cry in joy. She opens her arms to me, and I run into them, crying deeply as she holds me closely.

She whispers softly in my ear, "You're alive, it's a miracle."

It's not possible. They're alive.

Mythica releases me from her crushing hug, and I follow her and the others into a cave high up on the side of the mountain. The entrance is tight, barely more than a crack, but as I squeeze through the narrow tunnel opens and expands revealing a massive cavern in the center of the mountain.

Torches mark the paths through the cavern every few feet, casting a bright glow on the home my people have created for themselves. Children are running and laughing as they chase each other through freshly tilled raised gardens tended by their mothers and fathers. Tents dot the perimeter of the cavern.

"You rebuilt, here?" I don't mean for it to sound like a question, but from Mythica's soft chuckle I can tell she's picked up on my confusion.

"We needed a fresh start, someplace ... safe."

She guides me deeper into the cavern. As we pass families, they stop their work and stare at me in awe, a few shed tears. Their soft voices whisper thanks to Lady Hevastia for bringing me home safely. My gut twists in a knot.

Mythica stops in front of a simple tent, pulling the tattered cloth that serves as a makeshift door aside, ushering me inside. "Sit, make yourself comfortable."

She hands me a cup of water with crushed herbs swirling in the bottom. "It's for the pain." I take a deep sip, the bitter taste of the herbs catches me off guard, and I start coughing.

"Thank you." I say between coughs. Mythica laughs and takes the cup back.

She stares at me patiently, silent. Her gaze makes me uncomfortable, and I realize I've never spent more than a few minutes with her before. Her attention was always pulled to other places, she has been one of the most respected and loved elders in our clan.

"What happened?" I ask, quietly.

Mythica takes my right hand in hers and gives it a small squeeze. "We thought you died with the others, but we could never find you. I could ask you the same question, child."

I flinched at the word child. I have grown so much in these weeks away, and faced many truths.

She squeezes my hands again. "I meant it as a term of endearment, sweet girl, I can see how you have grown. You carry yourself with more strength, an inner fire has been lit in you."

"I'm sorry I left you." A tear slips down my cheek. "I should have stayed."

The guilt of seeing my people hidden away from the world, living in near darkness, cuts deeper than a knife, and I know if they asked I would abandon the idea of the reincarnations. My people need me.

Mythica smiles sadly and pats my hand.

"You did not return to us out of duty, but from guilt. And it's that same guilt that kept you from returning just as much as it urged you to come home. The fear is written all over your face. You fear never leaving again, even if guilt and duty whisper that you must stay.

"Eliana, you have always been destined for more than this small village. The wind calls you to run with it, the mountains challenge you to conquer them, and the world beyond our borders beckons you with every breath to answer their song."

"My mother is gone." I choke on the words but push on. "It is my honor to lead our people. I should have never left, I was wrong to turn my back on you. I chased petty vengeance against an enemy that sees our people as nothing more than the dirt they dust off their boots.

"I know we are stronger. I want to lead us back to that strength, as is my birth right and my responsibility. My mother would want this for me, it would honor Lady Hevastia."

Mythica stops me from continuing with a sharp glare. "Stop running. First you ran from the mantle of chieftess, now you run from the sacred duty of the god-blessed.

"Eliana, you are both daughters. You are your mother's heir, her guiding star, but you are also the heir of a far greater kingdom, a larger destiny. You are Lady Hevastia's Light, burning the darkness from our land and cleansing us of the evil that devours us."

I stare at Mythica, stunned from her casual mention of me being Hevastia's "chosen one." I open my mouth, hesitant, and then finally saying, "I'm not so sure I believe that." I sniffle. "I'm too weak."

Mythica squeezes my hand. "Eliana, you are anything but weak."

"I couldn't even avenge our people's deaths. I had several opportunities, but I wouldn't deliver the killing blow. I failed our people, and that is what I consider weakness."

Her nails bite into my chin as she raises my head to meet her eyes.

"Listen to me, Eliana, empathy is not weakness. You could have run your dagger through their hearts, you have the strength to do so, but you also have the heart to look beyond a person's deeds to the very core hiding deep within."

I stare into her eyes and swallow down my tears as she asks, "What did you see there?"

A solitary tear runs down my cheek. "I saw their fear, their grief, and their desire to change. They could have killed me, regained favor with the Haematites, but they chose to spare me, because

they desire a future free of bloodshed and pain, especially at their
own blades."

Mythica nods her head, urging me to continue.

"And, that's what I desire, too. I felt something deep within me
that resonated with what they claimed. I've just been too afraid to
accept it."

"That is precisely why you will be the one to lead us out of
this age of darkness and pain. You are Lady Hevastia's chosen
daughter." Her hands wrap tightly around mine.

"How did you know?" I whisper. My bottom lip quivers as I
draw in a shaky breath.

She smiles kindly at me, patting my hand. "I've always suspected,
but your mother did not want that life for you. She thought that
if she kept you hidden, kept you safe, that whatever happened
outside our valley would stay away. She was afraid of becoming like
her mother, Sarlaine."

"We never spoke of her. My mother left me some of my
grandmother's letters, but what happened to her?"

A shadow crosses over Mythica's face before she can compose
herself. She sits a little taller, placing her hands in her lap.

Her gaze softens. "Sarlaine went crazy after childbirth, obsessing
over the prophecy, pressuring your mother from a young age to
display magic. She insisted that Bellaema would be the chosen one,
and as the years went by and your mother never manifested a gift,
it twisted your grandmother, made her spiteful and cruel toward
your mother."

My gut clenches at the thought of everything my mother
endured at my grandmother's hands, and how much it must have
hurt her. I understand now why she wanted to protect me from

that same pressure and expectation, how it consumed her in a different way.

"Eventually Sarlaine grew so ill, she lost all touch with reality." Mythica takes a deep breath, taking my hands in her own. "She killed herself shortly after your mother became of age for the naming ceremony. Your mother has been our chieftess since the age of sixteen."

I regret all the times I thought my mother was weak for keeping us hidden. I realize now that her caution was one of her greatest strengths, that she was only trying to protect me from the mistakes of my grandmother, from being hurt by the burden placed on our family.

"Did my grandmother continue to journal after she went mad?"

Mythica shrugs. "If she did, your mother must have burned the letters long ago. Your grandmother used to disappear for a day or two at a time shortly before she passed. She would escape into the mountains, to this very cave system. No one ever discovered what she was doing on those trips. I followed her once, to try talking sense into her away from your mother's worried, watchful gaze, but I lost her in the maze of caverns."

"I wish my mother had written me more letters. I wish I had more time with her." The words are barely more than a whisper.

Tears run freely down my face, blurring my vision. Mythica pulls me close, and I settle my head into her chest letting the grief overtake me. I cry for my mother who is gone, for the people we lost, for those that remain and rebuild, and in fear of everything Mythica said—what I know to be true and have tried to run from.

She rubs my back, whispering calming words to me as I cry for everything I have lost, and for everything that lies ahead of me, the greater purpose I must accept.

I am the last reincarnation of Lady Hevastia, and I must save my people from darkness.

Mythica let me rest after I finished crying. It's hard to know what time of day it is, with very little light from the solari to illuminate the main antechamber of the cave.

When I awoke, she had left behind a change of clothes, my clothes from Hama ruined in my fight with Naomi's corpse, and a note on how to find the hot springs within the cave network.

I take the hastily scrawled directions and map, the fresh clothes, and the fruit she left and make my way to the baths. As I pass my old neighbors they touch me, whispering prayers and smiling at me. So far, no one has stopped to actually talk to me, and I am too afraid to start the conversation myself. I smile back at them as I wind my way through the camp, climbing a small hill out of the larger cavern and into a torchlit tunnel.

The soft whoosh of running water hits my ears before I see the baths, and when I enter the chamber it is so beautiful it takes my breath away. The torches illuminate the hot springs which roll with cleansing steam that hovers just above the surface of the small pools.

No one else is in the baths, and I sigh in relief. I won't have to make small talk with anyone. I walk to the small pool in the back corner, partially hidden in the shadows and far from the entrance.

Slipping off my blood-crusted clothes I sink deeply into the water, letting the heat soak into my aching muscles. I lean against the edge of the pool and take several deep breaths before dipping below the surface and letting the water muffle the sound of my beating heart.

I hold my breath for as long as I can before popping back up, scrubbing my scalp and body with a pumice stone and bath oils I find tucked into a crevice next to the pool. Hevastia's pendant and the purple gem from Atrya rest against my chest, I fiddle with them.

The memory of Hama making me a small bath in Wildewell flashes in my mind and a single tear falls into the pool.

I hope they're okay.

The thought catches me off guard, I don't know when I first came to trust Alana and Hama, or enjoy their company, but I find myself missing them now. They were like surrogate aunts, doting on me and helping me untangle the mess my life has become. I miss the late nights around the fire while we waited for Cire and Kai to return, the stories they would tell me of their adventures in Hevastia as part of the Morei—before the Haematites used them as a hellish army.

An ache spreads in my heart at the thought of Kai and Cire. I even miss them, despite everything.

Did they beat the monster? Did they survive?

Suddenly time alone with my thoughts feels like a trap, and I quickly exit the pool, drying myself off and pulling the basic white shift, black vest, and black pants on, before pulling on my boots. I re-tuck my daggers into their respective places on my belt and boot, realizing I left my sword in Mythica's tent.

I hurry out of the cavern following the torches back to the main cavern and to Mythica's tent. As I pull back the flap, I find her sitting and waiting for me, Fate's Guardian in her lap.

"How did you acquire the blade?" she asks, he hands tracing the design.

"It was a ... gift." I sit down across from her. "The men who helped me after I left Bellamere let me keep it. It's a complicated story."

Mythica nods her head, encouraging me to continue.

"The man that saved me from the dark beast in the mountains, he was there during the battle. He pushed me through a portal to the Thessimis Fields. He found me there, told me about the prophecy, and brought me to Wildewell where I stayed since I left. His aunts, Alana and Hama, watched over me, nursed me back to health from several different injuries.

"I found letters my mother left for me from my grandmother, Sarlaine, and from her. Mythica, I need to be honest about why I came back home. I had a vision that told me you might be able to give me answers, to help me understand the reincarnation and the prophecy."

"The pages of your grandmother's journal your mother gave you, they are part of a larger collection of letters and stories from our past chieftesses and elders. What your grandmother wrote about is true—a seer from Keladone did foretell the birth of a savior among our people. Though, they were a little vague about when that would happen." She laughs at her own joke.

Getting up, she goes to a small chest and rummages around before returning to me, setting a leatherbound book in my lap.

"The prophecy does not mention the Aceolevia or its greedy Council, but I imagine the darkness it refers to could be in any form. The Prophecy states that the Light embodied–you–overcome the darkness."

"But how do I do that?" I ask, exasperated.

Mythica shrugs her shoulders. "The writings are vague about what must be done. It feels as though we only have part of the story."

I sigh in frustration.

"Do not give up so easily, Eliana. Your vision, did it mention other god-touched children?"

"No, what do you mean other "god-touched"? In my vision, Atrya told me I needed to reopen the heart before 'He' returns." I take a sip of the bitter tea Mythica offers me. "Who is the 'He' that it's referring to?"

"Hmmm." Mythica mumbles to herself and takes the book from my lap flipping through the pages quickly. She earmarks a few pages and hands the book back to me, the first marked page flipped open.

"I think these passages may hold some of the answers we seek."

Lady Hevastia

The story as many know it is a false one. Lady Hevastia was not the first deity of our people's land, in fact it was not called Hevastia at all. Long before her time, our land was known as Soria, after its god, Soran.

Before the Time of Abandonment, the Gods of Odora walked the surface, hand in hand with their people, and Soran was the kindest of them all. He was a strong and righteous god, ruling over his people fairly. Soran taught them to harness their gift to command nature. He loved his people, and they loved him.

Soran was lonely, and so he went in search of an eternal partner amongst his people. In a small village, in the southern hills of the land, he found Hevastia, a young maiden of great beauty and quick wit. She was magnificent, and Soran's soul overflowed with the power of their connection and became truly whole the instant their eyes locked in the marketplace. He asked Hevastia to join him as his partner, promising her a life like no other for all of eternity.

Though Hevastia desired to be with Soran, she was also a woman of honor and integrity, and she refused Soran's offer.

Hevastia was promised to a cruel monster, the strongest in the village, named Vaiccar. Vaiccar was enraptured by Hevastia's beauty, and out of greed and jealousy, wanted it all to himself. When he saw that Soran, his god, wanted what was his, Vaiccar locked Hevastia away. He threatened her and her parents if she did not love him, and him alone. He told her that her beauty was not to be shared with the world, only he could enjoy her light.

Hevastia feared Vaiccar would harm her family and reluctantly accepted his terms, wishing only to spare her family, and Soran from harm. Vaiccar was satisfied in his victory, and gloated to all the surrounding villages how he outsmarted Soran. Little did he know, the god had heard his gloating, and devised a plan to rescue Hevastia.

Once, while Vaiccar was away, Soran snuck into his small castle, and freed Hevastia from her chains. He promised to protect her from Vaiccar and stole her away to his fortress in the north. Not long after, they performed the Envocia Amorei, the eternal bond of love, and as a gift to Hevastia he renamed the land in her honor.

Soran promised a life together for all of eternity, giving Hevastia some of his immortal soul in exchange for some of her mortal one. Hevastia was now a goddess, the first of her kind, a mortal gifted with eternal life and soul magic.

Hevastia's goddess gift manifested as the ability to influence life and death, one's very soul. Her magic gifted her descendents the ability to command life and death, and with Soran's gifts for nature the two magics blended so that each child born after their Envocia Amorei maintained balance in Hevastia, a link in a great cycle of magic that connected all beings of the land.

Hevastia and Soran lived happily, and peacefully in the north for a decade.

One day when Hevastia was attending a festival in a small village at the heart of the land, Vaiccar and a small army of his loyal followers moved against Soran. Soran was overrun by the sheer force of their might and could not overcome their attack, his eternal body weakened by Hevastia's mortal half. With his victory in sight, Vaiccar delivered the killing blow to Soran.

Vaiccar then laid in wait for Hevastia to return home.

When Hevastia returned from the festival and found Vaiccar sitting in Soran's throne, her partner's dead body at his feet, her heart shattered.

She attacked Vaiccar with her magic, cursing his soul to walk Hevastia for eternity, never to be loved, never to see beauty, or to hold it, never to experience joy.

Hevastia locked Vaiccar away, and forced him to watch the world from behind a veil.

Vaiccar has walked the veiled wall, trapped apart from Hevastia for centuries. It is foretold that there will come a day, when Vaiccar will rise again. Having cast a dark shadow over Hevastia's creation, he will break free, enslaving her people for his own use. He will harness the power of the Heart, overtaking all of Odora.

But, all hope is not lost for a child will be born, the last of her ladyship's line, and she will be said to be blessed by the Goddess Hevastia herself. To be the successor to the Goddess, the heir to Hevastia, its magic and its soul. Light embodied.

Vaiccar has been awaiting the day that the foretold reincarnation of Hevastia herself would return to her people, so that he may take her for his own and fulfill his dark desire to conquer Hevastia and all of Odora at last.

It is said that the girl Vaiccar hunts will be lost to her people, as if hope itself had been snuffed out, only to emerge out of the ashes, to take her rightful spot as the true ruler of all of Hevastia. The Light to unite them all, and free them from his darkness.

I was right, there is something blocking our magic, and I think Vaiccar must be involved somehow.

I flip to the last passage Mythica marked for me, pulling the book tighter to my chest as I fold my legs under me to rest the book in my lap.

The God-Touched

Odora's children were called to her sacred home in the sky many centuries ago in the Great Abandonment. Before leaving, each deity created an anchor, a living conduit between their eternal life and the mortal lives of their people. This child is known as the Auror, and they possess great magic acting as the key to the wellspring of their people's gifts.

"I see you finished your readings." Mythica offers me a piece of jerky before sitting across from me.

"I'm no closer to understanding any of this than when I started reading." My laugh sounds hollow.

Mythica smiles encouragingly at me, taking the book from my lap and setting it on the cot beside me. "I will do everything within my power to help you."

"Do you know soul magic? It said I should have the power of life and death." I swallow. "I read about the brutality of the Great War–I don't want to do that, I don't want to hurt people in that way."

"Magic does not have to be brutish, it can be a beautiful and gentle thing. I will show you what I know of the Old Ways, teach you the incantations and rituals."

"There is one more thing Atrya shared with me. Well, she gave it to Kai first, and he gave it to me–that's a long story. She told him that I would need this."

I pull the chain attached to the small purple gemstone, and it pulses gently in my hand, a small humming energy radiating from its core. "I don't know what it is."

Mythica takes the gem from my hand, and the soft glow emanating from its core dims.

"Interesting," she says in awe.

She hands it back to me and the glow returns. I hold the small gem closer to my face, scanning for any etchings I may have missed. I've run my fingers over it so many times, I know the curvature of every edge and rough chip as well as my own hand.

Mythica takes the small gem back from me, holding it to the firelight, the light inside it flashes ever so slightly.

"I've never seen magic like this, but it's not of Hevastia. Not entirely."

Mythica hands back the gem and leaves me alone with my thoughts. I turn the small purple rock over in my hand several times, not sure what to make of it. I pull my satchel close, grabbing the bundle of letters from my mother, and the scroll from Alana and Hama.

Unrolling the scroll from Alana and Hama, my fingers trace the same story they told me many weeks ago in the shop, the fall of the King and Queen, and the rise of the Haematitian Council. My anger rises in frustration. There are only dead-ends. I'm no closer to understanding what I need to do, or how to save my people.

I hold the scroll up higher, unrolling the very bottom, dismayed to find it's blank. I stop closing it when I see a faint shimmering in the large open space. I hold the scroll higher and closer to the fire, using the flame's light. As I raise the scroll, the shimmering spreads until a diagram appears at the bottom of the scroll followed by beautifully written text.

In the middle of the drawing is Hevastia's Heart, at each corner of the Heart are strange symbols I haven't seen before. One is a mountain range, across from it a person. Each of them has a dark stain above them, but I don't know what. The final symbol on the bottom is a mystery, it's not anything I've ever seen before.

I skip the text below the drawing, and my breath hitches in shock.

Fate's Guardian
Just as regrowth begins to bloom,
Tragedy will befall, making way for
Darkness and doom.

One hundred years shall pass,
Light diminished, but never gone,
Plagues and dark beasts amass,
The veiled one awaits his chance.

All hope is not lost,
Lady Hevastia will return,
Fate's Guardian to pay the cost.

A daughter of Light,
Born of bone and blood,
Forged in the flames, bright,
She will rise from the ashes.

Her Light the declaration,
Battle against blood and shadow,
She will lead the liberation.

The god-touched powers united,
Her touch burns true,
Darkness purged, ignited,
Balance and harmony renewed.

If these were hidden, then they must mean something, and I trace the shapes and the prophecy born from the fire's light into my journal for safe keeping. I reroll the scroll and slip it into my satchel.

Did Alana and Hama know of the hidden cipher and this version of the prophecy?

Kai

I t's been two days since the *craicabra* attack. Alana and I have worked alongside a few other Morei to recover the bodies of the dead. They lay piled in the center of the village, next to the rotting corpse of the monster.

Cire has not spoken to us since he awoke from blacking out after Hama smashed a rock on the back of his head. He helped gather the dead, understanding the urgency with which we collect their broken bodies. Even his anger cannot overcome the logic, the fear we all refuse to voice.

The torch in my hand is heavy as I stand beside Alana and Whalen, the self-appointed leader of the survivors, few that we are. On the count of three, we lower our torches, tossing them on to the monster's corpse and its victims, setting them ablaze.

I'm back standing in the remnants of Bellamere after our attack. I hold a torch. Next to me is the girl with glowing brown skin and dark black hair. We light the pyre. She smiles up at me while I hold her bleeding body in my arms.

My gut twists.

I step back, grimacing against the horrible smell that emanates from the pyre. Turning my back on the fire, I head away from the ruined *tehendra* in search of Cire. He and I need to settle a few things.

Whalen steps into my path and puts a hand on my chest.

"I just wanted to thank you for helping us with this ... mess. If you see your brother let him know I also send my thanks."

I nod my head, and step past him but he steps back into my path. I frown.

"I happened to notice that Alana's niece isn't counted among the survivors or the deceased. Do you know where she is?"

"Not that it's your business, but no, I do not."

He continues to block my path. "Kai, it would be unwise for you to hide her body. You know what happens in a few days' time, you put us all at risk."

I scoff. "Whalen, get out of my way. I am not harboring a potential dark beast."

I shove past him.

"I would have thought you smarter than that." I remark over my shoulder as I walk away. I shake my head, not interested in fighting.

Cire's back is to me as he sends his ax down on another log, cleaving it in two.

"Cire," I say loudly. "We need to talk."

He kicks the two halves out of his way, placing another log in front of him. "So, talk."

He sends the ax down again, with so much force it splits the log and wedges into the ground at his feet. He grunts and pulls it free, using his hand to pick off the mud and soot.

"Cire, stop," I yell, frustrated. "Put down the damn ax and talk to me."

I flinch as he flings the ax to the side, turning aggressively toward me. "What do you want me to say? 'Thank you' for knocking me unconscious, for dismissing my concerns about Eliana betraying us?"

"Whalen asked about her," I say. "He must have seen her while we were gone, he wants to know why she's not here, or burning with the others."

Cire's chest is heavy from breathing heavily, his anger dissipating.

"Whalen can be dealt with," Cire grumbles, turning his back to me.

"What is that supposed to mean?" I ask, frustration giving way to my own anger.

"It doesn't matter," a voice says from over my shoulder. "You won't be here to worry about it." Whalen emerges from the shadows.

He comes after Cire with the ax, and my brother dodges, rolling out of his path. He springs back up onto the balls of his feet, panting.

"Cire," I yell.

Whalen swings at Cire again with the ax, and he stumbles trying to dodge, falling to the ground. Whalen is on top of him in an instant, pinning Cire to the ground with the handle of the ax, trying to choke him.

I scramble for anything to grab, my fingers closing around a small rock. I bash it into his head and he growls, pressing hard on Cire's chest and neck.

"Stand down, Kai."

"Stop trying to kill him," I pull on Whalen's arms, trying to pull him off Kai. When that doesn't work I wrap my arms around Whalen's neck prepared to snap it.

Cire passes out from Whalen choking him. Whalen growls as I put pressure on his neck.

"Whalen, I don't want to kill you."

"You're dead either way, I'm only doing you a favor." He grunts, and head butts me, knocking me back into the dirt.

Whalen is on my chest, pressing the handle of the ax into my neck just as he did for Cire, and I buck, trying to throw him off. He presses harder, sweat pouring from his forehead and dripping onto my face.

"Stop struggling." His voice nearly a hiss.

The shadow of someone passes above us, and when I strain to see who is coming to my rescue my blood turns cold at the sight of High Priest Marius staring down at me, an evil smile on his face.

"It's time to go," he says, glancing disapprovingly at me.

"Bring them both along if you must, they could still be of use to us." He snaps his fingers, and turns to walk away.

The pressure of Whalen's body lifts from my chest, and when I glance back, the butt of Cire's ax smacks into my head, and the world goes dark.

I wake in a dark room, the smell of stale blood fills my nostrils and floods my senses. I call out, but no one answers. The door at the other end of my cell is open, faint light from the corridor spills in, casting shadows on the walls of my cell.

My hands are bound over my head, and I have been stripped of my weapons. There's no sign of Cire. I pull at my chains, and the metal cuffs dig into my wrists. The clang echoes in my cell, but they don't budge.

I strain against the chains again, a thin trail of blood running down my arms from where the cuffs cut into my skin. The pain bites, but I would rather lose my hands than be at the mercy of the High Priest and whatever sick games he has in store for me and Cire.

"Cire," I yell. "Cire, can you hear me?"

There's a faint grunt from beyond my cell. The sound of scraping on the stones echoes as someone tries to sit up, their chains rattling with the effort.

"Kai?" Cire's voice is faint. "Kai, what happened?"

"Whalen turned us into the Council," I growl. "Asshole."

"You said ... he asked about ... Eliana?"

"He knows something." I grunt, yanking on my chains again. I hiss with the bite of the metal, but I won't give up so easily. Eliana is at risk. I can only hope she is truly far from Wildewell and the Council.

The chains in Cire's cell rattle as he strains against them. The rattling almost masks the sound of footsteps coming down the corridor. They scrape the ground, shuffling along and growing closer. I sit up straight, staring at the door. The faint light from the hall is blocked by the body of a young boy as he scurries into my cell dropping a stale loaf of bread and small cup of water at my feet.

"Wait," I yell. "What is your name? Where are we?"

He stops and stares at me, but does not answer my questions. His eyes are wide with terror, and he scurries away, another loaf of bread and cup in his hand. The cup clatters to the dungeon floor as he drops the food in Cire's cell. Cire does not address him.

"Kai, where did Eliana go?" Cire asks. "Tell me she is safe."

"She's gone ... I don't know where." I sigh. I stare at the food placed at my feet, unable to reach it. My stomach growls, and I kick the food away.

"What do you think they will do to us, Cire?" I can't keep the fear out of my voice.

I have heard the rumors of the horrific things the Council has done to prisoners. There are horrors worse than the Krothesu.

"I'm not sure, Kai." Cire's voice is faint through the wall. "I imagine they will not be as kind to us as they were last time."

I chuckle. "Yes, running the death race thirteen times was very generous of them."

Cire barks out a hoarse laugh. The cup clanks against his cuffs as he sips water. "We can't tell them anything, Kai."

"Agreed, brother."

The young boy does not return for our cups, and after some time I close my eyes, my arms and body numbing.

I blink the bright light out of my eyes, squinting against the torch light so near to my face, flinching away from the nearness of the heat that threatens to singe my hair and face. I try to shift away, but my arms and legs are bolted to a table in the middle of a different room.

This room smells of fresh blood, and it glistens on the wall next to me. I strain against the bonds again, but I am stuck tight to the table.

Movement flashes to my right, revealing High Priest Marius sitting in the dark corner, watching me. I struggle again, desperation spiking in my body. The chains rattle, and the noise echoes in the small room. Fresh cuts on my arm weep blood, and I call the wind to me, dismayed when I cannot feel it. The High Priest smiles down at me, seeing the panic on my face as I fail to call magic to my aid.

"Don't bother, you've been blocked. You are no more powerful than the bleeders we gather in every village. *Giftless*."

Hearing the word on his tongue feels like a thousand knives stuck into me. The room spins as I strain to access my magic, sweat beading on my forehead.

"What a pity." High Priest Marius stands and approaches me. He's wearing a plain black robe in place of his red robes and adornments, his hands tucked away in his sleeves. He stares down at me with disdain.

"You had such potential, Kai, you could have done great things in the New Order." He clicks his tongue.

"All the same, you are still useful to us now." He smiles at me, sending a shiver down my back.

I struggle against my bonds, not bothering to respond in words. I glare at him.

"Are you not the least bit curious about what I have in store for you?" His words are a taunt, he smiles again.

"No?" He leans in close to my face, I can smell his breath, and it reeks of stale wine. "You will be something special, Kai."

He pulls a syringe from his sleeve, full of the same dark liquid I saw the nurse inject Cire with. I move away from him, shifting my weight against the cuffs that bolt my body in place. The movement cuts into my wrists and ankles, and I can feel the slow trickle of blood running from the wounds.

I try again to call wind or water to my aid, but nothing happens. It feels as though my hands are pounding against an invisible barrier, pulling at something that is no longer there.

High Priest Marius chuckles. He grips my arm in one hand, holding it still as he plunges the needle into my arm. The sensation that crashes through my body is like a cold embrace of death as it rushes through my veins.

I school my features, showing no reaction as he gazes expectantly at me.

"Hmmm." He grunts.

"We will resume again tomorrow."

A white cloth covers my nose and mouth, and as I suck in a breath the world goes dark around me. My last thought is that I need to stop passing out.

Eliana

T HREE WEEKS HAVE PASSED here in the hidden cavern, and
there is still no hint of my magic manifesting.

I have tasted every nasty concoction Mythica makes for me,
choking down thick herbal blends, eating raw flowers, and even
animal blood. Nothing has helped me tap into my powers, and I'm
no closer to understanding this than when I arrived.

I understand even more now why my mother did not want
this life for me. And I sympathize with my grandmother who
must have bore similar treatments pursuing the birth of the fated
daughter.

I have fallen into a simple routine: wake, bathe, eat, study,
practice, eat, study again, practice more, rest, and repeat. Our
warriors all perished in the battle with the Haematite mages. I
have been leading small lessons with some of the more capable
villagers, teaching them basic defensive moves and attacks. It has
been slow progress, especially when weapons are scarce without a
forge master to make more.

The gardens they have planted in the cavern thrive, surprising us
all. Today, I am leading a small group into an unexplored tunnel
system to see where it leads and what it may hide. Mythica wants
us to make sure we secure the cavern from any external threats

before the cold season pushes beasts into the caves for shelter. And I have a secret mission of searching for any remaining signs of my grandmother Sarlaine's, trips into the caverns beyond the large one we've remade our home in.

Mythica finally explained to me the absence of burials in our sacred hill. When my people returned to Wildewell after a week in hiding, they were too late to bury our dead. The surviving temple guardians had already built a pyre in the middle of the village and set our dead and theirs on fire. The pyre consumed the remainder of the village, leaving nothing but ash behind.

The bodies that were not burned rose again. It is just as Jasath warned us, there is no final death. Naomi was not consumed in the fire, and her spirit has been corrupted by the darkness that spread to our valley with the invasion of the Haematites, and now she and a few others roam the village perimeter as aimless, violent monsters. Dark beasts.

Mythica cannot be sure of my mother's fate, so I can only pray that she was burned with the other brave warriors who lost their lives protecting our people.

"Are you ready to leave?" Maendril interrupts my journaling, stepping into my small tent. My small tent is nestled in amongst the others. I am surrounded by my clanspeople on all sides.

I set down my quill and journal, smiling at Maendril. "Yes, let's gather the others." I drape my satchel over my shoulder, dropping in a small loaf of bread and canteen, my journal, and some flint. I hesitate for only a moment before strapping my sword on my back, just in case.

I pull the flap aside and step out of my tent. Five others are joining me on the excursion, all armed with a simple weapon and their own supplies. Maendril and I are the unofficial leaders of the group with Clyn, Raen, Tyr, and Tenya making up the remainder of our measly band of explorers.

Cutting through the cavern we pass the rest of the clan, and they wave as we walk by, the children, giddy and laughing, chase after us, only stopping when we leave the torch-marked paths. Without their laughter a silence falls over the group, and it sends a chill down my spine.

Tyr and Tenya walk side by side, they have been mates for nearly ten years now. Raen and Clyn are younger, not old enough to join the warriors but strong enough and old enough now to be trusted with weapons.

I walk in the middle of the group, surrounded by my people and yet apart from them, still alone.

Maendril brings up the rear, my old weapons master. He retired after a hunting injury from a dark beast attack left him with a permanent limp. I am silently thankful he did not fight in the battle, his familiar face and calm demeanor is a small blessing in this difficult time.

"Princess?" Raen asks, clearing his throat.

I glance back at him, smirking. He stares up at me with nervous eyes that widen when we make eye contact under the torch light.

"Call me Eliana, there are no princesses here."

He relaxes, a smile easily lighting up his young features. "Where are we going?"

I shrug. "I'm not sure, we will know when we get there."

That earns a chuckle from Maendril and Tyr.

Tyr signs to Tenya what's been said, and she winks at me. Tenya is nonverbal and deaf. Her sister, Pyria, is nonverbal.

I have not seen Pyria around the cavern, is she among the dead lost to us?

So many dead.

I sigh to myself, the dark thought pulling down my excitement at exploring the caves.

We venture deeper into the tunnel system, following every twist and turn. Our torches stay bright, lighting our way and I am thankful for the light. The two younger boys lead the way, their excitement growing the farther we venture from home, I can hear the conspiring whispers bounce off the tunnel walls and back to the rest of us a few paces behind.

A slight breeze tickles my face and neck, sending the torch lights flickering.

"Raen, Clyn come back." My shout echoes in the tunnel as their torchlight disappears around a corner and I no longer hear their soft, childish laughter.

The breeze grows, and as we round the corner we enter a large open cavern, a deep pit in the middle. The path we have been following crumbles and disappears along the edge. I search frantically for Clyn and Raen, and I spot a torch at the bottom of the cavern.

"Boys?"

"Help, princess!" Clyn yells.

I turn to the left and see his small body hunched on the ground, clinging desperately to Raen's hands as he dangles over the edge. I toss down my torch and run to them, wrapping my hands around Raen's arms and pulling. Together we pull him to safety, and I hug him close.

The poor boy is shaking, my shirt wet with his tears.

"I'm sorry, so sorry." He whispers into my chest, over and over. I rock him back and forth, soothing him as he shakes from his fear.

"It's okay, you're okay." I hug him tighter. "You will be okay, I won't let anything happen to you."

Maendril quietly scolds Clyn for getting too far ahead of us, and I can hear him sniffle, sucking down his tears and fear. "You must be more careful, son."

Tenya and Tyr stand to the side, relighting the torch I tossed away in my haste to save Raen. Tenya hands me the torch, and I take Raen's hand, pulling him along with me. At this moment I realize just how young twelve is. I give his hand a small squeeze and smile encouragingly at him.

We continue around the edge of the deep pit, searching for a safe way to descend. Up ahead, the path curves down into the pit.

"I can go ahead." I offer, trying to step past Maendril, but he puts his arm out to stop me.

"Absolutely not." His voice booms in the cavern.

"Tenya and I will lead." Tyr says and signs as he and Tenya step to the front of the group. Their boots send a few loose stones over the edge, and we hear the faint echo of the stone hitting the floor, after bouncing down the path.

Our torches barely penetrate the darkness of the hole as we slowly descend into its depths. A chill spreads up my arms and Raen holds my hand tighter. We continue forward for what feels like hours, further and further into the darkness. Tyr sighs in relief when he reaches the bottom.

"We made it," he shouts. "Let's rest."

We sit on the floor of the pit, eating our bread and sipping water. The breeze has dissipated, leaving an eerie stillness in the air.

Continuing deeper into the pit, we hold our torches out, scanning for more tunnel systems, but there are none. The pit is just that, a giant pit.

I step closer to one of the walls, and the fire illuminates markings etched into the stone. I hold the light closer, squinting to make out the symbol. It shimmers into view just as the cipher on the scroll.

"It's Hevastia's Heart," I whisper, the noise bouncing off the walls, drawing everyone's attention.

"Did you find something, Eliana?" Maendril asks, his voice a deep timber that rumbles like thunder in the tight space.

"I think so, can you lend me your torch?"

Tenya and Maendril hold their torches close, illuminating the wall in front of me. It's covered in symbols, Hevastia's Heart shows up multiple times, but there are others that I don't recognize.

I hand my torch off to Clyn, pulling my notebook and lead from my satchel. I copy down the symbols. Clyn steps out of my way, and the light shines on more of the pictures.

We circle the entire pit, it is covered in markings, like a story written down to be discovered later.

Is this the work of my grandmother, Sarlaine?

I frantically copy the markings, filling my note book with the drawings on the walls. Our torches dim as I finish the last section of the wall.

"It's getting late, we are running low on light. We need to leave, Eliana." Maendril's hand rests easily on my shoulder as he pulls my attention from my notebook.

I nod my head, tucking my notebook away. I got everything I need.

"Time to go home," Tyr says, leading us out of the pit and back to the cavern and our people.

That night around the fire, Raen and Clyn tell the tale of my heroic rescue of Raen from certain death, really playing up the story. Many of the other adults laugh at their antics, the children sit enthralled in the story, some even staring at me as they repeat the tale.

My nose is firmly in my notebook, studying the symbols. A torn page rests on my knee as I decipher the other symbols, creating a key. So far, I only recognize Hevastia's Heart, the rest are a mystery. I pull Mythica's book into my lap, flipping to the story about Hevastia and Soran.

Suddenly, it all clicks into place. It's Hevastia's story. The solari is Soran, the dark cloud that was angrily, deeply etched into the wall of the pit is Vaiccar, and as I follow the notes of Hevastia's story the rest of the symbols follow along.

When the mention of the god-touched appears in the story, one of the final symbols is revealed, Hevastia's symbol with a sword drawn through the middle

That's me, the Hevastian Auror.

I slip to the next page of drawings, my fingers greedily tracing the sketches. My symbol continues to appear, suddenly accompanied by the same dark scribble of Vaiccar, but with a small light traced in it. *The Shadows.*

We appear next to the Hevastia symbol–the same knot as the etching of my necklace.

It looks like a gate, holding back Vaiccar.

In the next sketch the gate is broken, and the symbol for Vaiccar is larger, more emphasized by the deep grooves I traced into the paper, mimicking the sketches on the cave wall.

What happens, how is he released?

My symbol and the shadows are swallowed by the darkness, consumed by it. I flip ahead, scanning for any sign of my symbol reappearing. There are other strange symbols like mine, other elements with swords drawn through them– the other god-touched. Vaiccar fights them, and devours them one by one.

This can't be right, he can't be allowed to conquer all of Odora.

I flip ahead again, remembering a line that was drawn in the cave separating this set of markings from a different version. My symbol and the shadows at Hevastia's gate appear again, a small symbol like a droplet of water beside mine.

Instead of the gate breaking open and releasing Vaiccar, a big circle surrounds me, and my symbol is drawn larger, as big as Vaiccar. The two of us battle, and instead of being absorbed by his darkness, I kill him. I am surrounded by the other god-touched, each of them drawn larger as well.

I jump up from my seat, making Clyn and Raen jump as well, fear glistening in their eyes as they glance nervously toward the cave entrance. Beneath their bravado, they're both still children, and they've seen so much death and darkness.

"I'm just going to get a second notebook, everything's okay. You both did a great job today."

Hearing my praise their faces light up with pride and excitement, the fear of the dark beyond the safety of the cave momentarily forgotten.

I leave the warmth of the fire and slip into my tent, pulling the scroll into my lap. I unroll it, holding it to the flames, and the hidden cipher comes into view once more. Comparing the newly decoded drawings from the cave, the similarities are obvious.

The scroll shows the regenerative cycle of Hevastia's magic, how it balances nature and magic, creating life and honoring death. The symbol at the bottom, Hevastia with a sword drawn through it–it's me. I'm a key piece of the magic cycle, without the god-touched there's no anchor to the land or the people. The water droplet, it's blood–Hevastia's blood, my blood as her descendent.

My blood is the key to unlocking our magic. I need to get to the Heart. It's finally time I make good on my promise to storm the Aceolevia.

I smile ruthlessly to myself, a new energy coursing through my body at the thought of finally having my vengeance for the death of my mother and our people, and the chance to unlock the magic that was stolen from us.

Mythica and Maendril helped me pack the few belongings I am bringing with me. I explained everything to her two nights ago, after I finished piecing together the drawings from the cavern. She was impressed with my translation, hugging me tightly before arguing that I stay longer and practice the incantations more, but we both know that time is of the essence, and the longer I delay, the more powerful Vaiccar may become.

"I'm coming with you," Maendril says, confidently. "You shouldn't go back alone."

I turn to him, the argument on the tip of my tongue. His face is drawn in a serious line, determined. He looks so much like my mother when she would make up her mind, and my heart aches for her. I nod my head.

"I would be grateful for your company."

"Then I hope you don't mind some more." Tyr's voice is light, a soft laugh. The familiar giggle of Clyn and Raen reaches me from behind.

"Oh no." I turn to them, hands on my hips. "I cannot allow you all to come with me, no way."

"I don't think you have a choice in the matter, Princess." Raen's voice is confident as he stands tall with his chest puffed out. "We are your self-appointed guardians, you can't go without us."

I smile at him, but shake my head no. "I appreciate the sentiment, but don't you think our people could use your help here?"

Clyn frowns, he and Raen stand tightly together, a united front against me. Maendril chuckles, the sound like thunder.

"There's no use arguing with them, I already tried." Maendril places a hand on my shoulder. "Please, Eliana."

I sigh and stare up at him, his deep eyes gazing patiently back at me. "I don't want you to get hurt."

He smiles softly at me, and pulls me in for a hug I didn't even know I needed. I relax into his embrace, and soon more arms hold me tightly as my friends encircle me.

"We can't let anything happen to you. It would be our honor to stand beside you, no matter what." Tyr and Tenya are holding hands, Raen and Clyn standing beside them. They all smile at me, and the matter is settled.

"If you're joining me, then we need a plan."

Tyr signs to Tenya what was said and she leaves to gather wood and build a small fire.

We huddle around it, and they listen as I tell them my idea. Maendril and Tyr interject to argue at some points, but eventually we all agree with my strategy.

"Then it's settled, we travel to Wildewell in the morning" I pull out the traveler's stones from my pocket.

"I will take you there using this."

I hand the second traveler's stone to Mythica. "Just in case we're not back in a week's time, send someone to search for Alana and Hama of Wildewell. They will help you."

We go over the plan one more time, and then they depart to say goodbye to their families, leaving me and Mythica alone by the fire.

Her hands are warm on mine as she gives them a squeeze. "Your mother would be proud of you."

"Do you want to practice using the stone again?" I ask, changing the subject.

She shakes her head no, tucking it into her pocket. "I think I can manage. You were very thorough in your instructions."

It's my turn to laugh, I remember drilling her on the motion of how to trace on the stone, the importance of envisioning your destination.

"You are a strict teacher," she says with a wink.

I nudge her with my shoulder, resting my head on hers. "I learned from the best."

She pulls me close and hugs me tightly.

"I will miss you, Mythica," I say softly.

"I will miss you too, child, but I will never be far from you. Your people will always be close in your heart."

I nod my head, closing my eyes as the fire warms my face and hands. She tucks a blanket around both of us and lets me sleep as she strokes my hair like my mother once did. I dream of my mother that night, we are lying in the fields outside our village gazing at the stars.

"I am so proud of how you have grown, my little star. You have become so brave and strong."

My mother is younger, the weight of being a tess no longer marking her face and aging her. She looks so free.

"Are you at peace where you are, Mother?"

"Yes, I am, child," she says, smiling brightly at me, before turning back to the stars.

"I'm afraid," I whisper.

My mother rolls onto her side and chuckles. "I would be more worried if you said you were not afraid. It's natural to be nervous."

"What if I fail?"

Her arms open, and I tuck into them, letting the familiarity comfort me. "You only fail if you give up. And I did not raise a quitter. No matter what, Eliana, never stop trying. Promise me."

I hug her closely, closing my eyes. "I promise."

When I open my eyes it's morning, and Mythica is roasting vegetables over the fire.

"Good morning, Eliana. Are you ready?"

Stretching my arms over my head, I scan the cavern and see everyone, my family, milling about, falling into their normal routines as they make breakfast and start chores. My heart aches at the idea of leaving this easy life behind, the comfort of a simple routine and the familiarity of my people. But I know that they can only continue to have this relative peace if I am successful in stopping Vaiccar.

"Yes," I say confidently, standing up. "I'm ready."

Breakfast passes quickly, and too soon, it's time for me to go. I hug Mythica goodbye, waving to everyone else who gathered by my tent to see us off.

"Thank you," I whisper in Mythica's ear as I pull back from our hug. She smiles and squeezes my hands.

"May Hevastia's Light protect you." Mythica says, and the prayer is echoed by everyone else as they wave to us. I hold the traveler's stone in my pocket, tracing the pattern and closing my eyes as I picture the gate to Wildewell.

Maendril steps back, wary of the portal that opened right in front of him. Tyr and Tenya are holding hands with Clyn and Raen who are ready to dive head first into the portal, the excitement evident on their faces. Maendril swallows deeply, giving me a quick glance for confirmation before stepping through, followed closely by Clyn who turns just before stepping through to stick his tongue out at Raen. Tenya and Tyr follow them, and I am left by myself.

The air ripples around me as I step through, never glancing back at my people. I will see them again, I tell myself, wrapping that promise around my heart. The breeze of the fields outside the village ruffles my hair, and I open my eyes.

"What happened here?" I gasp in shock. The beautiful stone huts stand no longer, all that remains of Wildewell has been burnt to the ground, just like Bellamere. I stumble back, tripping on a root sticking up in the path. I hit the ground, ash kicking up and coating my arms and legs. My hands are blackened by the soot that sticks to me.

Tyr offers me his hand, pulling me to my feet.

"It's just like home," Raen says, his words a whispered whimper. He hugs Tenya's arm, drawing closer to her. She pats his head, her eyes meeting Tyr's over Raen's head.

"Where do we go next?" Tyr asks, throwing as much confidence into his voice as he can muster.

My friends all wear mixed looks of apprehension and fear. We wander through the remnants of the village, searching for any sign of survivors.

Am I too late? Did Kai and Cire not defeat the great beast?

The *tehendra* is completely gone, and as we walk further into the village, toward Kai and Cire's home the buildings are less damaged, but still destroyed. There is nothing left standing.

"Eliana, is that you?"

Hama stands behind me, carrying a sword. The sword is so out of place on their person– I've grown so accustomed to seeing them holding colorful bolts of fabric and sewing needles. They stand strong, a warrior once again.

"Hama, what happened here?" I ask.

They gaze fearfully at my companions, holding the sword out to keep us at a distance.

"These are my friends, survivors from Bellamere, my home. They can be trusted."

Hama hesitates before slipping the sword back into their scabbard. They grab my hand and tow me behind them, weaving through the wreckage and the ruins.

"We must go, it's not safe here."

We follow them out of Wildewell and into the Hilwe Wildes. As we near the edge of the forest, I hesitate, my shoulder throbbing with the memory of the first time I ventured into the darkness of the forest. Hama glances back at me, extending their hand for me to take again.

"Please, Eliana, we can't be caught out here." I grab ahold of their hand and follow, quickening my pace to keep up with them as they dart through the trees, weaving us deeper and deeper into the Wildes.

Maendril grunts, his large frame catching on all the low branches and brambles as we dart through the thickets. Tenya and Tyr are trying their best to keep up, their charges having a hard time navigating forest terrain for the first time in their lives. We were never allowed to leave the valley perimeter back home. I can only imagine how thrilling and terrifying this must be for the boys.

We finally stopped in front of a large tree. Hama scans the area before kneeling down, dusting away a layer of leaves and twigs to reveal a small, wooden trap door. They open the door, ushering us all inside. Maendril insists on going first, and I follow last, descending a ladder into the dimly lit corridor, as Hama follows me down and closes the hatch. The tunnel goes completely dark. I suck in a surprised breath.

"It's okay, we won't be in the dark for long." Their hand closes around mine, as we all link up to follow Hama.

They lead us deeper underground, the tunnel slanting under my boots.

"Duck."

I crouch down, feeling soft dirt rain onto my hair where I did not crouch low enough, and I hit my head on the ceiling. I crawl behind them in the darkness for a short while, before the tunnel opens up and the light of a torch illuminates a series of passage ways.

Hama stands in front of the first one on the right, holding the torch. They beckon us forward without a word, and we follow, my head buzzing with so many questions.

The tunnel opens up to a large cavern much like the one we just left behind. There are only a handful of people in the cavern, huddled around a small fire.

Hama glances back at me, frowning. Sorrowfully they say, "Welcome to Wildewell."

I wind my way deeper into the cavern toward the group of people and the fire. I scan their faces, and my heart twist as I realize that Kai and Cire are not among the survivors. The young girl I rescued waves to me, sandwiched between two adults, one holding her baby brother.

"Where are they?" I ask Hama. "You keep dodging my questions. Tell me what happened."

"Enough." Alana steps away from the group and comes toward us.

"Who are these people?" She points at my friends.

Alana has her swords on her back. In fact, all of the survivors around the fire are carrying weapons. They sit hunched over, staring into the flames. Very few of them are speaking, the rest too defeated and exhausted.

"They're survivors from Bellamere, my home. I brought them with me because–" I stop myself, peering at the group crowded around the fire. "I brought them with me because there's something I need their help with. We came searching for you. Is there somewhere we can go to talk?"

Hama steps up, and motions for Maendril, and the rest to follow them.

"Your friends can follow me this way for a seat around the fire." Hama smiles encouragingly at them.

With a wink they say, "I might even have a treat for the two strapping young lads you've brought along."

At the mention of them, and sweets, Raen and Clyn eagerly follow Hama, grinning to each other.

Alana motions for me to follow her away from the others, and I turn, descending deeper into the cavern after her, toward a small ledge overlooking an underground pool. If it weren't for the somber mood, the view would be beautiful and peaceful. The pool catches the reflection of our torches turning a golden orange in the firelight.

She sits on the ledge, dangling her legs over the water. Alana peeks over at me and pats the ground beside her.

"Sit," she commands.

I sit beside her, my feet nearly touching the pool below. I stare down at the water and see my reflection, my face covered in ash and grime from the village.

"We lost nearly everyone when the *craicabra* attacked," she whispers. "It took out half of the village, destroyed all the homes with its fiery breath.

"Kai and Cire miraculously took it down, but not before almost everyone was caught in its destruction, its fire burned the entire village down. The retired Morei of the village couldn't repair the damage with our gifts. You ran with the others that fled."

She motions back to the small group sitting around the fire we just left. "Some of them did not make it through the night. Beast attacks."

I sit quietly, too afraid to speak, too saddened by the loss to find the right words. Guilt sucks me toward the depths of the pools.

If I had stayed back, if I hadn't abandoned them too, then maybe lives would have been spared.

"The survivors had to recover the dead from the rubble, it took several days to find all the bodies, some of them already burnt beyond recognition. We had to be sure they wouldn't rise again." She chokes back a sob. "We had to burn them all. The pyre for our fallen and for the beast's body was so large we couldn't control the flames and they consumed the rest of what was not already burned down in the attack. We lost everything."

I touch her shoulder, lightly squeezing it. "I'm so sorry for your loss."

"We're survivors." She sniffles, gazing at me with hopeful eyes. "I'm glad to see you're safe. Cire worried you had perished in the fire. Where did you go?"

"I went home to seek answers. I'm sorry it meant not being here to help you."

"It's better that you left, it wasn't safe for you here. We moved underground afterward, there's nothing left of the Wildewell, and no one left to rebuild it."

She throws a stone into the pool, sending ripples that distort our reflections and darken the glow of the torchlight in the water.

I tell her about my time in Bellamere, of returning home and everything I learned. Alana listens closely, nodding along. I show her my notebook and the drawings, explaining to her the symbols and reading the prophecy out loud to her.

"The scroll Hama gave me, did you know about the hidden cipher?" I ask. "Held to the flames, it showed a depiction of Lady Hevastia's connection to all of us, with me as a key, an anchor. I need to find the Heart. Do you know where it is?"

If she's surprised by anything I've told her, she does a good job of hiding it. She shakes her head no. "Only the most trusted within High Priest Marius's inner circle have ever seen the Heart. Its location within the Temple is hidden."

"But, Cire knew what it looked like ... he identified it immediately on my necklace. It's what convinced him I'm the chosen one. How would he know?"

"I'm not sure. After we set the pyre ablaze, Kai and Cire vanished from the village. There's been no word from them in several weeks. I worry something happened to them."

We sit in silence for a long time, just staring out over the water. Hama joins us some time later, sitting on my right, nestling me between them and Alana. They take my hand in theirs and squeeze it.

"We're glad you're back dear, we missed you."

Hama doesn't mention Cire or Kai's absence but I know we all feel it. The heat of the torch staked in the ground behind us warms me despite the chill creeping into my body as I stare into the darkness. I fear something terrible has happened to them.

"I will get them back, I promise," I say to Alana and Hama, to the darkness that surrounds us.

It's a promise I plan to keep, no matter what.

Kai

I PARTIALLY OPEN MY eyes, the swelling preventing me from seeing much past my hand in front of my face. My arms are no longer chained above my head, instead my leg is weighed down by a heavy chain around my ankle, bolted into the ground.

I am weak from blood loss, and my vision swims with each pulse of my pounding headache. The sound of footsteps shuffling beyond the threshold of my cell echoes on the stone floor, but I don't bother calling for help.

They took Cire away some time ago, I have not heard him come back. I sit against the wall. My head hangs, and I wheeze in a breath. I close my eyes, closing out the horror my life has become.

A loud scream erupts from somewhere beyond my cell and my eyes dart open, pain searing my face as I push past the swelling that stretches my skin. Cire screams again, the sound guttural, pained.

"Cire," I yell, my throat sore and voice hoarse. "Cire!"

I crawl toward the door, banging my fists weakly against the heavy wood door.

"Let me out you bastards. Let my brother go."

Cire cries out again, but it's cut short, and my breath hitches in my throat.

Please don't be dead, I cannot go on without you. I need you, Eliana needs us.

I picture her face in my mind, and my strength briefly swells. The thought of her is the only thing that keeps me going. I pray she is still safe and far from the Council's grasp. I bang against the door again.

Cire's body smacks the ground as he's dumped back into his cell, his breath coming in short wheezes.

"Kai," he moans.

"Cire, I'm here," I say, crawling to the wall that separates us.

"Kai, help me," he moans in pain again. "Please."

"What can I do to help?" I ask, desperation in my voice. "Shall I distract you from the pain?"

Cire chuckles, but it ends in a coughing fit. The coughs are wet with blood.

"Kai, they torture me for information. I haven't told them ... anything." Cire wheezes. "Please tell me Eliana is safe."

This is a game we have played many times, almost a mantra between us to keep our faith. We will not break. While Cire has been gone, I have been reflecting on our time with Eliana, however brief, and everything Alana and Hama told me of their time with her while we were away.

She had been seeking answers about the prophecy, as we all were. If she left us, I can only believe it was because she had a lead she had not shared with anyone. Elaina was distrustful of us, but the only thing that could have kept her from saying anything, even to taunt, would be if she believed it put someone at risk.

"She went home," I whisper quietly.

Alana mentioned that Eliana had a vision after her injury from the *severn*. She wouldn't tell Alana or Hama the details, just that she was feeling very guilty over the ordeal. She gave up avenging her people's deaths, there is no greater guilt than forsaking her people if she believed she owed them a blood debt. Because she did not kill us, she couldn't return home.

"Of course." I gasp, it all makes sense.

"Kai, what is it?" Cire's voice sounds stronger, more urgent.

"Cire, she went home," I say confidently. Hope swells in my chest, hope that she found the answer to stopping the Council, that maybe she is on her way back here right now.

"Are you sure?" Cire asks, his voice showing more life than it has in days.

"Yes, it's what I would have done. I would even bet she knows more than she's led us to believe."

Cire laughs, no longer sounding in pain at all. His boots step confidently, without struggle, on the stone floor as he walks from his cell, and to mine. He stands on the threshold of my cell, the door between us, just outside of my reach, staring down at me.

"Thank you, Kai, for finally being of some use." He smiles cruelly down at me.

"What?" I breathe out, confused. "Cire, what's going on?"

High Priest Marius steps into the light, standing beside Cire.

"Good work, son." He peers down at me, resting a hand proudly on Cire's shoulder. "You have done well."

Cire frowns, but does not say anything, just stares down at me in the dirt, covered in my dried blood and grime. He is clean, not a speck of dirt or blood on him, he was never injured or tortured.

"You tricked me," I scream and lunge at him, the chain around my ankle pulling taunt and hurling me into the dirt.

"You liar. How could you?" I throw dirt at him, tears running freely down my face.

My own brother betrayed me.

High Priest Marius turns away, flicking the dirt off his red robe, striding down the corridor. Cire turns without a backward glance to me and follows him out.

The door at the end of the hall thuds closed behind them, and I am left truly alone for the first time since being thrown in this cell.

I'm not certain how much time has passed since Cire walked away, leaving me to bleed in the dirt. I have not seen him since.

The young boy continues to bring me food and water once a day. Just enough to keep me awake and alive. I sit with my back on one wall and stare at the wall across from me, counting the bricks to pass the time.

Thirty-seven, thirty-eight, thirty-nine...

The door at the end of the hall opens, heavy footfalls echo in the corridor stopping at my cell. High Priest Marius stares at me through the cell door.

"Stand up, Kai."

When I don't move he sucks in deep breath. "I said, stand up," he snaps.

I don't move.

He growls and opens the cell door, stepping inside. He stays close to the doorway, careful not to come too far into the cell.

"Get up this instance," he yells. His face reddens as his temper rises. "Larsus," he snaps.

The young boy scurries forward, bowing to the High Priest. "Yes, sir?"

"Unlock him."

The jangle of keys accompanies Larsus as he moves to undo the cuff around my outstretched ankle. There's a soft click, and then the cuff loosens and unhooks, freeing me.

I jump up immediately, lunging at the cell door, reaching for the High Priest. He ducks behind the door, shutting it firmly closed behind him, out of my grasp. I stagger on my weakened legs, stumbling back from the doorway.

There is a soft whimper of a scared child behind me. Larsus did not escape with the High Priest. I stumble toward him and he tries to dart away, but he's not nimble enough, and I seize his arm. I pull Larsus against me, tightening my arm around his neck.

"Let me out, or I will kill him." I stare at Marius, daring him. He barely glances at the boy, disinterested.

"Go ahead, kill him." He turns away from me. "There are more young acolytes, he's nothing special."

Larsus squeaks, his tears wet my sleeve as he cries in my arms. I release him and he runs to the door, and I stand back, letting him escape. Marius opens the door for the child, and snaps it closed behind him, locking it.

"You're not as strong as you think," Marius jeers. "Pathetic."

He tucks his hands back into his red robe and walks away as Larsus follows, his head hanging as he shuffles his feet, leaving me alone once again. The door shuts firmly at the end of the hall, and only then do I sit back down, pulling the keys I stole from Larsus out of my pocket.

"You're not as smart as you think you are, High Priest."

I stumble to the doorway, and try each key in the cell lock. The third key clicks and turns, opening the door. I relock it and sit back against the wall, waiting.

Eliana

T HE NEXT MORNING, ALANA leads me, Maendril, , and Tyr through the Hilwe Wildes to the base of the Dartneau Hills, where the Aceolevia is hidden.

Raen and Clyn stayed with Hama and the other refugees from Wildewell to help gather supplies and protect them from beasts. Maendril gave them a very rousing speech before we left, and when I passed them they were still standing with their chests puffed out and huge grins spread across their faces. Hama was holding back a laugh behind their backs.

Maendril cuts a large path through the undergrowth, parting all the bramble and small trees with ease. Alana follows closely behind him, giving him directions, the rest fall in line behind her with Tyr bringing up the rear.

The traveler's stone burns in my pocket, but we don't know where Kai or Cire are within the Temple, or what we might find stepping out of the portal unplanned. It will, however, come in very handy if we find ourselves in need of a quick getaway.

Alana signals Maendril to stop as she crouches lower into the brush. My heart rate beats wildly. *We're here.*

Alana slips past Maendril, stalking through the shadows of the forest until she nears the temple, darting across the lawn. I hold my breath as she turns a corner, slipping out of view. Minutes go by, the only noise, the thumping of my own heart in my ears. I'm not sure I've even breathed since she left.

Tenya grows restless beside me–she keeps glancing at Tyr and scanning the bright lawn surrounding the temple, on alert for any trouble. Maendril grips his sword tightly, his breathing slow and even, but his sharp gaze never leaves the temple.

The temple grounds are pristine, the flowerbeds surrounding the building are well maintained, the trees planted in neat rows. It's beautiful like a castle out of a fairytale mother would read to me as a child. I sneak past Maendril, gasping in awe at the stone statues that decorate the grand entrance.

They're all of Lady Hevastia.

The Haematites may no longer worship Her, and their use of unnatural magic tarnishes her world and legacy, but it's clear that whatever their goals, they are inexplicably bound to her, as we all are. She is within all of us, even if our magic is locked away.

My fingers curl around the pendant hanging from my neck, and I whisper a prayer for strength and luck, "There is promise in the Light."

Movement to the right startles us all, and Maedril pulls me closely behind him, pushing me to the ground to shield me even further. I want to argue that I can take care of myself, but my pride's not worth getting caught. The tension is so high, I almost throw up when Alana comes into view, crouching low to slink through the shadows of the forest back to us. Clenched in her fist is a set of keys on a thick iron ring. She smiles triumphantly, and Maendril claps her on the back with pride, sending her reeling to the ground.

We follow Alana across the lawn, and I spot a smear of blood on the bright green grass. Alana glances sideways at the blood stain, guilt shadowing her face, and I decide not to ask what she did to get the keys. She quickens our pace, darting into the gated courtyard, closing the gate behind us.

A collective gasp echoes through our small group as we take in the beauty of the hidden garden surrounding this part of the temple. There are flowers in vibrant shades I can't name, varieties I've never seen. My fingers itch to pull out my sketchbook and study every flower in the garden. In the center is a large shade tree, flowering vines of yellow and light pink cascading down from its high branches.

I step closer, when a deep voice echoes from across the garden.

"Is he ready?" an authoritative voice asks.

"Not yet, sir, but I think he will be after today," says a second, quieter voice.

Could they be talking about Kai or Cire?

I move closer, keeping to the shadows and out of sight.

"Excellent, bring him to the Heart," says the first voice. "Make sure he's awake this time."

"Are you sure, sir?" whispers the second voice. "Won't he be able to fight back?"

"What are you implying?" growls the first voice. I hear the sound of a chair scrape against the stone path before clattering to the ground.

"Nothing, sir. It was my mistake." The second voice yelps in pain.

Quieter they say, "I graciously accept your punishment, High Priest. I will go and fetch him for you now."

Two men leave the garden, a gangly boy of fifteen, and a man dressed in all red with long, trailing sleeves–*the High Priest*. My blood boils, and I fight the urge to spring from my hiding spot and end him right there.

You'll get what's coming for you once I find Cire and Kai. I swear it.

Maendril's strong hand rests on my shoulder, and glancing back, he wears the same fiery, vengeance on his face. I'm grateful to have my family with me, their strength bolsters my own.

"He's going to the Heart," I whisper. "I'm following him, I need to find it."

Tyr looks ready to object, but Maendril interrupts, "It's a good idea, Tyr."

"Tenya and I will follow the High Priest. Alana, can you lead Maendril to the dungeon? You can free Cire and Kai, and rendezvous with me at the Heart. Tenya, when you deliver me there safely, return here to Tyr. You will be our eyes and ears for movement in the temple." My voice is confident as I give the orders. It's the most I've ever sounded like a leader.

I sign the plan to Tenya who nods, smiling mischievously to herself.

"Use this to find Cire and Kai." I hand the traveler's stone to Alana.

"You know I am the one who gave these to them, right?" She smiles.

I shake my head, no, I had no idea. "Let's plan to meet back here."

Everyone nods in agreement, and with those final words, Tenya and I leave, trailing a safe distance behind the High Priest. He winds his way further into the temple, the hallways doubling back on one another, forming an intricate labyrinth, all but ensuring no one could find their way in or out without knowing the way.

I worry for Tenya finding her way back safely to Tyr, but she assures me with a confident squeeze of my hand that she's not worried about it.

It seems like we have been trailing him for hours when he finally stops in front of a beautiful, ornate wood door in the middle of a plain hallway, deep within the maze. Reaching deep into his red robe, the High Priest pulls out an ornate key, and unlocks the door.

I wait with baited breath for him to open the door, my anxiety sucking me down, rooting me to my spot. Tenya places an encouraging hand on my shoulder, and I give her fingers a small squeeze.

Her warmth leaves my back as she moves to stand farther down the hallway, her hood covering her face. Her hand barely moves, but she gestures to me to stay hidden before she turns and pulls the large vase away from the wall, sending it crashing.

"What are you doing?" the High Priest yells, spotting Tenya as his face turns red and furious.

His eyes lock onto Tenya, mouth open, ready to shout again as she turns and runs. The High Priest follows her down the hallway, abandoning the door.

I pause, listening as his heavy footsteps fade down the hallway, accented by his huffing breath as he prepares to shout at Tenya again.

Lady of Light, please keep Tenya's feet swift, don't let her be caught.

One... two... three deep breaths before I dart across the hall and open the heavy wood door, shutting it quietly behind me. Carved into the floor of the hall is the pattern I cannot get out of my head, the one I wear around my neck–Hevastia's Heart. The floor is stained dark brown, the smell in the room is metallic, like old blood. My own blood runs cold in my body.

What's happened here?

At the center of the Heart is a large purple gemstone that stands nearly as tall as me. As I draw closer the purple stone in my pocket seems to pulse, and I'm pulled toward the large one. Reaching out to touch it, I'm thrown back to the floor, and my vision goes dark before bright flames surround me on every side.

Through the flames and smoke, Atrya emerges like a vengeful spirit.

"Princess," I say, my voice breathy from the force of being knocked flat. "I'm ready to restore my connection to the Amorei, the Heart."

"You shouldn't be here," she says, her voice small yet powerful and strong like that of a blue flame. "It's not safe for you to be here, you risk everything."

"I don't understand. I need to be here, I need to restore my connection to the Heart." I pull my favorite dagger from my boot. "My blood will unlock everyone's magic."

I'm struck to the floor by an intense blast, my dagger skidding across the stone, out of reach. Atrya stands above me holding another ball of flame, ready to strike me once again.

"How are you doing that?" I ask.

She's never been able to touch me before.

"Are you *insane*?" she hisses. "You'll get everyone killed. You need to leave immediately, he cannot possess you."

"Not until I free Hevastia. Our people are defenseless without magic, I need to reconnect to the Heart."

I stand back up, striding toward Atrya and the purple gem in the center of the Heart.

"Get out of my way, Atrya. My blood is the key."

"You're the *Auror*, your blood is also the lock. With it, Vaiccar will not need to siphon magic," she says as she points to the purple gem on the Heart, and to more along the edge of the hall that I had not noticed before.

All of them pulse with the same soft inner glow as the small shard in my pocket.

"He'll be completely free, and you will doom us all."

"I don't understand–why did you give me this gem, why lead me here if I'm not supposed to free our people's magic? What chance do we stand against Vaiccar without it?"

"I gave the gem shard to Kai hoping he would find the Heart himself and destroy these siphons. You don't need the gem, you need the light inside it–that's the magic of Hevastia."

She takes the gem shard from my hand and crushes it into my hand. There's a shocking jolt, and a searing pain like liquid fire has spread through my veins.

The room comes into a sharper focus, and I can see Atrya in true light–she's sixteen, only a few years younger than me, hiding behind the visage of our Lady of Light, Hevastia. Her form pulses stronger here, stronger than when I saw her in the Hilwe Wildes. It's as if she is able to harness the lingering magic here.

"Leave–quickly! It's not safe for you here, he's coming. I sense his sickly darkness drawing close." She whispers, her eyes wide in fright. "If he catches you, Hevastia's Light will fade to darkness forever and all will perish."

"How did you escape him?" I ask, frantic.

"Help me, please, Atrya." I grab her hand but the fire burns my skin, and I have to let go.

"There's no time, I will visit you again when it's safe. I must go before he finds me," she says, turning to return to the flames, her shape already fading to smoke.

"Hide," Atrya's voice whispers loudly in my ear, her form already gone from my view.

I duck behind a large pillar at the edge of the hall, concealed by one of the siphon gems. Voices draw closer, and the sound of a struggle echoes across the hall as the door opens and a small group of men enter, the High Priest in the lead, a man dragged by Haematian guards close behind.

"I couldn't find the spy, but I have several guardians searching for the culprit. We will not be disturbed, I promise, sir," the High Priest proclaims in a loud voice.

"For your sake, I hope that is true," growls a familiar voice with a strange edge. "Bring the prisoner forward."

A low groan escapes the lips of the half-conscious man as he's strung up on a hook near the edge of the Heart where the rusted blood stains are worst. I peek around the gem, trying to see past the guards to who they have on the hook. As they pull the chain to lift him off the ground, I choke down a scream at the sight of Kai's bruised and broken body dangling in the air.

"Leave us," the strangely familiar voice says. "Marius, you stay, I want you to witness this."

The High Priest shifts uncomfortably, glancing longingly at the guards as they leave and shut the heavy door behind them with an echoing thud. "Are you sure, sir? I could be of more use in the search for the spy."

I stretch around the other side of the pillar, trying to see the source of the other voice, but they're standing in the shadows, hiding from the light of the sconces surrounding the hall. High Priest Marius dances from foot to foot, nervous. Kai's head hangs limp to the side, and he hasn't stirred since they hung him on the hook.

The man in the shadows finally steps into the light, the dagger in his hand glinting.

My dagger.

"Eliana, I know you're here, come out from hiding," Cire says. "Every minute you stay hidden I will plunge your dagger into Kai. And, from the looks of it, he doesn't have that many minutes left."

I swallow down my fear, trying to process what I'm seeing.

Cire is standing next to the High Priest ... something isn't right. He'd never hurt Kai.

"Don't believe I'll do it?" He taunts.

He drives my dagger, all the way to the hilt, into Kai's side, blood gushing out of the gaping wound as he pulls it free.

"Don't test me, Eliana."

The siphon gem pulses under my fingertips, the magic inside screaming to be set free. I lay my palm flat on the gem and whisper, "There is promise in the Light."

A white-hot pain sears into my skin as the magic trapped within the siphon leaks out and covers my hand, white flames burning intensely on my skin before vanishing, a thin blue smoke trail hovering just before my eyes.

The magic surges through my body, chaotic, uncontrollable. It feels as though I might explode at any moment from the pressure. Squeezing my eyes shut I concentrate on my breathing, finding my center and cooling the fiery magic burning throughout my body like avenging flames.

I have magic. I can't believe it–it's real!

My body is alight with excitement, pure joy coursing through me. Momentarily I forget the world around me, as I savor the rightness, the completeness of magic. But, there's no time to focus on what having magic means, or what to do with it.

Have I successfully connected with the Heart? Am I strong enough now to face what's to come?

"Eliana, I am not a patient man," Cire growls. "I have waited a very long time for this."

He stabs Kai again, twisting the dagger. "Come out now, or I will be forced to kill him."

One ... two ... three deep breaths as I slow my beating heart.

I step out from behind the pillar, holding my head high, my heart thumping in my throat and thundering in my ears. Each step toward Cire echoes across the hall, and I fight the urge to panic. The magic writhes under my skin, but I hold it down, waiting for an opportunity. I slowly move my hand to my hip, reaching for one of my hidden daggers.

"Don't even think about it," Cire snarls.

He flourishes my dagger, holding it close to Kai's neck.

"Try something stupid, and he will bleed to death before your dagger even hits its mark."

He laughs, and it sounds wrong.

"Drop your daggers where you stand, all of them."

He keeps the dagger to Kai's neck, and a single hot tear slides down my cheek.

I can't sacrifice him.

The sound of my daggers hitting the ground sounds like the cannons my people fired against the Morei guardians, now shot directly into my chest. The weight of failure threatens to suck me down, and another tear slides down my cheek.

I finish closing the distance between myself and Cire. And as I draw closer, the air chills, and an inky darkness settles on my skin. The magic within me shrinks away from the darkness, gathering itself in my heart.

"I trusted you." My voice is barely more than a whisper. "Cire, what have you done?"

Cire turns to me and smiles cruelly. "You were right all along, Eliana, you should have never trusted me."

He grabs me, pulling me close to him. The coldness jolts through my body, and it feels like the chilled grip of death itself holding me.

"What did you do?" I yell and kick, trying to break free.

He laughs and the sound sends chills down my spine.

"It wasn't hard to trick you, you were so blinded by the need for revenge I just played along. I didn't need you to trust me. You gave up your ambitions of finding the Aceolevia and decided to 'understand who you are.'

"You learned to trust me all on your own. Not very smart of you." He says the last words in a mocking tone dripping with disdain. "You're weak, and pathetic—that's what you are."

He waves his hands around the great hall we are standing in.

"You hand delivered yourself to me. It was all too easy. I was ready to send men all the way to Bellamere to hunt you down, and you strolled right in."

He ties my hands, handing me off to the High Priest before lowering Kai's body to the ground, blood still dripping slowly from the dagger wound.

"Pathetic." Cire kicks Kai's body. "So much wasted potential."

He beckons the High Priest forward. "Marius," he orders. "Come closer."

Cire pulls my arms over my head, and hoists me up on the hook hanging from the ceiling, my feet barely dangling off the ground, my toes just able to touch. I scream with the pain of being lifted as my arms stretch above me.

"Why are you helping the Haematites? What about everything you said before? About wanting to free Hevastia from the Council?" My voice strains, as I fight to talk through the pain.

"You wanted to do good, what happened?"

The High Priest smiles at me, and my stomach rolls in disgust.

"I'm afraid that's my doing. The man you see before you is not Cire. He's using Cire's body as a vessel now. The Cire you knew, the boy you trusted, is gone."

My voice grows quiet. "What do you mean he's gone?"

"Say hello to Vaiccar. He's inhabiting your friend now," the High Priest declares as Cire does a dramatic bow and flashes another evil smile before speaking.

"Marius, you ruin my fun. I wanted her to believe her friend had truly betrayed her after she finally learned to trust her enemy."

He flashes another disgusting smile. "I was trying to teach her a lesson."

"Enough games, Vaiccar. You have the girl, do what you must so that you may remain on this side of the veil. A deal is a deal."

Vaiccar huffs, glaring at Marius. He flicks his hand, dismissing him from the room. "Leave us, I need a moment alone with her."

Marius opens his mouth to interject, but Vaiccar glares at him, his cold stare cutting off Marius's argument.

"Leave."

Marius bows and turns to leave.

I push away from Vaiccar as he draws closer. When he reaches out to touch my face, I turn away, flinching as his cold hands caress my cheek. His touch sickens me, and my stomach rolls.

"Shhh, there's no need to be shy," he whispers in my ear.

I bite my lip, but a small whimper escapes. I squeeze my eyes shut.

His cold fingers grip my cheeks tightly in his hand, forcing me to open my eyes and look at him.

"I won't help you." I spit in his face.

He snarls and shoves my face away, making my body sway and wrenching my arms. I cry out from the pain.

"You have no choice, you have no power to stop me. And without your magic, you are nothing."

"Why?" I ask, curious, stalling.

Now would be a great time for my magic to do something.

I think back to all of the incantations I practiced with Mythica, but my magic is nothing like we expected–it's fiery, uncontrollable, and wild. It's not the soft, strong, calming presence Mythica believed it to be.

"Revenge. Freedom. Power." He ticks each reason on his fingers, his smile growing wider and more revolting.

He turns to me and sneers.

"I needed Hevastia's magic out of my way. So, I had to weaken it, and eventually destroy it. Without your people's magic charging the Heart, keeping the veil strong, I was able to step over from the otherside, at first only for brief moments, then long enough to meddle with your affairs, toy with the balance.

"It wasn't long before I found a few souls susceptible to my manipulation, I sunk my claws into them, and I used them for my gain. I have been plotting this for centuries my dear, far longer than you can contemplate.

"Every move calculated, every pawn perfectly executed, so that I could stand before you and take your life to secure my rule of Hevastia. The darkness, the plagues, the rising dead and dark beasts–they're all me. They are my creations meant to weaken your magic.

"Only a century or so ago, did I discover something even more powerful than the small nuisances and perversions of your magic I had been toying with all these years. A soul stone, something that could harvest and contain Lady Hevastia's magic and very being."

I follow his hand as it gestures to the large stone in the center of the hall and the circle of stones surrounding the hall.

"It's taken a lot of stones to siphon and contain Hevastia's magic, but it is nearly complete. Your blood will give me the ability to harness this magic as my own."

I strain away from him, pleading, "No, you don't need to do this."

"But I do. An eternity, damned to watch your people flourish, seeing everything Soran and Hevastia created together thrive–it made me sick. She was MINE, she was ALL MINE! And now you will be too."

His back is to me, as he holds his arms wide with pride, standing so close to me. I quietly whimper as I swing my body, my arms burning as I swing one more time, and draw my legs over his shoulders, pulling him under me, taking him by surprise.

I squeeze my legs around his head, trying to choke him. My dagger drops from his hands as he reaches to pull me off of him, but gravity is on my side. I leverage his height to pull my arms off the hook and reach into my braid to pull my thin blade free.

I plunge the blade into his shoulder, at the base of his neck. He thrashes wildly, and I lose my balance, tumbling to the ground, my arms still bound, the thin blade clattering away. I struggle to roll to my knees, clawing at the ground, trying to crawl to my dagger.

A boot presses me to the ground, and I cry out. Rough hands turn me over, and Cire's weight is on top of me as Vaiccar pins me to the ground, holding my dagger to my throat. He smiles at me, an evil expression that shows no trace of Cire. My blood runs cold.

He leans down, his breath hot on my cheek. "You will be mine, with me always."

I squirm beneath him, trying to escape. My legs kick uselessly under him, and my arms remain tied. I'm without any leverage. I try desperately to call forth my magic, but there's nothing. The surge of energy I felt before is gone, and I don't know how to bring it back.

The dagger stabs into my gut, the sharp pain as he twists it deeper, my blood pouring out over his hands and onto the floor.

He leaves the dagger in, letting my blood drip onto the floor. Vaiccar stands up, and steps back, watching with satisfaction as I bleed out.

"You're sick." I growl. "You'll never get away with this."

He laughs. "That's the best part–I already have. I promised Marius I would make him a god in my new world, in turn he handed over the one thing ensuring its very protection."

He throws his arms up and turns in a circle, indicating the Heart and the soul siphons. "There is literally nothing standing in my way now that I have the Auror's blood."

My vision blurs from blood loss, distorting my sight as Cire's body is tackled to the ground, and he tumbles with someone.

Kai yells over the noise of the struggle. "Get her out of here. Go!"

"Stay with me Eliana," a scared voice whispers over me, repeatedly.

I black out.

Kai

I WAKE UP IN time to see Cire twisting a knife into Eliana's stomach.

No, not Cire, something else.

I throw myself at him, tackling my brother's body to the ground before punching him square in the jaw.

Footsteps ricochet off the stone floor and Eliana's body is lifted from where she was lying, Alana gathering her in her arms.

"Get her out of here. Go!" I yell as Not-Cire struggles beneath me.

I punch him again, sending his head snapping back onto the ground with a sickening thud.

He laughs at me. "Go ahead, kill me. You'll be killing your friend, too."

I sneer at him, landing another punch to his face.

"That's funny, I don't need to kill you. You may be in Cire's body, but you're not him, and therefore you're no match for me or my training."

I grab Not-Cire's body by the shoulder slamming him down into the ground with all my strength, knocking the imposter out cold. I notice the giant purple crystal like the one Princess Atrya gave me in the gauntlet sitting in the center of the room, more surrounding the hall. Eliana's blood is being absorbed into the largest one as it pulses and glows.

"That can't be good," I mutter to myself.

I draw Cire's sword and with all my remaining strength I strike the gemstone, shattering it. Shards blast out in all directions as all the gems in the hall explode and the pulsing glow fades. The blast knocks me back, and I tumble to the floor, the sword clattering from my hand and out of reach.

A bright light floods the hall as the deep grooves etched in the floor, Hevastia's Heart, glow, sending streaks of blinding light into the ceiling along the lines of the design. Eliana stands on the edge of the Heart, in a pool of her own blood. She's glowing like the Heart, cloaked in white, ethereal flames.

Eliana strides forward, her hair whipping wildly, the flames rippling around her as she walks to the center of the Heart. I watch her scan the room, her black eyes landing on me for a moment, twin pools of darkest night. A shiver runs down my spine.

"Blood has been spilt, the veiled one released, the prophecy awoken. She who is known by many names–the Chosen of Hevastia, the Auror, Fate's Guardian–has arisen from the ashes. Her Light is the candle flame standing against the devouring night. Her blood is the Hope everlasting, borne of the same sacred vein as Hevastia, the binding tie. She is the Truth destined, her burning touch shall cleanse this land of its wicked darkness."

The white flames encircling Eliana disappear, and she drops unconscious to the floor. I scramble to my feet, rushing to her side.

Not-Cire collides with me knocking me to the ground as I reach for Eliana.

"I won't let you near her." I growl.

I grunt against his weight on my chest, struggling to grip his neck in a chokehold with my bare hands while keeping his hands off my own neck.

Alana shouts my name, holding Eliana's limp body, she stands in a portal next to a large man with imposing features, and another man and woman holding hands.

"Go," I shout, punching Not-Cire in the face as he snaps his attention toward Alana.

Distracted, I am able to roll him off of me, instead pinning him to the ground. "Alana, go!"

"Kai, I can't keep this portal much longer, you have to come with us." Alana yells, her eyes full of desperation, and the confusion of watching me beat my brother to near-death.

I bash Not-Cire's head into the ground once more, and launch off of him, sprinting for Alana's outstretched hand. The portal wavers, and I run faster. My fingertips graze hers before the portal blinks out and she disappears.

"No," I yell, collapsing to the ground.

Bootsteps crunch across the gem shards scattered on the floor.

"It appears your friends left you behind."

I turn to make a sharp remark, but instead catch a boot to the face. I bring my hand to my nose, my blood dripping down my fingers.

My body hums with energy.

Eliana's blood.

It sings to me, and in this moment, I realize I have the upper hand now. I pull on the strength from my own blood, and that of Eliana's blood on the ground. It surges into my body and I stand taller, fists raised in front of me, beckoning Not-Cire to attack.

His eyes turn murderous. Not-Cire tries to pull essence from Eliana's blood, but it doesn't respond to him in the same way, the imposter is reliant on Cire's limited gifts. He yells in frustration, grabbing the dagger he used on Eliana and throwing it at me. I dodge it easily, calling the wind to redirect it.

"Let my brother go!" I yell, sending a burst of air at this imposter. He rolls out of the way.

His laugh echoes through the chamber.

"Gladly. Just as soon as I can have you instead. You will make a much better vessel than this *weakling*." He spits out the insult.

"Would you so willingly give your life to save his?"

"I would. Cire is better than me, he didn't deserve this. He was good, he wanted peace."

I send another burst of air at him and this time it hits him dead on, knocking him into the air before sending him crashing down to the ground.

"I will get my brother back."

"Better you say? Interesting." He laughs. "Because if I recall, your brother resented you, so full of hatred for your gifts, your recognition. It made it so easy to influence him, he practically gave me this body."

"Liar." I growl.

The wind swirls around me, and I use it to throw a gemstone from the corner of the room at him.

He laughs. "I should be thanking you, you're the reason I have this body. After living in your shadow all this time, Cire was so desperate for strength, power, significance. This sacrifice has meaning and purpose, unlike his blood shed for your glory."

The raw pain and bitter truth of his words hits me as hard as the large gemstone shards I've been hurtling at him. I hesitate too long before throwing the next, as he surprises me with a stone of his own, knocking me to the ground. I struggle to get up, lying among the shards of the gemstones. His boot comes down on my chest, pinning me in place.

I call to the earth to rise under me, but nothing responds. It's as if all of the energy within me has suddenly been sucked away, I reach for my magic, but ... there's nothing.

"This isn't the end." I growl.

He smiles, showing all of his teeth. Dark tendrils curl around his body, like snakes made of shadow. Somehow Cire's gentle smile comes across warped and evil, showing the monster hiding behind Cire's kind eyes.

He bends close, his hot breath brushing against my cheek as he whispers a sinister promise in my ear.

"This is only the beginning. I have big plans for you."

Acknowledgements

To my husband, Brandon, thank you for always cheering me on, and for allowing me to spoil the entire series so that I could have someone to bounce ideas off of. You are my rubber ducky, and my rock. I am so grateful to have a partner that supports me chasing my dreams and gives me a front row seat to the pursuit of their own dreams. I love you, and I wouldn't want to do life with anyone else. And, I quote, "It's hard to be both a rubber duck and a rock at the same time, because one sinks and one floats."

To my parents, Bryan and Tricia, thank you for your support and love. Thank you, momma, for reading my shitty first draft, and several other versions after. And daddy, I promise to buy you the best spot in the theatre if this ever becomes a movie. Thank you for helping me to dream bigger. I love you.

To Brooklyn, thank you for being my author Yoda. For every 10 p.m. video call, late night message, and countless questions—thank you. I am a better writer because of your feedback and support. *Prophecy of Blood and Flames* is the best version of itself because of your edit suggestions and feedback.

Thank you for letting me stand on your shoulders so I could see the finish line for myself, I owe you.

To my beta readers, Kelly, Morgan, Megan, and Sara, thank you for being such amazing friends and harsh (but supportive) critics. Your questions challenged me to see my book from different perspectives. *Prophecy of Blood and Flames* would not be the book it is today without your feedback.

To my Grandma Mary, who was the very first person to read my shitty first draft of *Prophecy of Blood and Flames* in 2018 when it went by a different name, and an entirely different plot. I will always cherish your random phone calls asking me questions and telling me where you got stuck while reading. I still have the 8x11 printed copy I mailed you where you left notes in the margins. You were the first to be all-in on my dream, and you never doubted me for a second. It may have taken me a little over five years to finally publish, but I did it. I love you.

To my chonky cat, Esme, thank you for doing nothing. Just kidding, thank you for being my constant shadow and leg warmer. I love you—even if you only see me as a means for getting cheese and stealing popcorn.

To my readers, thank you from the bottom of my heart for reading *Prophecy of Blood and Flames*. Whether it was through a purchase, a library loan, or maybe you found it somewhere free on the internet (I'm not mad)—thank you for supporting an indie author's dreams. It's my sincere hope that you enjoy the story, and that you see at least a little of yourself in my characters. This one's for you, too.

About the Author

Author Lacie M. Lou makes her novel debut with *Prophecy of Blood and Flames*, the first book in a dark fantasy trilogy, The *Aurorian Trilogy*.

Lacie is a cat mom to a chonky cat named Esme. On a typical evening you can find them both curled up on the couch while Lacie writes, eats popcorn, and drinks caffeine past a "reasonable hour."

Growing up Lacie devoured series such as R.L. Stine's *Goosebumps*, James Patterson's murder mystery novels, and countless fantasy series. *Prophecy of Blood and Flames* also drew inspiration from the author's own experiences with self doubt, anxiety, and grief over the loss of loved ones, as well as her desire for more diverse representation of identities in the fantasy genre.

Made in the USA
Monee, IL
01 April 2025

14670140R00204